Barbarian Prize

'May Poseidon pierce your entrails with his trident,' she hissed as she caught sight of him. 'And stand up when I'm talking to you. After all, you are a slave, although you seem to forget that far too easily of late.'

'On the contrary,' he replied, as he rose to his feet. 'I remember it every moment of the day and night. Nevertheless, I should not have acted as I did. I'm sorry.'

'Sorry is not good enough, Taranis,' she shouted, as she ripped off her dress and threw it at him.

'I don't expect it is,' he agreed, as he stepped over the dress and walked towards her. 'I embarrassed you in front of your friends, even more than you embarrassed me it seems.'

'Embarrassed!' she repeated furiously. 'Slaves aren't allowed to feel embarrassed. If I order you to walk around the city stark naked, your cock strung with jewels, you do it. That's what slaves do, they follow orders.'

By the same author

Savage Surrender
Wild Kingdom
Doctor's Orders

Barbarian Prize
Deanna Ashford

Black Lace books contain sexual fantasies.
In real life, always practise safe sex.

First published in 2006 by
Black Lace
Thames Wharf Studios
Rainville Road
London W6 9HA

Design by Smith & Gilmour, London
Printed and bound by Mackays of Chatham PLC

ISBN 0 352 34017 7
ISBN 9 780352 340177

1

AD79

It was hot, far hotter than usual for late June, the month named for the goddess Juno, and the sun hung like a glittering ball of pure gold in the cloudless blue sky. Not even the hint of a breeze rippled the glassy green surface of the sea as the Roman warship, a liburnian with a high curving prow, glided forwards propelled by two dozen oars either side of the vessel. Each oar was manned by two wide-chested slaves, with hugely muscled arms. On days such as this, when there was no wind to fill the sails of the liburnian, they would be forced to row for hours and hours, each oarstroke controlled by the relentless beat of the drum.

As soon as the helmsman saw the island of Prochyta on the starboard bow, he leant hard on the huge oar at the rear, which served as a rudder. The boards of the vessel creaked as it slowly changed direction, rounding the headland into the Bay of Neapolis. The liburnian was not heading for the harbour at Misenum, the headquarters of the western imperial fleet where at least forty huge triremes were moored, but for a city further across the bay. Captain Cornelius was under orders from Governor Agricola to convey the captives in the hold to Pompeii.

Deep in the bowels of the vessel, Sirona stirred restlessly as the steady drumbeat coming from the oardeck above changed pace. 'The ship is slowing,' she whispered to Taranis, who lay beside her. 'Do you think we are pulling into port again?'

'There could be many reasons,' he said. 'Perhaps we are heading into more treacherous waters,' he added, pulling her closer to him, the chains that held him clanking as he moved his arms. 'Don't be concerned, my love.'

She tried not to be frightened but she didn't find it easy to be as brave and steadfast as Taranis was. They had no idea of their destination or what the future held for them. Most likely they faced either death or slavery; the Romans were quick to punish those who dared to rise against them. When the Roman General Agricola and his legions had marched into northern Brittania, Sirona's father Borus had led an army made up of a number of different northern tribes against the invaders. They'd fought long and hard against superior forces, yet despite all their prayers and sacrifices the gods had been far from kind. She, along with Borus, his second-in-command Taranis and many of their men, had been captured.

At the express order of Emperor Vespasian, her father and most of the other prisoners had been taken from the vessel at Ostia. They were to be paraded in chains through the streets of Rome before being sent to their execution.

Sirona had no idea why she, Taranis and a few others had been spared for a time and left on board this vessel. 'I just thank the goddess Andrasta that she answered my prayers and allowed me to be with you, at least for a short while longer,' she said to Taranis.

During the long overland march south, Sirona, the only female captive, had been kept apart from the other prisoners. When they'd boarded the military liburnian at the port of Narbo in Southern Gaul, she'd been confined alone in a small aft cabin. Three days earlier, extra passengers had come aboard, a corpulent Roman general and his wife, and she'd been moved to the hold, but she had not been chained like the other prisoners. The few Roman females she'd known in Brittania were weak and submissive creatures, compelled to obey their fathers or their husbands at all times, so the captain must have thought that leaving her unfettered posed no threat to the safety of this vessel. He clearly did not know that Celtic women were also warriors; even so, she cursed her weakness, as no matter how hard she tried she could find no way to free Taranis and the other prisoners from their manacles.

She caressed her lover's muscular chest. The heat in the dark hold was oppressive and his skin was slick with perspiration. The air around them was thick with the foul odours of stale sweat and excrement; yet she could still detect the familiar musky masculine scent of his body as she ran her hands over the grubby fabric of his loincloth. Beneath the thin layer of linen she felt his cock stir. The coarsely woven tunic her captors had given her to wear stuck to her hot flesh and the rough boards of the floor of the hold dug into her hip, but none of this mattered; all she could feel was her rising desire for Taranis.

He was a renowned warrior and military strategist whom Borus respected enough to make his second-in-command, even though Taranis came from Gaul and not Brittania. The first time she'd laid eyes on him she'd thought him the most amazingly attractive man she had ever seen. He was tall, at least a head taller than her fellow Icene, and most of his life he had been a mercenary, fighting against the Romans in far-flung lands. His skin had been darkened by the sun to a deep golden brown. His hair was the colour of ripe wheat, his

3

eyes as blue as the clear skies of summer and, with his square jaw and masculine features, he was amazingly handsome.

She felt the hard contours of his belly tremble as she brushed her fingers across his hot, damp skin. Taranis gave a muffled moan as she leant forwards and traced the outline of his nipples with the tip of her tongue. The salty taste of his perspiration sharpened her desire for him. She pulled one of his nipples between her lips and sucked on it gently.

His muscles tensed, those on his arms cording, as he pulled her half across his body. 'I want you,' Taranis said softly, as a prisoner a few feet away coughed noisily, his chains clanking as he tried to move into a more comfortable position.

'Are you never satisfied?' she teased. Over the last three days, she had learnt to virtually ignore the presence of the other prisoners and concentrate only on this brief, bitter-sweet reunion with her lover.

Taranis meshed his fingers in her tangled hair as he kissed Sirona. The hot wetness of his mouth increased her need for him, as her pussy grew warm and moist. He continued to kiss her while he cupped her left breast with one large hand, kneading it sensuously through the coarse linen of her tunic. The rough fabric chafed the sensitive tip, making her moan with pleasure. She pressed her fingers against his belly, then slid them beneath his loincloth. Curving her fingers around his cock, she massaged it gently.

'Slowly,' he begged. 'Every touch of your fingertips sends me wilder than the god of war, Mars, in the thick of battle.'

'Not too slowly,' she said as she pulled off her filthy tunic.

She wanted him naked also, desperate to enjoy the

tactile pleasure of his hot skin pressed close to hers. Unfastening his loincloth, she released his cock. Even though it was too dark for her to see it properly, she knew how beautiful it looked, so magnificently large, rearing stiffly out of its bed of golden hair.

The first time she'd seen his body totally unclothed had been in front of the altar of the goddess Andrasta. They'd made love in the ring of ancient stones, believing that the gift of her virginity would please their goddess of victory. At that moment Sirona had realised how much she loved him and had vowed to be his forever.

Curving her palm around his shaft, she pumped it slowly, feeling his erection grow harder as the moisture between her pussy lips increased. There was a certain kind of raw power in turning him on until he became so desperate to fuck her that he would do anything she wanted. Especially as this magnificent warrior had slain at least two dozen Roman soldiers in a vain effort to protect her in the final battle before they were captured.

Nevertheless, he was in no mood to be patient today as he grabbed hold of her waist and swung her astride him. As she ground her wet sex against his muscular belly, savouring the slick heat of his skin against her open pussy, she felt the hard line of his cock brush her buttocks. His large hands cupped her breasts, kneading them roughly before his fingers focused on her nipples, pulling and squeezing them until she gasped with pleasure. Then he captured one teat, sucking on it hungrily.

'Now,' she gasped.

Sirona barely heard the loud groan uttered by a nearby prisoner and the rattle of his chains as, excited by the sounds of their lovemaking, he began to masturbate vigorously.

Having lifted her high in the air, Taranis eased her

backwards until her sex was poised over his groin. He held her there with his strong arms as if she weighed next to nothing, letting the damp tip of his cock-head press erotically against her sex lips. Sirona struggled, giving a soft whimper of frustration, now desperate to fuck him. 'Please,' she begged, as he toyed with her senses, holding her tightly, only letting her body move downwards a hair's breadth at a time.

'Slowly, my love,' he whispered. 'I know how much you want this.'

As he spoke, he eased her down on to him. His thick shaft slid smoothly into her; the hot, hard, delicious length of it invading her cunt, filling her completely. Tightening her inner muscles around him, she started to move, rocking her hips backwards and forwards, lifting her body, and then grinding it hard down against his groin. The weight of his chains fell across her widely spread thighs as his hands slid down to grasp her waist. His fingers dug into her flesh and she leant back, increasing the depth of his penetration, fucking him in the self-same rhythm as the drumbeat guiding the oars-men above them.

Sirona felt the pleasurable sensations building inside her, spreading outwards like an all-consuming fire. It didn't matter that it was too dark to see Taranis clearly. In her mind's eye she saw his handsome face – his eyes glazed, his lips curved in a rictus of pleasure as she rode him hard. Her movements gradually became faster and faster until she was no longer in time with the slow thump of the drum, but following the accelerated beating of her own heart.

Taranis muttered her name as his hand moved between her widely spread thighs. He brushed the rough pad of his thumb against her clit and she gasped and jerked in response. He increased the pressure, rubbing harder and the combination of sensations spiralled totally out of control. Her internal muscles contracted around his cock shaft in powerful waves as the orgasm swept through her body.

As the intense sensations died away and the trembling of her limbs ceased, she realised to her surprise that Taranis was still engorged and erect inside her. 'What's wrong?' she whispered.

'Nothing,' he said softly. 'I want to feel your sweet lips sucking me dry.'

Lifting her hips, she let his shaft slide slowly out of her, then she edged backwards, ignoring the splintered, salt-encrusted wood that dug into her knees as she crouched over Taranis. She could smell his arousal as her mouth lovingly nuzzled his groin. She lapped at his swollen prick that was still slick with the juices of her cunt. At first, all she could taste was the musky flavour of her body's leavings. But, as she eased the tip of her tongue into the tiny slit at the top, she detected the familiar saltiness of his pre-come as it seeped from the opening.

'Take it fully into your mouth,' he moaned, as she brushed her lips up and down his veined shaft, then ran her tongue sensuously around the rim of the engorged head.

'Take mine instead,' begged a disembodied voice in the darkness.

'Quiet, Ramus,' Leod, a young warrior she'd known since childhood, shouted. 'Let them have the pleasure of forgetting this hell for a moment.'

Sirona was barely conscious of this brief exchange of words as she concentrated all her attentions on Taranis. She pressed her hand on his belly, feeling his stomach flexing as her lips encircled his cock. The smooth texture of the large glans was arousing and his powerful sex odour filled her nostrils, making her pussy grow hot with need again. She used her tongue, swirling and feathering his tightly stretched flesh as she tried to swallow even more of his huge shaft.

Driven wild with desire, Taranis gave a strangled groan. His cock twitched and Sirona knew he was agonisingly close to coming but she didn't want him to climax just yet. After easing her mouth away from his cock, she gently lifted his scrotum, lapping at it with the tip of her tongue. Taranis gave a strangled groan as she pulled one ball into her mouth, feeling the soft down covering the sac tickle her lips. Curving her tongue round the smooth hard stone, she sucked on it gently.

'Oh, yes,' Taranis gasped.

Ramus, who'd been quiet for a few moments, began to clank his chains agitatedly as he shouted a jealous string of obscenities. This time he was forced into silence by a well-placed kick from the prisoner next to him.

Immune to everything but her lover's imminent pleasure, Sirona played teasingly with his testicles, while she ran her fingers up and down his rampant cock, feeling it twitch excitedly.

'Please now,' Taranis begged. 'Let me come.'

Sirona slid her lips around the thick shaft, swallowing as much of him as she could until she felt his cock-head hit the back of her throat. Suppressing the brief urge to gag, she sucked greedily on the organ. Her heart was racing now, her body filled with desire for him again. Her nipples contracted into two sharp points and her pussy became even moister as she slid her lips smoothly up and down his cock, squeezing them tight to increase the pressure. Roughly, she scraped a ragged fingernail across the strip of skin between his balls and anus. Taranis grabbed her hair, forcing her down harder on to him as he grunted loudly and bucked his hips. His balls tightened as the hot creamy seed spurted into her mouth. Sirona hungrily swallowed every drop of the life essence of his body until he was totally drained and lay limply beneath her, gasping for breath.

Taranis pulled her body across his so that she was cushioned from the rough planks, which served as their bed. Cradling her in his arms, he whispered tender words of love in her ear assuring her that, even though they might be destined to be parted for a while, the gods would one day allow them to be together again. Sirona rested her head on his broad chest, letting herself believe his reassuring words, feeling exhausted and for a brief moment happily replete.

She drifted off to sleep for a while, for how long she didn't know. She was jerked into wakefulness when the relentless thump of the drum on the oardeck above suddenly ceased. Orders were being shouted to the oarsmen. They were still moving, but very slowly, and waves were slapping loudly against the sides of the vessel. From what she'd heard on previous occasions, she was led to believe that they must be pulling into a harbour again. 'Where do you think we are?' she anxiously asked Taranis.

'Hush.' He eased her sideways, supporting her in the curve of his arm. 'Let's not think of that.'

Sirona's breasts were still a little tender and when his hand moved to gently caress her hot, slippery flesh she gave a soft gasp. At first he concentrated on squeezing and pulling at her teats until her nipples hardened and her breasts ached with pleasure. How easily he could arouse her, she thought, as moisture pooled stickily between her thighs. Her body felt overripe and still sensitive from their last bout of sex, yet her clit ached to feel the touch of his fingers again.

Slowly, Taranis moved his hand downwards, lovingly

stroking her perspiration-covered flesh. His callused fingers brushed the curve of her belly and she moaned and trembled, desperate for them to reach the copper curls covering her pubis. She wanted them to explore the burning valley of her sex, and gently ease their way inside her. Suddenly, he thrust his bunched fingers deep inside her pussy, moving them hard and fast, finger-fucking her with a rough kind of desperation that he had never displayed before. Sirona's breathing grew ragged, as she moved her hips to meet each thrust, and she gave a strangled moan as he rubbed his callused thumb against her clit. The combination of sensations became more intense until she reached the peak, but she was unprepared for the force of her climax as it came; this time the pleasure was even harder and sharper than before.

Sirona blinked, half-blinded by the bright sunshine, as she was led on to the deck of the liburnian. At first, all she could see was a misty haze of azure, ochre and gold, then slowly her surroundings came into focus. They had entered a busy port. On higher ground some distance away was a large fortress city. Sirona had visited a few Roman towns in Brittania but they were far smaller and much less impressive than this place. Even on their long journey through Gaul, which had been ruled by the Romans for many years, she'd seen nothing as imposing.

Beyond and below the protective ramparts, she could see many dwellings, so it was clear that the occupants of the city no longer feared invasion. The wide terraces were covered in palm and Cyprus trees and a number of the villas were very large, obviously the homes of wealthy and influential citizens. Above the line of flat red roofs she could see a temple with gleaming white pillars, which faced out to sea. In the distance, some way behind the city, was a high mountain. The lower slopes were covered in vegetation but the sharply pointed peak looked grey and forbidding.

There were ships of all shapes and sizes tied up at the dockside and so many people. The port was crowded, as were the roads leading to the city gates. Some travellers were on foot, some on horseback, while others were in carts or ornate chariots.

A small group of citizens had gathered to watch the liburnian dock. With Roman military precision, the long oars were shipped and they glided alongside the wharf. Some of the sailors jumped ashore carrying the thick mooring cables, which were then wound tightly around the huge stone bollards lining the dockside. The cables tightened with a sharp snap and the ship jerked wildly. Sirona might have fallen if one of her soldier escorts hadn't grabbed her arm to steady her.

The vessel came to rest, parallel to the shore, almost motionless now in the still waters of the harbour. The gangplank was laid in place. Immediately, both soldiers took an even firmer hold on Sirona's arms and escorted her down to the dockside.

The two men led her through the small ring of chattering onlookers, who stared at her with evident curiosity, most probably wondering why a pathetic-looking female prisoner needed two soldiers to guard her. However, they did not know that she was an Icene princess, whom Governor Agricola considered his special prize.

Sirona felt weak from a combination of insufficient food and water, the terrible conditions in the hold and a lack of exercise. She had no wish for this escort but she was glad that they were holding on to her so tightly, otherwise she might have stumbled and fallen. It would not be seemly for the only daughter of King Borus to show weakness of any kind.

It was a hot afternoon, almost as hot out here as it was in the hold, but Sirona still enjoyed the feel of the warm sun on her skin and fresh air at last to fill her lungs. Her first few breaths were fine, as most ports smelt the same. It was a musty mixture of seawater, the caulk used on the vessels and hot stale bodies – all mingled with the exotic odours of the different cargoes from far-flung lands. Then the faint breeze wafted towards her a foul odour of rotting flesh. She swallowed, willing her stomach not to heave in disgust. She was not aware that the smell came from the fish sauce factory close to the docks. Tons of fish-guts were left to decompose in huge vats, ready to be made into Garum, a favourite Roman condiment.

The port of Pompeii was a hub of activity, visited by merchant ships from all corners of the ever-expanding Roman Empire and beyond. Practically anything could be purchased here: spices such as Chinese cinnamon, treasures like Egyptian glass and amber and marble from Greece. There were even animals like wolves and bears from Brittania and leopards and monkeys from Africa.

'I hear that there are at least thirty brothels in Pompeii.' The soldier to Sirona's left addressed his companion. 'I've a mind to try one tonight.'

'The one off the Via Stabiana, near the baths, is the best,' the other said with a wide grin, which revealed his lack of four front teeth. 'Most of the whores there are Orientals and renowned for their exotic foreign tricks.'

Sirona was curious to hear more. What sexual tricks she wondered? Rich and influential Roman citizens had slaves to serve their every whim and lived a life of indolent, sensual luxury, so perhaps there were many erotic pleasures that she knew nothing about. Also she was curious about this city the soldiers had called Pompeii. She knew little of her captors' homeland, but she had heard tales of the splendour of Rome. It was said to be a massive, truly awe-inspiring place. Emperor Vespasian resided there and had numerous palaces filled with gold, silver and precious stones. That wasn't surprising, as the Romans had huge armies and were an incredibly rich, powerful and widely feared nation, which had conquered almost a third of the known world and beyond.

She had to admit that Pompeii was an interesting city and, for a moment, fear for her own fate receded a little, as she was overwhelmed by the sights and sounds around her. All the citizens looked prosperous and there was an amazing mass of goods piled outside the many warehouses they walked past.

Her green eyes grew wide with astonishment as she spotted a large cage. Inside was a strange, but truly magnificent animal with golden fur and a thick ruff of darker hair around its neck. The lion paced his cage and gave a loud roar, which made Sirona jump nervously, as her escorts hustled her past the noble creature.

'Wonder how long he'll last in the arena?' the first soldier commented.

'Probably grow fat on Christians and criminals,' his companion joked, as they reached the paved road which led to the city gates.

Further on, to the left of the road, stood a large stone building. It was bigger than the warehouses and had an embellished portico with two stone columns and a large wooden door decorated with thick bronze studs.

One of the soldiers rapped on the door, which was pulled open by a man with skin as black as pitch.

'We come from Captain Cornelius of the warship *Cronus*,' announced her escort.

'You are expected.' The servant's voice was deep and he spoke Latin with a strange accent.

Sirona was hustled inside. Many Roman buildings were constructed around a central open courtyard and had no windows in their outer walls; this place appeared to be designed in a similar manner. After passing through a small entrance chamber, they entered a large paved area, open to the sky, with a raised platform at the far end. All the Roman-style villas she'd seen in her homeland had statues, fountains and plants decorating the central garden, or peristyle as they called it, but this area was totally bare apart from a pile of low benches stacked in one corner.

An elderly woman hurried forwards. Her grey hair was pulled back in a bun and, although she wore a plain blue tunic, it was made of a fine fabric and she had ornate silver bracelets on both wrists. 'The master has asked me to attend to the girl,' she said, taking the small roll of papyrus one of the soldiers handed to her.

'You're welcome to her,' one of the soldiers said, pushing Sirona forwards. 'She doesn't look much like a princess to me.' He glanced disparagingly at his charge. 'I'd much prefer to fuck one of those oriental whores you mentioned,' he added, turning to grin lewdly at his companion.

Pointedly ignoring his crude words, the woman said in a dismissive tone, 'You may go now. Nubius will show you out.'

She nodded to the black gatekeeper who immediately led the two men towards the door. As they departed, they exchanged very loud, obscene comments about the whorehouse they planned to visit later in the evening.

'Come,' the woman said to Sirona. She didn't respond, staring blankly at her as if she did not understand the simple Latin word, even though she spoke the language fluently. Borus had told her that it was wiser to know one's enemies, but to let them know as little of yourself as possible. When she had been captured by Agricola's men, it had been presumed that, as a barbarian, who had not experienced the benefits of their civilisation, she would not understand their tongue. So she'd let the Romans believe she was just an ignorant savage. She'd continued this subterfuge when she had discovered that her captors often spoke more freely in front of her, wrongly believing that she could not understand them.

The woman shook her head in irritation. 'This way,' she said in a firm voice, as if talking loudly would help the new arrival understand what she said. She took Sirona's hand and led her hurriedly through the paved courtyard, then turned left through a small archway into another courtyard. This one had a fountain at its centre surrounded by tall statues and pots of brightly coloured flowers. 'You're filthy, you poor thing,' the woman chatted on to herself, as she led Sirona into a tiny cubicle, which contained a narrow cot. The only other furniture was a small side table on which reposed a basin filled with warm scented water.

'You smell like you've been shut in a foul brothel for weeks.' The woman wrinkled her nose in disgust. She picked up a damp sponge and began to vigorously wipe the dirt from Sirona's arms and face. 'You really need a bath but this will have to do. The senator wants to see you right away.' She lifted Sirona's arms, tutting as she saw the cluster of hair in her armpits. 'A heathen through and through,' she muttered to herself, rinsing the sponge out in the basin before energetically washing the offending armpits. 'They should have warned me you would need a change of clothing,' she said anxiously, as she threw the sponge into the basin of, now filthy, water. 'I dare not pause to find one. He will become angry if he has to wait any longer.' She took hold of Sirona's hand, pulling her towards the door again. 'Come,' she said, concern sharpening her tone.

She led Sirona out of the cubicle, whereupon they turned left and entered a larger room, which had elaborately painted walls and, like most Roman houses, was sparingly but elegantly furnished. All Sirona's attention was immediately drawn to a man seated on a chair in the centre of the room. She knew that he was important because he was wearing the purple-bordered toga of a Roman senator. His much younger companion was wearing a short blue tunic, which told her that he was most probably a slave or a servant.

The senator's cold grey eyes examined her thoughtfully and Sirona repressed an unconscious shiver as a trickle of fear slid down her spine. She couldn't explain her instinctive reaction as his expression wasn't unkind, just thoughtful and there was nothing repellent about him. On the contrary, although he was well into middle age, he was still good-looking. His angular features and long straight, slightly overlarge nose were softened by the short iron-grey hair carefully arranged in curls either side of his face, a style favoured by the late Emperor Nero.

'So this is the barbarian princess.' His tone was harsh. 'Bring her closer.'

The woman led Sirona forwards until she was standing in front of him, barely an arm's breadth away. 'She appears not to understand what I say to her, my lord,' she explained nervously, then she bowed her head fearfully, as if she might be punished for speaking out of turn.

'You may go,' he said and the woman immediately scurried from the room. The man glanced back at his young companion. 'A savage, Tiro. And she stinks,' he added in disgust, as he lifted an ampoule of scented oil to his nose.

'You wanted to see her immediately, Senator,' the young man cautiously reminded him. 'There was no time to have her properly bathed and perfumed.'

Sirona hoped that she was managing to appear quite unafraid as the senator stared at her. He took another sniff of the perfumed ampoule. 'You're from Brittania, Tiro, have you ever taken one of these savages to your bed?'

'No, Senator,' Tiro replied.

The Romans had ruled southern Brittania for over thirty years, but their efforts to conquer the rest of the large island were slow and hampered by resistance from many of the individual Celtic tribes. Governor Agricola had yet to begin his advance further north towards Caledonia.

'Fucking her might prove interesting,' the older man said thoughtfully. His narrow lips curved in a cold hard smile that turned Sirona's blood to water. She had been raised as a warrior, taught to fear nothing, yet all her instincts told her to fear this man. 'As you can speak her barbarian tongue, you can tell her to take off that filthy rag.'

Fighting the urge to stiffen defensively, Sirona stared blankly at her captor.

'Remove your tunic, girl.' Tiro spoke her language haltingly, but well enough for her to understand. 'You must obey Senator Aulus Vettius at all times.'

'I'm no girl,' Sirona spat proudly. 'I'm Sirona, Princess of the Icene.'

'The Icene, the Brigantes – all the remnants of the tribes that fought under your father's command have now surrendered to Governor Agricola,' Tiro reminded Sirona as he stepped towards her. 'Rome is now your master as it is mine.'

'What's wrong?' Aulus snapped, clearly irritated by the fact that he could not understand what was being said.

'Nothing, master,' Tiro replied rather anxiously in Latin. He tugged at Sirona's filthy tunic. 'Take it off now or you'll be punished.'

'What are you saying?' Aulus asked angrily.

'I told her to strip,' Tiro nervously explained.

'Is she stupid?' Aulus growled. 'If she doesn't obey immediately, make her!'

Having no wish to be forcibly stripped, Sirona angrily pulled off her tunic and with a proud toss of her head flung it at the senator's feet.

'She has spirit.' Aulus gave a harsh laugh as he stared at her naked body. 'Good tits too and nice legs.'

Like most of her tribe Sirona was naturally fair skinned and, since her capture, she'd grown even paler, as she'd barely seen the sunlight. The male prisoners had been forced to march across Gaul, but she'd been almost permanently confined in the baggage wagon. She was unaware that her ivory skin would be envied by most Roman women who plastered their faces with creams containing white lead to lighten their sallow complexions.

'Her hair colour is unusual.' Aulus wasn't looking at her hair, which, when clean, was the colour of burnished copper, he was staring at her pubes.

'All shades of red hair are common in her land,' Tiro told his master.

'Then we should import more female slaves from Brittania – the brothels here need to provide more variety.' Aulus pointed at her groin, curling his lips in disgust. 'The body hair is quite offensive, is it not?'

Aulus had all his body hair removed by regular pluck-ing, an uncomfortable procedure considered a necessity by most high-ranking citizens.

'That is no problem,' Tiro said quickly. 'I'll have her sent to the Venus baths with the other female slaves.'

'No.' Aulus shook his head. 'She'll use my household baths. I've no wish for anyone to lay eyes on her just yet. Bring her nearer, so that I can examine her more closely.'

Tiro pushed Sirona forwards until she was close enough to the senator to smell the rose oil that scented his skin, and see the pulse beating in his neck. She wished she was holding the bone-handled knife her father had given her when she reached womanhood, then she could have leant forwards and slit his throat. However, she could do nothing and she was forced to endure his long fingers probing and pinching her flesh. She tried not to flinch as he touched her breasts, pulled at her nipples and then stroked her flat belly.

'Too muscular for a woman – but then she is a barbarian.' He pushed his fingers between her thighs.

Tiro stared at Sirona as if he felt some kinship for her and pitied her plight. They were both from Brittania but there the likeness ended. To her, he was as much a Roman as this vile senator, Aulus Vettius, was. 'I think that a well-schooled whore would prove to be far more enjoyable for you, master,' he said cautiously.

'Whorish tricks bore me, as do the simpering atten-tions of sex-starved Roman matrons,' Aulus snapped, cruelly thrusting his finger inside Sirona.

She tensed and bit her lip. The brutal probing was both painful and demeaning. Yet, suddenly and ashamedly, she felt another darker emotion arise within her, almost akin to sexual arousal, an incomprehensible reaction she could not even begin to explain, especially when the only man that had ever touched her so intimately before was Taranis.

'She's barely moist.' Aulus removed his finger and delicately sniffed it. 'Yet she stinks of sex.'

'That's unlikely,' Tiro quickly replied. 'The captain of the *Cronus* had orders to keep her confined apart from the other prisoners.'

'Do you think Captain Cornelius fucked her?' Aulus grinned. 'I confess I would be surprised as he's said to be only interested in young boys.'

Tiro glanced at the papyrus the soldiers had delivered, which Aulus had left unrolled on a nearby table. 'I would not think he would dare to. It is written here that Governor Agricola issued specific orders to deliver her here untouched and unharmed.'

'She must be at least nineteen or twenty,' Aulus commented thoughtfully, as he continued to run his hands over Sirona's body. 'So I doubt she'll be a virgin ... more's the pity.' He pinched and squeezed her buttocks, feeling them tense at his touch. 'I've a mind to test her skill.' Aulus looked at Tiro. 'Tell her to kneel and pleasure me. Even a barbarian should know how to do that.'

Sirona had to force herself not to react with horror to his words, as Tiro stepped behind her and placed a firm hand on each of her shoulders. 'Kneel and take my master's cock in your mouth,' he ordered curtly. 'He desires you to pleasure him.'

Her instinctive response was to refuse but she knew how unwise that would be. Fearfully, she watched Aulus part his legs and lean his head back against the chair. He stared expectantly at her. When Sirona made no move to follow his instructions, Tiro roughly shoved her forwards until she was standing between the senator's wide-spread thighs.

'Kneel,' Tiro hissed in her ear, as he pressed his hands down hard on her shoulders. He was stronger than he looked and easily forced her to sink to her knees. 'Touch him, pleasure him with your mouth, any fool can do that, girl.'

Sirona knelt on the cold floor staring fixedly at the lower folds of the pure white toga, unable to bring herself to do as she'd been ordered.

Sighing anxiously, Tiro pulled aside the folds of the heavy fabric and lifted the senator's short tunic. Aulus wore no undergarments, and Sirona found herself facing a surprisingly well-honed form with a flat muscular stomach. She'd expected a sagging, flabby body but Aulus looked strong and firm. His flaccid cock lay there on his hairless groin, curled up like a pale sleeping snake. She found it both repulsive and yet oddly fascinating.

When the soldiers had come down to the hold to take her away, Taranis had begged her to do everything in her power to survive. He'd vowed that if he lived he would somehow find a way to come for her and they would flee to a land far from Roman domination. She remembered his words all too clearly as she stared at the senator's naked sex.

'You know what to do,' Tiro worriedly prompted.

Sirona glanced nervously up at Tiro. He was clearly concerned, not for her of course, but his master might blame him for her failure to do as she was told. Sirona didn't care what happened to Tiro but she intended to try and keep the promise she had made to Taranis. Cautiously, she touched the senator's cock, trying not to show her abhorrence as she curved her fingers around the flaccid shaft. Aulus tensed, almost as though her callused fingers with their ragged, dirty nails repelled him. Yet he was still obviously aroused by her touch because to her amazement the organ immediately began to stiffen.

There was a massive void between pleasuring this man and having sex with her betrothed. She loved touching his cock and bringing him to a climax in any way he wanted, but this was totally different. Yet she had to do it, she reminded herself, as she began to gently rub the senator's long slim shaft, employing the same rhythmic movements she used when milking live-stock at home. Sirona felt the pale crinkled flesh start to harden and she heard him give a groan of pleasure. She wasn't that skilled in sexual matters, yet it appeared that where their cocks were concerned men were the same the world over.

Trying to ignore her conflicting emotions, she moved her hand more briskly, wanking him harder. The skin on the domed head grew tight and shiny, as a small drop of pre-come seeped from the slit.

'Her efforts are crude, but effective,' Aulus grunted, his face reddening. 'Tell her to use her mouth, I want her to suck me.'

'Take it into your mouth,' Tiro bent forwards and hissed in her ear. 'You surely know how to do that?'

She had no intention of taking the senator's cock between her lips, the idea was utterly repulsive, so she had to find a way to make him climax as quickly as possible. Anxiously, she began to pump his shaft harder, while at the same time fondling his pale hairless balls.

'No!' Aulus gripped the arms of his chair, wincing in discomfort. 'Tell the bitch to use her mouth!'

'Jupiter defend me! Girl, are you stupid?' Tiro anxiously remonstrated. 'Use your mouth on him, now.'

Ignoring Tiro, Sirona continued to wank Aulus with a brutal enthusiasm she would never have thought to use on her beloved Taranis.

'By the breath of Hades!' Aulus gasped. 'She doesn't know what she's doing,' he shouted angrily. 'She's clearly too stupid to even follow an order properly. Get the bitch off me.' He lashed out at Sirona, catching her hard across the face with the flat of his hand. Then he roughly kicked her away from him.

Sirona fell back on the cold mosaic floor with a hard smack, barely feeling the pain. She hoped that this man, whom she could only presume was now her owner, had obtained little satisfaction from their brief sexual encounter. The thought of having to permanently provide such intimate services for him appalled her. Perhaps, if she continued to appear as clumsy and stupid in future, he'd ignore her and turn to his other slaves who were doubtless more skilled in attending to his vile demands.

She expected some immediate form of punishment or at least the threat of one later. Yet, to her surprise, Aulus just glared over at Tiro and said, 'Show the bitch how to do it properly; she's clearly an imbecile and totally unskilled.'

To Sirona's total amazement, Tiro stepped forwards and sank to his knees between his master's thighs. She stared in surprised fascination as he reached out and touched Aulus's cock, handling it as he would a revered object. Tenderly, he stroked the rigid member. There was a strange kind of erotic servility in this moment as he began to masturbate Aulus.

In Brittania, men did not pleasure other men, well, as far as she knew they did not, but she had heard tales of such Roman depravity. She had found the idea disgusting, but now that she was here witnessing the lecherous act, strangely enough it was exciting her.

Both senator and slave appeared to have forgotten her presence, so she moved, edging to her left, filled with curiosity and wanting to get a better view of the intimate encounter.

Tiro leant forwards and tenderly kissed the taut head of Aulus's penis, running the tip of his tongue round the clearly defined rim, until the entire tip glistened with his saliva. 'Take it in your mouth,' Aulus demanded.

Sliding his lips over the head, Tiro pulled the cock deep into his mouth. Aulus arched his neck and gave a loud grunt of pleasure as Tiro slid his lips further down the shaft, almost swallowing it to the root.

Sirona had never watched anyone having sex before and she was surprised at how titillating voyeurism could be. She slid her hand between her thighs and pressed it to her pussy as the erotic feelings grew stronger.

Aulus smiled and leant back in his chair, watching Tiro with heavy-lidded eyes as the slave crouched between his widely stretched thighs, mouthing his cock. Tenderly, he stroked Tiro's short brown hair. 'I don't want to come yet, use your mouth as you know I like it.'

After letting the rigid cock slip from his mouth, Tiro began to kiss and lick his master's denuded balls. Sirona found his immediate obedience rather unsettling. Would she grow to be like that, worn down by servility to a point where she would always do exactly as she was ordered, she wondered, as she saw Aulus grip the arms of his chair, his entire body tensing as Tiro's moist tongue moved downwards. The slave slowly licked the tender skin of his master's perineum and Aulus shifted in his seat, sliding further down the chair. He looped his legs over the slave's shoulders so that the tip of Tiro's tongue could easily reach the taut brown ring of his anus.

Her pussy was now tingling with excitement and she pressed her hand harder against it, hardly able to believe what she was seeing, as Tiro's tongue touched, then gently probed the forbidden opening. She was certain that she could see the tongue sliding deeper into a place none should ever venture and moisture pooled between her thighs. Aulus grunted and bore down against the questing tongue. His cock looked as hard as it could be, the shaft a deep red, the head slowly turning a purplish colour. It stood out stiffly from his groin, as another bead of pre-come seeped from the tip and rolled slowly down the side of the glans. The sharp scent of their sexual desire drifted towards her, and Sirona found herself moving her hand unconsciously, rubbing the heel of her palm against her clit, as she wondered what it would feel like to be touched in that secret part of her body.

Aulus shifted in his chair, breathing heavily. 'Now,' he ordered, lowering his legs. He meshed his hands in Tiro's hair, forcing the slave's face towards his cock, which looked ready to explode at any moment. She heard his groan of bliss as Tiro's mouth hungrily swallowed the shaft. Keeping a firm hold on Tiro, Aulus lifted his buttocks and thrust vigorously into the slave's mouth.

Sirona was so tempted to slide her fingers between her pussy lips and stimulate the small bud of her clit, just as she had done in the past when Taranis hadn't been around to pleasure her. Fighting her desires, she pulled her hand away from her sex and clenched it tightly, ignoring the aching need in her groin. She knew that she could not succumb to such temptations, because the senator might suddenly see what she was doing and try to force her into another sexual encounter.

Still, she couldn't resist continuing to watch the two

men as she wondered what Tiro was feeling. One of his hands had reached beneath his tunic and he was masturbating himself while servicing his master. While his lips worked steadily on Aulus's cock, Tiro was wanking himself off.

She was captivated by the strange sensuality of this moment and, when Aulus threw back his head and gave a loud grunt of pleasure, she jumped nervously. The senator's face was suffused with blood and his eyes were bulging. He gave another, even louder grunt as he climaxed in Tiro's mouth. The slave's throat contracted as he swallowed every last drop of his master's semen.

Pulling back his head, Tiro took a deep unsteady breath, but he had yet to climax himself. Awkwardly, he pulled down his tunic in order to hide his erection. Leaning forwards, Aulus gave a chilling smile as he lifted the slave's garment and stared disdainfully at the engorged penis. 'Please, master –' Tiro started to say.

'Finish it,' Aulus interjected, then leant back in his chair, making no attempt to cover his own sex. He kept his gaze fastened on Tiro, watching the slave curve his nervous fingers around his cock and start to masturbate himself.

2

Julia Felix was feeling in an extraordinarily good mood today. It had been almost two months since the official period of mourning for her hated husband Sutoneus had finished and she was finding the freedom of widowhood exhilarating. All her business ventures were doing well and she no longer had to endure a life of looking after a bad-tempered old man, who often appeared to despise her as much as she despised him. Now she could do exactly as she wished.

The festival of Fortuna had just ended and it felt even hotter than usual for the time of year. The market in the forum had been packed with people and filled with dust from the ongoing renovations of the temple of Apollo. Not that the Via dell'Abbondanza was any less crowded but at least here she could walk along the pavement on the shady side of the street.

Julia crossed the Via Stabiana, stepping on the row of raised stones that were placed there to prevent pedestrians getting their feet wet during the rainy seasons of the year. At present, it also protected them from the horse-shit and rubbish ground down into the paved road by the iron-shod wheels of the chariots. She decided to send a letter of complaint to Gaius Cuspius, one of the four magistrates elected to run the city. After all, it was his responsibility as an aedile to make sure the slaves employed to keep the streets clean did their job properly.

Her thoughts were suddenly disturbed by a cacophony of whistles coming from a group of workmen on the other side of the road, who were repairing a derelict building damaged by the terrible earthquake almost seventeen years earlier. To Julia's surprise, they appeared to be whistling at her. Blushing awkwardly, but secretly flattered by the unexpected attention, she hurried on towards the bakery.

Julia had only been a child when the earthquake hit Pompeii. It had been one of the most terrifying days of her life; the other had been when her stepfather Aulus Vettius had taken her to Rome to marry the elderly senator, Sutoneus. She had never even met him; all she knew of her future husband at the time was that he had already outlived two previous wives.

The smell of freshly baked bread mingled with the delicious odour of lentil stew from the thermopilia, which sold food to passers-by. Suddenly feeling a little peckish, she glanced back to see if there was any sign of her maid Sabine, who she'd left at the forum to collect some grey mullet for dinner from the fishery in the centre of town. Not looking where she was going, Julia almost collided with two burly seamen who were standing on the pavement outside the tavern of Sotencus. They were staring up at the balcony where a young woman, one of the many pretty waitresses, stood. She was exchanging greetings with the men who, judging by their lewd comments, were regular customers of the tavern. On the outside walls of the establishment were painted crude slogans and obscene graffiti all praising the many talents of the waitresses, who also provided sexual services for their customers. They were often far cheaper than the whores of the official brothels, the lupanaris.

Realising that they might have offended a lady of some standing, the two men muttered a hurried apology to Julia and strode inside the tavern.

Longing to get home, sit down and have a cool drink, Julia walked swiftly onwards. As she descended the hill, the pavements became less crowded. There were only a few shops here; mostly the road was lined with homes belonging to private residents of the city. The door of Octavius Quoro's house was open and she could smell the sweet scent of the roses and jasmine that filled his large garden. However, only a few steps further on, the sweet odour was overwhelmed by the unpleasant stink of stale urine.

Just ahead, Julia saw a man lift his tunic and pee into a large red amphora standing by the entrance to the fullery. The man was sturdily built with muscular thighs and he had an impressive cock. Julia felt little embarrassment as she stared at him because it was usual to see male passers-by relieving themselves in the amphoras set outside fulleries.

He grinned and winked at Julia, as he dropped his tunic. With a casual wave of his hand, he turned and walked in the direction of the Sarno Gate. Julia was certain he was one of the gladiators who had fought in the arena last week and her heart gave a nervous flutter. Many Roman matrons paid good money to bed a gladiator and most young females had a crush on one or other of these men.

Togas were generally worn by most citizens and the long lengths of woollen fabric were not easy to wash at home. Most of the urine, which was an important component in the laundering process, came from animals and public urinals but all fulleries also relied on the fresh supplies obtained from the amphoras placed outside their entrances.

Julia lifted her skirt not wanting to soil the hem of her stola in the dust surrounding the amphora as she walked past it. Many drunks from the taverns used the jars and their aim was often far from true. Increasing her pace, she hurried on towards her house, relieved to be moving further away from the sour odour.

'Mistress,' she heard Sabine call.

Julia turned to see a red-faced Sabine scurrying down the road, trying desperately to catch up with her mistress. 'You were a long time,' she gently scolded as the maid reached her. 'Were you flirting with Musa again?'

Sabine coloured even more. 'Of course not,' she said hesitantly, still struggling to regain her breath.

Julia gave a soft laugh. Musa was a young freed man who ran the fishery for its wealthy owner. 'I don't mind you spending time chatting to the young man, just as long as you've completed all the tasks I've given you. He's good looking and quite charming. If you wish it, I'll allow you time off one evening so that you can meet him.'

Sabine lowered her eyes. 'I'm not sure about meeting Musa,' she stuttered as she accompanied her mistress through the wide entranceway of Julia's house. The doorman shut the heavy wood door and the noise of the street outside faded as they walked through a short corridor into the atrium.

'It is your choice, Sabine. Think on it as you take the fish to the kitchen,' Julia told her. 'And don't forget to tell the cook to prepare the special herb sauce I like.'

She was luckier than most of her friends and acquaintances, in that she had a house slave who was a very good cook. A large number of them were always complaining that none of their slaves could cook a decent meal. Some of the richer citizens paid vast sums to import decent chefs from Rome or even further afield.

As Sabine hurried off to the kitchen, Julia handed her packages to a young male house slave. Then she walked down the corridor to her favourite place of all, her garden. Julia's establishment was much larger than those of her neighbours. As well as a large villa and a huge garden, there was also an extensive bath complex set aside from the main house and a long row of workshops. The baths were considered one of the cornerstones of Roman civilisation. Cleanliness was a necessity for its citizens, while in contrast it was said that most barbarians lived in filth and squalor. At present, there was only one working public bath in the city, as the other had been damaged by the earthquake and never repaired. There was a new, far more luxurious bath complex currently under construction but it would not be ready for some time yet. Because of this, Sutoneus, when he was alive, had been persuaded to let out their bathhouse to a few special friends and acquaintances. He had a close business involvement with Maecenus, the largest slave dealer in the city. Julia didn't like the man, but she continued to allow him unlimited access to the baths mainly because he paid generously for the privilege. Also he was rich, very influential and someone she had no wish to cross.

Julia might not have liked her late husband but she was appreciative of the luxuries his wealth had provided her with during their ten-year marriage, even though she'd had little chance to truly appreciate them until now.

She loved this house more than anything else in her life, she thought, as she stepped into the sunny garden. In front of her was a long colonnaded swimming pool, its marble-faced pillars wrapped with climbing plants covered with crimson blooms. At the head of the pool was a large fountain and to its left a tablinum for receiving visitors which was flanked by statues of Apollo and Aphrodite. Only last year Sutoneus had imported these statues from Greece. She could hear birdsong and the air was sweet with the scent of roses, her favourite flowers. Skirting the pool, she walked over the low bridge which crossed the man-made stream running through the grounds. Water from the stream eventually fed the huge beds of fruit and vegetables at the far end of the garden.

Julia sat down on a stone bench beneath a tall Cyprus tree and relaxed, just enjoying the peace and tranquillity of her surroundings. Her servants were well trained and immediately a slave hurried towards her and handed her a cup of wine mixed with water and flavoured with honey.

Behind the slave came her steward, Borax. In his will, Sutoneus had freed the steward in return for his many years of loyal service, but Borax had chosen to continue to work for her. Dangling from the belt at Borax's waist was a heavy bunch of keys and in his hand was a wax tablet and stylus, so that he could make notes about any household problems which needed his attention.

'Mistress.' Borax smiled warmly.

'I trust the mullet Sabine purchased will make a good supper?'

When she was on her own Julia rarely ate her main meal, *cena*, at the usual time of three o'clock. She preferred to eat later in the cool of the evening.

'Musa always provides us with good fish,' he replied. 'Not surprising now that he has taken such a liking to Sabine.'

'I've told Sabine that I am happy for her to spend time with the young man if she so chooses,' Julia said thoughtfully as she sipped her wine. 'The baths, are they occupied today?'

'Maecenus has brought three special slaves to be prepared for his weekly auction tomorrow,' Borax replied.

The slave dealer had a reputation for finding most unusual goods that often commanded high prices at auction. A couple of months ago there had been two young and very beautiful identical twin sisters from Egypt. Also there had been a pretty blond Greek boy who had caused something of a sensation. He had barely reached puberty, yet he was supposedly trained in every conceivable sexual technique. A bidding war had erupted at the auction between three high-ranking citizens. The price eventually paid by Gaius Cuspius was one of the highest ever for a young male slave.

'Anything interesting today?' Julia asked curiously.

'I think you will be *very* interested.' Borax consulted his wax tablet. 'The slaves he's sent today are part of the batch shipped here by Governor Agricola. These three are all warriors who took part in the uprising in northern Brittania. Maecenus thinks he'll definitely be able to sell two, who are good fighters, for gladiatorial training.'

'And the third?'

'Maecenus says he's the best prize of all and would be wasted in the arena. His name is Taranis ... he's from Gaul. He was one of the leaders of the uprising. For some reason – I know not what – Governor Agricola chose not to have him sent to Rome with most of the other prisoners.' Borax paused and sighed. 'Although executing him would have been a waste. Even I was a little overcome when I first saw him, my lady. The slave-trader is right, he's quite the best specimen I've laid eyes on for a very long time. Taranis is tall, blond, very muscular and extremely good looking.'

'Perhaps I should see him for myself.' Julia put down her cup and stood up, her heart beating a little faster. Her friend, Poppaea, had suggested only yesterday that she should find herself a house slave she could take to her bed. Sutoneus had watched over her carefully, so she'd never had the opportunity to bed any other man but her ageing husband. Sex with Sutoneus had been a very unpleasant experience. Now, though, as a widow, she had a measure of sexual freedom and she felt more than ready to take full advantage of this. She knew that Borax rarely showed much interest in Maecenus's merchandise and she was eager to see this slave he found so attractive.

Feeling excited, while hoping she wouldn't be disappointed by what she was about to see, Julia accompanied Borax through the garden. The bath complex was some distance from her villa. It had an outside entrance that led on to a road at the rear of the property, so she suffered no loss of privacy. However, there was also a private entrance from her garden that was always kept locked when clients were using the establishment.

Julia loved the warm humidity of the baths and the all-pervading odour of the sweet-scented oils that were used. She was not short of money, as Sutoneus had left her well provided for, but renting out the baths had proven to be very economic. Even so, it wasn't cheap to keep them in good working order. She needed a large number of slaves to run the place and feed the huge underground furnace. It heated the water and the air which flowed through the underfloor spaces to warm the rooms above.

Borax used his key to open the heavy wooden door which led to the Venus Baths. They entered a narrow corridor, where they took off their shoes and put on wooden-soled sandals that protected their feet from the intense heat of the floor.

The moist warmth of the air made Julia feel a little light-headed as they reached a narrow arch which led into the tepidarium. She could hardly contain her excitement as Borax pulled aside the heavy curtain. If she were careful, she could spy on those inside without being seen. In order to keep the room temperature at a constant comfortable heat, it was necessary to have no windows in the bath complex. The large room with its mosaic-tiled walls and floor was lit by torches and oil lamps. There were a number of marble tables to accommodate clients as well as seats round the edge of the walls. On the furthest tables were two tall, well-built red-headed men. The bath slaves had already rubbed oil into their skins, now they were scraping off the dirt mixed with oil with a delicately fashioned instrument called a strigil.

'There,' whispered Borax.

All Julia's attention was immediately focused on the other man in the room. He was lying on his stomach so she couldn't see his face, but she hoped that it matched the rest of his body. He was tall and as well muscled as a gladiator, with smooth tanned skin. Unlike most soldiers, his hair wasn't cropped short, but was long, well past shoulder length, and an attractive golden blond. Her heart missed a beat. Borax was right, the slave was truly a magnificent creature.

The other two men had risen to their feet and a slave was leading them through a doorway into the caladarium. There they would soak in the hot bath for a while before moving back into the cooler rooms of the complex.

Taranis was left alone with the female slave who was massaging him. She was rubbing scented oil into his muscular back and taut buttocks. Julia recognised her, but she had so many slaves she couldn't recall her name. The girl was young and pretty and, like most female slaves in the bathhouse, naked apart from a thin linen skirt tied round her hips, which barely covered her sex.

Perspiration covered her skin, making it gleam in the flickering light, as small beads of moisture rolled down her small tits and flat belly.

As she rubbed the oil vigorously into Taranis's back, her small round breasts bounced up and down enticingly. Julia noticed that the girl's nipples were stiffly erect. So she too was aroused by the sight of the naked god, Julia thought, wishing that she could take the slave's place and be free to run her hands over his glorious body.

The girl whispered something in Taranis's ear and he immediately rolled on to his back and relaxed back on the marble slab. Julia caught her breath and clutched on to her steward's arm. 'By the gods,' she gasped. Not only was the blond slave very good-looking, but also his cock, even un-aroused, was an impressive sight.

'A gift indeed,' Borax growled softly. 'No wonder the governor of Brittania did not send him to Rome to be executed. It would be such a waste to destroy such physical beauty.'

Taranis was pleased to be rid of his facial hair, which had grown quite profusely during the long journey from Brittania. Also it was good to feel really clean again, especially after the days he'd spent in the dirt and squalor of the hold. He could not recall how many months it had been since he'd been able to savour the warmth and pleasure of the baths. He might despise the Romans, but he didn't despise the comforts they brought with them. Even though he now fought against them, he still retained many of the Roman ways and customs he had learnt in his youth.

He was the only son of a centurion, a man of Gaul who'd fought for the Empire for many years and earned his Roman citizenship. His father hadn't been rich but he was wealthy enough to employ tutors to educate Taranis as well as any young Roman nobleman. They had lived in Vesuna in southern Gaul and, when he wasn't studying, Taranis had spent his time exercising in the gymnasium, enjoying the pleasures of the baths, and drinking and whoring with his young Roman friends.

He had hoped to follow his father into the army where, as a Roman citizen, he would fight to defend the power of the Empire. However, his ideas had begun to change when, at the age of eighteen, he'd met Paul, a man who followed the teachings of the Galilean and preached the Christian faith. Taranis had always had the heart of a warrior and there were sides to this new religion he found hard to accept, so he couldn't bring himself to promise to serve this new god. However, a lot of what Paul preached made perfect sense, including the precept that in God's eyes all men were born equal. Taranis started to question various aspects of his Roman upbringing, especially where slavery was concerned.

Then one terrible day his plans for the future had fallen apart. It had all started when a slave belonging to a city magistrate murdered his master. The law decreed that not only must this slave be put to death, but also every one of the slaves in the magistrate's household: that was well over thirty innocent men, women and children. Angered and appalled by such cruelty, Taranis protested and ended up leading a crowd of irate citizens to the steps of the local forum to demand that the inhumane law be repealed. The governor of the province sent the local militia to deal with the uprising, and Taranis, along with many others, had been arrested and charged with sedition.

With Paul's help, Taranis had escaped from prison but had then been forced to flee his homeland. In order to survive, he'd become a mercenary, fighting on the side of those that opposed Rome. His upbringing and his excellent knowledge of Roman soldiery and strategy had made Taranis a huge asset to those he chose to serve.

Taranis gave a soft sigh of pleasure as his thoughts were drawn back from the past and fully into the present again. The girl was better at her job than most bath slaves he'd known. She was small and slight but her fingers were surprisingly strong, reaching deep into his tense muscles, working away at the knots in his shoulders, back and buttocks.

When she asked him, in a soft shy voice, to turn over, he rolled on to his back and watched her as she carefully poured more of the delicately scented oil on to his chest. She leant forwards, giving him a coy smile as, whether deliberately or not, her small breasts brushed teasingly against his upper right arm. The touch of her naked tits excited him. Taranis fought to contain his sudden arousal as she began to massage each arm in turn. He made a conscious effort to relax, trying to ignore the sexual need she had awakened, as she worked on the well-honed muscles of his chest.

Taking up the small glass container, she slowly dribbled the perfumed oil across his flat belly, then down each muscular thigh. He tensed expectantly as her soothing fingers slid sensuously across his skin. First, she concentrated on his legs, digging hard into the firm muscles of his thigh. As she stroked and massaged his tanned flesh, her fingers began to slide upwards, getting teasingly closer to, but never quite reaching, his groin.

Despite himself and all his concerns for Sirona, Taranis still felt the sexual desire grow stronger, creeping insidiously through his entire body. Controlling his lustful thoughts as much as he could, Taranis closed his eyes and tried to focus his mind solely on his beloved Sirona. Where was she now? What had happened to her, he wondered worriedly.

The Romans probably considered that a barbarian princess was a prize of some worth. He thought it unlikely that they would consider killing her; if they had planned to do that, she would have been sent to Rome with her father. Probably she was destined to be the slave of some rich, very influential citizen. However, that thought didn't settle his concerns, on the contrary it magnified them. She might be kept alive but she was doubtless destined to suffer. In his youth, Taranis had seen for himself how most rich citizens treated their slaves. Sirona was stunningly beautiful and he dreaded the sexual indignities she might be forced to suffer. He could only pray that her new master would be kind to her, perhaps then she might come to care for him and be able to accept the fate the gods had decreed for her, at least for the time being. Whatever, he was still determined to find a way to escape and somehow rescue his beloved Sirona.

Once again, the slave girl's fingers drifted towards his groin, just brushing his pubes. In the past, such intimacies had been an inherent part of the bathhouse experience, although he was a little surprised that the slave girl was being so forward with him today. After all, he wasn't a regular paying customer, he was only a slave being prepared for sale on the auction block. However, he did not have the will to protest as he lay there enjoying the gentle sexual stimulation.

She began to stroke his flat stomach, her movements becoming bolder as her fingers threaded their way through the golden hair at his groin and pressed sensuously on the sensitive triangle of flesh just above his

39

penis. Her warm breath brushed his belly, as she leant closer, her fingers gently stroking and caressing the root of his cock.

His arousal increasing, he opened his eyes and stared at her. The slave girl was attractive, there was no doubt about that, with her slim figure, large dark eyes and full mouth. Perspiration beaded her smooth olive skin, rolling down her neck on to her pert breasts where it lay twinkling like precious stones in the lamplight. Her tits were a little small for his taste and would not sit comfortably in his hands like Sirona's full breasts did, but they were firm and quite pleasing to the eye. Her small brown nipples were stiffly erect and, judging by her expression, she was becoming excited just by massaging him.

The girl gnawed nervously at her full bottom lip as she looked enquiringly at him, her fingers just brushing the root of his penis again. Taranis gave a soft groan. '*Certe*,' he murmured, nodding his head as his cock stirred in unconscious response.

He laid his head back on to the piece of folded linen that served as a pillow, as her soft fingers encircled his cock. He felt the warm tingling sensation of growing arousal as the girl ran her fingers up and down his shaft. The moist perfumed air, the warmth of the tepidarium and the feel of the girl's fingers were so comforting, so very familiar. The pleasure grew as she began to wank him expertly, making the blood flow even more vigorously through his veins.

Taranis heard her gasp of surprise as his cock grew harder. He knew that the gods had blessed him, and compared to most men he was very well endowed. Women liked big cocks, it was as simple as that, and he'd never had any problem attracting them so he had rarely resorted to visiting brothels. The women seemed to like not only his cock but also his muscular body and his looks, so in the past he'd become a little full of himself and made a point of seducing as many as he could. That had all stopped when he'd met and fallen desperately in love with Sirona. Even so, at present he had no problem in separating these sort of sexual pleasures from his love for Sirona, especially as the slaves who worked in bathhouses were often almost as skilled at pleasuring a man as whores were.

Her grip tightened, her oiled fingers sliding smoothly up and down his shaft. Taranis gave a soft groan as her other hand moved to touch his balls, gently kneading the scrotal sac. Then he felt a warm wet tongue lapping at his cock-head, rimming the large glans. She pulled the head into her mouth, sucking on it gently.

She must have released her long dark hair, which had been tied back with a strip of leather, because he felt it brush teasingly against his belly and legs, as she continued to expertly fellate him with her mouth. The warm wetness engulfed his sex and for a moment Taranis was tempted to reach out and touch her also, but this wasn't Sirona so he clenched his fists and kept his arms stiffly at his sides. Yet he was still achingly aware of the soft, seductive body of the young half-naked slave. Her slick belly was pressed against the side of his thigh. He could smell the musky odour clinging to her skin, hear the muffled noise of her breathing and the soft sucking sounds she was making as she did her best to swallow as much of his cock as she could. Her mouth was working hard, expertly fucking him; the pressure of her lips increasing and decreasing as she slid them up and down his shaft. Still, all the time, her fingers played teasingly with his balls.

Suddenly, a small hand crept across his chest to tug at one of his nipples, squeezing and pulling at the pap, while the pressure she was applying to his shaft increased. Taranis's heart pounded out of control, all his senses now focused on his impending release. He was panting, the heat and humidity in the room seeming to increase with every breath he took. She was employing every tantalising technique, her tongue flicking up and down his shaft and over the sensitive head, her mouth making every effort to suck him dry. All the while, her fingers worked on his nipples and squeezed and caressed his balls.

He conjured up a vision of Sirona in his mind, managing to convince himself that it was her glorious copper-coloured hair brushing his belly, her lips working their magic on his senses. As he did so, his pleasure peaked. There was a loud roaring sound in his ears as he spurted his seed into the slave girl's willing mouth.

Drained by the strength of his orgasm, it took him a few brief moments to catch his breath and regain full control of his senses. He opened his eyes to see the slave girl smiling provocatively at him as she rubbed one hand over her small breasts. She plucked at one firm brown nipple while lifting her linen skirt to expose her sex to his gaze. The message was clear: she wanted him. In times gone by, Taranis might have accepted the invitation and taken the girl into a private cubicle to pleasure her just as she'd pleasured him, but he had no desire to do so today.

Taranis sat up, studiously ignoring her entreating looks. He pointed to a damp cloth that she'd left on one of the low seats surrounding the edges of the room. Doing her best to hide her disappointment, she picked it up and handed it to him, waiting while he cleansed himself. Rising to his feet, he grabbed a clean linen towel from a nearby pile.

As he wrapped it around his waist, to his far left, in

the flickering lamplight, he caught sight of a short, quite pretty woman peering round a curtain which appeared to cover a narrow alcove. He noticed that her cheeks were very flushed from the warmth and her light-brown hair was a little dishevelled. She certainly wasn't dressed for the baths, and when she realised he'd spotted her she tensed nervously and then suddenly disappeared behind the curtain. He was confused. It was not usual to have opposite sexes using the baths at the same time. Also, judging by her elaborate hairstyle and fine garments, she was a lady of quality.

His curiosity aroused by her unexpected presence and the fact that she might have been watching what had just happened between him and the slave girl, he strode forwards and pulled aside the curtain. He was just in time to see the woman, accompanied by a tall man, disappear through a heavy wooden door at the end of the narrow corridor.

Sirona, now wearing a clean tunic, was led from the building by two burly slaves. Judging by the position of the sun, it was late afternoon, yet it was still very hot. The senator had totally ignored her both during and after watching Tiro bring himself to a swift climax. However, when Aulus had left the room, she had heard him issuing orders to have her taken to his house.

She could only presume that they were taking her there now, as she was bundled unceremoniously into a litter. The thick side curtains were fastened tightly down, before she even had a chance to look towards the harbour and see if the *Cronus* was still there. She wondered what had happened to Taranis, as she sat in the stifling, swaying darkness.

It seemed like ages before they stopped, and the curtains were pulled back. She saw that they were in a narrow paved street, lined by buildings on both sides. One of the slaves immediately took hold of her arm, pulled her out of the litter and through a plain-looking doorway into the senator's house. The inside was luxurious. She caught brief glimpses of elaborate furniture and magnificent wall paintings as she was led to the rear of the building and into the small private bathhouse. There she was stripped by two surly-faced female slaves, her skin was oiled and then scraped until it stung and glowed bright pink. Her hair was vigorously washed a number of times with a strong-smelling substance, presumably to rid it of any lice. Then it was piled on top of her head while she was immersed in a pool of near-scalding water.

She was relieved that they had made no attempt to remove the body hair that the senator had found so repulsive. Surely, if he had wanted any sort of sexual relationship with her, he would most likely have ordered it removed. That reassuring thought and the heat of the water gradually made her relax and she began to feel a little better, hoping that they had almost finished with her and she would soon perhaps have a chance to rest, as she felt emotionally if not physically exhausted. Yet it appeared that there was to be no respite for her yet, as she was urged from the bath and handed over to a menacing-looking very muscular woman. She made Sirona lie down on a marble slab that had been covered with linen towels. The woman then massaged her vigorously with sweet-scented oils until her skin was as smooth as it could be and her muscles felt as though they could take no more abuse.

Feeling remarkably clean, Sirona was taken to a smaller less well-decorated part of the large house which she presumed must be the slaves' quarters. By now, not only was she hungry, but also desperately thirsty. After her confrontation with the senator, she felt she had to continue in her subterfuge of not being able to speak Latin, so she was forced to resort to pointing to her mouth and simulating swallowing, hoping they would understand that she wanted a drink. Much to her relief, a few moments later, a mug of water flavoured with lemon and honey was thrust into her hand and she was given a couple of minutes to gulp it down.

Then one of the slave girls began to scrape any remaining dirt from under her fingernails, before manicuring and buffing them until they shone. Another girl started on her hair, working on the tangles and knots that had formed in her long locks since she'd become a prisoner of the Romans many weeks earlier. Sirona could not repress a few squeals of pain as they pulled roughly at her scalp. Eventually, every single knot and tangle was removed and her hair hung down her back in shimmering copper waves.

She had no idea why they were taking such care over a new house slave. Once again, she began to fear that the senator might have ordered all this because he still intended to bed her. She sat there mutely, trying not to think about him, let alone imagine what sex with him might be like, as she listened to the women's chatter. They made no attempt to be friendly or communicate with her in any way and she began to feel even more fearful and totally alone in this alien land.

They dressed her in a long tunic of fine green linen that was almost the same colour as her eyes, and a plain white girdle was knotted around her narrow waist. Not more, Sirona thought wearily, as one of the women picked up a wooden cosmetic box. She was just about to outline Sirona's eyes with black antimony when Tiro entered the room.

The servants immediately ceased their near-constant

chatter and turned to look at him. 'No, no make-up,' he said firmly. 'It is not necessary. Stand up, Sirona, let me see you,' he continued in her language.

She stood up and slowly turned to face him.

'An improvement beyond belief,' he said. Tiro smiled at the women who had been attending Sirona. 'Well done,' he added, switching again to Latin. 'Now, you may leave and get on with your other duties.' He waved his hand dismissively.

They all did as they were told in a quiet but cheerful manner, as if they liked and respected him. So Tiro was a man of some influence in this household, Sirona thought, although she was unable to forget her previous sight of him meekly pleasuring his master.

'It is good to feel clean,' she said, relieved to be able to communicate with someone. 'You may consider me a barbarian, but despite what you think of us we don't enjoy wallowing in filth and squalor.' She paused, then added, 'However, I must admit I do not understand why they took such care over my appearance.'

'The master considers neatness and cleanliness a necessity for all members of his household,' Tiro replied, as if the care they'd taken of her was nothing out of the ordinary. 'Now, come with me and I will show you around the house and acquaint you with your duties. Usually, that task would have fallen to one of your fellow slaves. However, I have decided to honour you with my attention because you appear not to understand Latin. I'm not a fool, Sirona. You are of noble birth so I am certain that you must know at least a smattering of our language, despite your mute behaviour earlier this afternoon. Heed my advice. It would not be wise to display such obvious reluctance and disobedience in future.' He smiled wryly. 'I suspect your actions stemmed more from a desire to resist than a lack of understanding. Now you have to concentrate on your survival. I'm certain you will soon become proficient enough in Latin to enable you to follow orders quickly and obediently.'

'With your help, I am sure I will,' she conceded sweetly, deciding it would not be wise to make an enemy of Tiro.

3

Taranis paced his small cell, ignoring his companions Leod and Olin. They were slumped on a straw-stuffed mattress in the corner, snoring softly, with their bellies full for the first time in many weeks.

The barred door of the cell faced the large peristyle, which was lit by flickering torches. When they were led into the building, Taranis had caught sight of a notice advertising a slave auction the following morning. They were preparing for it now, as servants laid out lines of chairs and benches. The chairs at the front were for the wealthiest and most respected citizens. The less influential would be seated on the benches, while the rest would be standing crowded together behind them.

Taranis was no stranger to slave auctions, and had attended some with his father. His family owned slaves just like everyone else and, when they died or became too old to work, they had to be replaced. As he grew older, he had gone to the auctions with his friends, not always to buy slaves but sometimes out of curiosity, most notably when it was advertised that they were selling prime pieces of female merchandise, as often such women were displayed totally naked. At the time, he had not even bothered to consider how the slaves might be feeling, let alone imagine that he might be forced one day to endure a similar indignity.

Compared to some of the establishments he had seen, conditions here were not too bad. The cells were clean, they had adequate bedding and they had been well fed.

Nevertheless, Taranis was filled with apprehension, fearing what would happen the following day – death on the battlefield would be far preferable to the humiliation of being sold on the block.

Suddenly, he heard imperious Roman voices speaking, as they usually did, far too loudly. He stepped back in the shadows as a number of well-dressed citizens were led past his cell. Soon more guests arrived, laughing and joking, as they were escorted across the peristyle. A small niggling concern formed in his mind. Was it possible that there was to be a pre-auction viewing? He recalled the many rumours that he had heard about them, as he tried to convince himself that neither he nor his companions would merit such an event.

Leod awoke, disturbed by the shrill giggles coming from a couple of women as they walked past the cell. 'What's happening?' he asked, stretching his arms and yawning.

'Looks like there is some kind of party going on,' Taranis replied casually. His two red-headed companions were simple men – warriors who had been raised far from Roman domination. They knew little of their captors' ways. Taranis had no wish to increase their concerns; after all, he might be wrong about tonight. It was possible that the slave trader was just having a private party. 'Go back to sleep, you need your rest.'

More guests strolled past the cell. Judging by their pure-white togas and fine jewellery, they were all wealthy. The majority were male but there were a few women as well, rich Roman matrons wearing fancy dresses, with their hair elaborately dressed. One man wore a senatorial toga; it was unusual to find such an important man so far from Rome.

Eventually, it appeared that the last guests had

arrived and for a time there was silence. The peristyle was left in near total darkness and Taranis began to wonder if his uneasy presumptions were wrong as he stood there listening to the soothing sounds of the crickets, interspersed now and then with one of Olin's loud snores. He stiffened as he caught sight of a number of flickering torches across the other side of the peristyle. The lights moved closer as the small group of guards advanced towards the cell.

The cell door made an ugly grating sound as it was pulled open and a gruff voice said, 'The prisoners are to step forwards – the man from Gaul last.'

'What?' Leod mumbled, as he and his bleary-eyed companion sat up. They both understood only a little very basic Latin.

'We are to stand up and move outside,' Taranis explained. 'One at a time. You go first, Leod.'

He stood back to let Leod leave first, then watched as the slave accompanying the guards took a pair of ankle irons, joined together by a short length of chain, from the basket he had placed on the ground beside him. The slave knelt and fastened them securely around Leod's ankles. Then another pair of irons were used to fasten Leod's hands together.

Olin stepped forwards nervously. As he was being shackled in a similar manner, Leod glanced question-ingly back at Taranis, who was still standing inside the cell. He had no intention of even trying to explain that they were most likely to be displayed at a pre-auction viewing, where they would be prodded, poked and per-haps intimately examined by any number of the wealthy guests. Swallowing uneasily, Taranis forced himself to smile reassuringly at his two friends.

Then it was his turn to leave the relative security of his cell. Taranis was immediately chained as well, but unlike his companions his arms were not fastened in front of him but securely behind his back. 'Let's go,' the man said gruffly, as he roughly grabbed hold of Taranis's shoulder.

It proved difficult to walk in anything but a slow ungainly shuffle as they were led through the peristyle, then through another smaller courtyard and into a large brightly illuminated chamber. Taranis blinked as his eyes adjusted to the light. The walls of the room were covered in brilliantly coloured paintings and the air was heavy with a sweet cornucopia of rich perfumes. A small group of musicians was playing an unfamiliar tune, which had a strangely compelling beat. The guests reclined on couches set around three sides of the room, watching two naked, large-breasted women performing an erotic dance in time to the music. Scantily clad male and female slaves stood by each couch ready to serve the visitors food and drink.

They were led to a spot just behind the dancers, close to the only empty wall in the room. This area was even more brightly illuminated and the heat from the lamps and torches made Taranis break out in a slight sweat.

'What's happening?' Olin asked anxiously, as they were lined up.

Taranis was positioned between his two companions and one of the soldiers knelt to securely fasten their ankle chains to iron rings set in the mosaic-tiled floor.

'Be strong, it will be over soon,' Taranis whispered reassuringly, as the dancers moved out of sight and the music ceased.

All eyes were on the three men as the slave trader, Maecenas, walked towards them. He was a portly man with a large belly. His heavy features, scar-pitted skin and bulbous nose most likely made him repellent to women. Taranis knew that wouldn't matter to him, as he must have many slaves who would be forced to pleasure him in every way he wanted. Judging by his ostentatious garments and heavy gold jewellery, he was as rich as Croesus himself. His long dark hair was oiled and hung in ringlets round his thick neck, and Taranis thought that he had never laid eyes on a more unattractive creature.

'The tunic,' Maecenus snapped.

A slave stepped behind the three men and unfastened the shoulder ties of Leod's short blue tunic.

'No,' Leod protested, as the tunic fell at his feet, leaving him clad in only a brief white linen loincloth.

'Steady,' Taranis hissed. 'Don't move, Leod. Trust me, it will be even worse if you fight them. Hold your head high and ignore them all. It will be over soon enough,' he added reassuringly.

Well used to obeying his commander, Leod stiffened and stared straight ahead. The slave then removed Olin's garment, and he too stood to attention and stared straight ahead. The two men had strong muscular physiques, but their skin looked extraordinarily pale in the bright light. Romans often exercised in the nude but the Celts rarely uncovered their flesh. Both Leod and Olin had uncommonly pale, heavily freckled skin, which contrasted even more strongly with their red hair. In Brittania, like most of the Celts, they had both sported heavy beards and long moustaches but despite their protests all their facial hair had been removed earlier in the day in the bathhouse.

Maecenus began to point out the various virtues of the two warriors he was selling, making much of their many fighting skills. Leod and Olin didn't really understand all he said, so they both looked questioningly at Taranis, as Maecenus politely invited his guests to examine the two slaves more closely.

'They want to see what they are buying – most likely you'll end up in the arena,' Taranis said, as that was the only positive thing he could think of which might help to reassure them a little. Life or even death as a gladiator would be a far better fate for a warrior than being sold as a lowly slave.

Taranis felt proud of his companions as they stood there, not moving a muscle, never betraying their disgust or embarrassment as a number of the male guests crowded forwards to examine them both.

It was clear from the conversation that his assumptions were correct and both Britons were most probably destined for the arena. Taranis hoped that he too might be sold for gladiatorial training. He'd been well schooled in all methods of combat, and could best most men with either sword or spear. Gladiators, if they survived, could often earn enough wealth to eventually purchase their freedom. Some had become so loved and respected that they'd been welcomed into the upper strata of society. The majority of gladiators were slaves, or prisoners of war but it was not that uncommon for poorer citizens, drawn by the promise of untold wealth, to sell themselves to a gladiatorial school in order to help their families survive.

Fortunately for Leod and Olin, none of those present overstepped the bounds and examined them in an embarrassingly intimate manner. In fact, they all appeared more interested in gauging the strength of their muscles and their stamina, as they tried to estimate how well the Britons might fare in the arena.

Eventually, Maecenus stepped forwards. 'Honoured guests, if you have all finished?' he said with an oily grin.

They nodded and smiled, then began to move away, chatting among themselves as they returned to their seats. Maecenus, meanwhile, beckoned forwards a couple of the guards who had been waiting by the doorway. They strode forwards, released Leod and Olin from the rings set in the floor, thrust their discarded tunics in their chained hands, and then escorted the young men from the room.

Taranis didn't like being left to face these people without his companions, but at least Leod and Olin wouldn't be here to witness whatever humiliation was in store for him. It was strange, he thought, he had been born and raised a Roman yet he felt not even the faintest affinity with any of the people in this room. Even before his capture, he had resided in a different world completely. Often he prayed now to the gods of his barbarian ancestors, fearing that Jupiter and the other Roman gods had deserted him.

Maecenus waited until the guests had been served more refreshments, then he turned to stare coldly at Taranis. 'They tell me that you were once a Roman citizen. That you turned against your people and betrayed your heritage,' he hissed. 'Now you will receive your just desserts for such treachery,' he added with immense satisfaction. 'The tunic, Nubius.'

Taranis felt the slave's hands brush his shoulders as they unfastened the ties of his tunic, and the fabric fell in a pool at his feet. He had been dreading this moment because the loincloth they'd made him wear was much briefer than those given to Leod and Olin.

A thin strip of fabric encircled his lean waist. Attached to that was an even thinner strip which threaded tightly between the crack of his buttock cheeks. The front piece was very small and just cupped his cock and balls, barely serving to cover them at all. Taranis had no idea how appealing he looked standing there almost naked and in chains. He was as handsome as a Greek god with his chiselled features and long golden hair. His skin, still lightly tanned, was covered with a thin film of perspiration, making it gleam in the flickering light.

Maecenus started talking, pointing out the physical perfection of the merchandise and the strength and ability of this powerful warrior who had been raised as a Roman but who had turned against his own and betrayed his heritage. Once he had finished his short sales pitch, he invited a number of the guests to examine the slave, pointedly listing them by name. Presumably, they were the wealthiest and most influential citizens who might be persuaded to make the highest bids at the auction tomorrow morning.

Taranis saw a number of the guests stand up. There were a couple of women among them and also the senator. He was certain that he would rather face an entire Roman army in battle than he would these people walking towards him.

Sweat beaded his brow, rolling into his eyes, and he blinked uncomfortably, not even able to wipe it from his face. Standing here, chained to the floor, he could barely move and was unable to do anything to protect himself from what was to come. He had never felt so helpless, as the small group of people surrounded him. Their hands touched his arms, legs, chest and back, and he wanted to close his eyes and block everything out but he didn't, as that would appear cowardly. So he stared straight ahead, trying not to move or flinch, as they poked and prodded him again and again.

The guests all wore strongly scented oils and perfumes. As they crowded around him, the sweet odours started to make his head spin. He didn't mind so much when the women touched him, as their hands were gentle and somehow it didn't feel quite so demeaning.

What would it be like to be sold to a woman of standing? Judging by the expression on their faces, these Roman matrons had only one thing in mind for him. None of them was unattractive and he tried to convince himself that it wouldn't be so bad to become a rich woman's plaything and spend his nights in her bed attending to her sexual needs.

These thoughts were still filling his mind when he felt soft, pudgy fingers stroking his chest. 'He is so handsome,' said a lisping male voice, as the fat fingers rubbed and squeezed his nipples. Taranis fought to repress his automatic shudder of disgust as the short, pot-bellied Roman pressed his body closer. 'So enchanting,' he cooed softly. 'With that arse what man wouldn't want him?'

'Have you tired of your pretty young Greek boy already, Gaius?' The senator, a tall man with grey hair, spoke.

'No, of course not,' Gaius said petulantly. 'But this one is so different – so masculine.' He continued to paw Taranis, his hands moving down to stroke his flat stomach.

'Masculine?' the senator repeated. 'By any chance, are you considering offering *your* arse to him instead of the other way around?' he continued with a scornful smile.

Taranis could feel other hands touching his buttocks but they didn't concern him so much, as he knew that they belonged to a woman. He could feel her full breasts pressed against his back and the soft fabric of her silk gown brushing his legs.

'You are being unfair, Aulus. Even you enjoy fucking young men on occasions,' Gaius snapped. In contrast to his irritation, his touch was very gentle as he stroked the bulge of Taranis's sex.

'Maybe so,' the senator said in a low voice. 'But to

freely admit that you desire to offer your arse to a slave –'

'I never said that,' Gaius protested. 'I'm not turning into a cinaedi! You presume too much.' The cinaedi were Roman men who enjoyed being the passive member of a homoerotic act. To publicly infer that an influential citizen would desire this was considered demeaning, even though such acts went on often enough behind closed doors.

'Perhaps I do,' the senator agreed, watching Gaius continue to paw Taranis. 'Forgive my presumptions, my friend,' he added with a wry smile.

The loathsome slug's hands began to slide under the scrap of fabric covering his male organs and Taranis swallowed his automatic groan of disgust.

'Please.' Maecenus placed a hand on the man's arm. 'I would ask you to desist.'

'You are spoiling Gaius Cuspius's pleasure, Maecenus,' the senator pointed out, sounding more amused than angered. 'He has been looking forward to this all evening.'

'I have no such intention,' Maecenus replied hurriedly. 'You will discover why a little later, my most honoured and esteemed guests. If I could ask you all to return to your seats,' he added, looking pointedly at the woman who was still standing behind Taranis, fondling his buttocks. 'I have a small surprise that I'm sure you will all enjoy.'

'Come, Poppaea, let me escort you back to your couch,' Aulus said to her, gallantly holding out his arm.

'Of course, Aulus,' the woman agreed in a low husky voice, as she smiled and stepped towards the senator.

'He's not usually so protective of his merchandise,' Gaius complained loudly as he reluctantly accompanied the other guests back to their couches.

Taranis watched them, hoping that his humiliation was at an end, although he didn't believe it was. He tried to recall what it was like to recline on a couch dressed in a toga being attended by slaves, eating, drinking and laughing, perhaps discussing politics or the state of the Empire, but he couldn't. That former life seemed only part of a half-remembered dream.

Maecenus clapped his hands, then sat down on the chair one of the slaves had brought him. The musicians began playing an eastern tune with a hypnotic beat and a dancer glided on to the floor. She was slightly built but with unusually large, firm breasts for such a slim figure. Her skin was the colour of amber and she had long straight, black hair, which brushed her buttocks as she swayed in time to the music.

Her nipples were painted gold and she was totally naked apart from a narrow, flat-linked gold chain around her hips. As she glided closer to Taranis, he saw that another chain was attached to it. The chain was barely visible, hidden between the cleft of her buttocks, threaded between her naked pussy lips, only reappearing where it dissected the mound of her denuded sex.

She moved closer to him, swaying her hips and making strange voluptuous movements of her belly in time to the slow evocative rhythm of the music. She was pretty, very pretty, and so close to him now that he could see the delicate beads of perspiration on her dusky flesh.

She appeared to be dancing just for him and not the guests. He couldn't help remembering the Roman parties he had attended, where slaves had been forced to put on erotic sexual displays to entertain their guests. Was he expected to play a central part in a similar lewd indignity?

The dancer began to touch him, brushing her fingers

sensually over his naked flesh, and, despite his nervous trepidation, his body responded and he started to become aroused. Still moving in time to the music, she sank to her knees. Leaning back, she opened her thighs wide, so that he had a near-perfect view of her naked pussy. Between her sex lips, he could see the gold chain digging into her moist rosy flesh. The gold links pressed against her clitoris and every time she moved they rubbed erotically against the entrance to her tight little cunt.

She rose gracefully to her feet and pressed herself close to him again, rubbing her gold-painted nipples against his lower chest. 'You want me, don't you?' she said huskily, as she reached round him to squeeze his buttock cheek. 'My master was told by the bathhouse slave that the generous size of your cock would please him, especially when it was fully aroused,' she added, as she unfastened his scanty loincloth and pulled it off. 'I want to see it, as do his honoured guests.'

As she stepped away from him, she dropped the small piece of fabric on the floor, leaving him naked and exposed. Filled with impotent fury, he glared at Maecenus as he pulled uselessly at his chains.

The girl wasn't finished with him yet, however. She moved closer again and ground her pelvis against his body and he felt a strange mixture of despair and excitement well up inside him. Still swaying in time to the music, she slid to her knees and gently took hold of his cock. Sensuously, she licked the tip, then slid her lips over the domed head. The warm wetness of her mouth increased the fire in his veins and he felt the organ start to stiffen.

Despite his fears and his shame, his body still automatically responded to the pleasurable sensations of the girl's soft lips and he felt his cock grow harder. He became even more aroused as she pulled his shaft deeper into her mouth and gently caressed his balls. He couldn't move, couldn't pull away, all he could do was stand there and submit to this lecherous indignity.

'No,' he groaned as her tongue flicked over the taut skin of his cock-head.

At first he was so bound up in all this that he didn't realise what else was happening, not until he felt other soft hands caressing his body. Maecenus had ordered the other two dancers to join their companion. The women rubbed their huge breasts against his naked flesh, their hands stroking every part of him. Surely no man, not even the great Jupiter himself, could withstand this, he thought, as he felt them squeeze and caress his balls. Slim fingers slid between his buttock cheeks and gently circled his anus. The women's hands seemed to be touching every inch of his flesh, invading every nook and cranny of his body. Yet still he fought his arousal, willing himself not to respond. But the battle was useless, as his sexual excitement grew stronger and stronger.

Lust overwhelmed him, and he knew without a doubt that he was agonisingly close to coming. He felt his belly contract and his balls begin to tighten as the dark pleasure overcame his will to resist. Suddenly, to his surprise, all three women stepped away from him and knelt submissively in front of Maecenus.

The blood sang in his ears, his body screamed out for fulfilment and at first he wasn't really totally aware why this was happening, as Maecenus dismissed the women, then stood up and stepped over to him. 'Magnificent, is it not?' Maecenus pointed at Taranis's erection. 'Almost as large as the god, Priapus, himself,' he added with leering pride. 'Lords and ladies, who wouldn't want to own this pleasure giver? Is it not worth any price?'

How vulnerable and exposed he was now with his erect cock standing stiffly out from his groin. Maecenus touched the rampant organ, tapping it gently so that it swayed and caught the light, gleaming with the remains of saliva from the dancer's mouth. Taranis had never been forced to face such abject humiliation as this. He willed his erection to subside but for some bizarre reason his degradation served to make it remain frustratingly erect.

'Come, Senator, come, Aedile,' Maecenus invited, looking towards the couches where Aulus Vettius and Gaius Cuspius were reclining. 'You wished to examine the merchandise more closely and this is your opportunity.' He gave a lascivious chuckle as he glanced back at Taranis, whose cheeks had turned scarlet with embarrassment.

Gaius, with a slave's help, struggled to his feet and waddled forwards, red faced and sweating profusely. 'By the gods,' he said breathlessly as he reached Taranis. 'My cock is almost as hard as the slave's.'

'But not half as generously sized,' Aulus rejoined as he followed him. 'Gaius got so excited he almost came on his couch.' He winked slyly at Maecenus. 'You old goat, you certainly know how to display your merchandise to the best effect. I wager that they'll be fighting to bid for this one at the auction tomorrow.'

'Indeed, I hope they will,' the slave trader replied, stepping aside to allow the two men to get closer to Taranis.

'Come, Gaius, you can do what you like to him now – touch his cock, examine his nether mouth – the choice is yours, is it not,' Aulus said derisively. Yet there was a strange look of cold lust in his eyes that decried his contempt.

Hold fast, Taranis told himself, the two warriors you

admire above all else, Achilles and Alexander, both welcomed men as well as women into their beds. However, that didn't serve to reassure him at all, because he had never ever felt even the slightest desire for another man, let along a fat slug like Gaius Cuspius.

He did his best to remain steadfast but he still gave a slight, almost imperceptible shudder as Gaius's damp pudgy hand took hold of his cock. His erection had started to diminish a fraction, so Gaius began to pump the organ enthusiastically. Up to this moment, Taranis had thought he'd reached his lowest level of degradation, now he knew that was not so. He clenched his jaw and stared straight ahead, focusing his eyes on nothing, trying to pretend that it was Sirona's hands on him not this loathsome slug's.

The trouble was that only made his cock stiffen fully again, and he heard Gaius's soft sigh of bliss. 'You and I could be so good together. You've no need to fear me, barbarian. I would treat you kindly if you pleased me, very well.' The pumping turned into a slow sensual caress as he whispered softly, 'Your cock looks so delicious I could take it in my mouth right now.'

Taranis was appalled. His erection should have sunk like a stone but, to his eternal damnation, it didn't. He was even more terrified because he'd begun to find a dark unexplainable pleasure in being abused by this man.

'You would have to be very careful if you ever decided to let this man fuck you, Gaius. You are unaccustomed to such strange pleasures, because in the past it is you who has always done the fucking,' Aulus said. 'Judging by the massive size of this slave's cock, he'd probably split you in two at the first attempt,' he mocked, his cold grey eyes focused on the erect member.

'It is far safer for you to consider fucking him, at least for the time being,' he continued, casually fondling Taranis's buttocks.

'He is very large,' Gaius agreed, this time not appearing to take offence at the senator's deliberately derogatory comments. 'That bitch in eternal heat, Poppaea, would love to buy him. She's had so many lovers, her cunt must be as big as the Aqua Augusta by now. But I've no intention of letting her get her greedy hands on this prize.'

'Poppaea can afford to outbid you if she wishes,' Aulus pointed out. 'Unless you intend to bankrupt yourself, of course.'

'You are rich enough to outbid both of us,' Gaius retorted jealously, as he continued to stroke Taranis's cock.

'If by some chance I decided to purchase this slave, would you expect me to allow *you* to have use of him as well?' Aulus raised one eyebrow questioningly. His hand slid in the crack of Taranis's buttocks and stroked the entrance to his anus. 'You expect much from me, old friend.'

'I expect nothing you are not prepared to give,' Gaius protested.

'Maybe so.' Aulus seemed unconcerned. 'However, I wager this slave would much prefer to service a woman. These barbarians from Gaul have plebeian tastes.'

'Don't forget that he was born and bred a Roman,' Gaius muttered. 'He might prefer female flesh at first, but over time I can persuade him to think very differently.'

'What manner of persuasion were you thinking of?' Aulus asked, surreptitiously easing his finger into the tight brown ring of Taranis's anus.

Taranis clenched his teeth, trying not to move or

betray any emotion at all. This intimate intrusion into his body was a totally unfamiliar occurrence and he had never experienced a sensation quite like it before.

'Kind or cruel, whatever proves necessary,' Gaius continued, unaware of what Aulus was doing to Taranis. 'He'd soon learn to enjoy the pleasure I have in store for him. After all, one hole is much like another – both gratifying in their different ways.'

'Would you think that, slave?' Aulus whispered huskily in Taranis's ear, pushing the finger even deeper for a moment. Taranis tensed, certain his cock had grown even harder still because the sensation was so strangely intense. Then, to his relief, Aulus removed the offending digit and stepped towards Gaius. 'I think that is enough for now.' He gently eased his friend's hand from Taranis's cock, then smiled broadly at Gaius. 'On reflection, perhaps I should bid for him. He is a little too mature for my taste, but I might well enjoy chaining him down and fucking him. Once I've had my fill, and tamed him adequately, I would be more than happy to pass him over to you for a time, old friend.'

'Knowing how cold and cruel you can be, Aulus, even to those of your own blood,' Gaius said, lust still distending his pudgy features, as he watched Aulus take hold of the captive's engorged shaft, 'I'm certain that you could tame him with consummate ease.'

'Precisely!' Aulus said, his fingers feeling as cold as ice to Taranis. 'I demonstrate.' Aulus pinched the end of the organ between his thumb and forefinger in such a way that it made the unwanted erection immediately begin to subside. He looked challengingly at Taranis for a brief moment then turned to address Maecenus. 'I think we've all seen enough, don't you?'

'If you say so, Senator,' the slave trader immediately

agreed in a very obsequious manner, as if Aulus Vettius was not to be upset at any cost.

Julia was feeling flustered and rather nervous by the time she and Borax arrived at the auction house the following morning.

'We are quite safe, my lady,' Borax assured her, knowing that she was concerned because this area had a rather shady reputation. 'Half the nobility of Pompeii is here it seems,' he said, glancing at the litters and chariots parked at the front of the establishment. 'This auction has prompted a lot of interest,' he continued, as he led her inside the building. 'It appears that everyone is curious to see the barbarian warriors from Brittania and their leader.'

Maecenus had arranged to auction off all the inferior merchandise first, and saved the best for last, hoping that the richer attendees would perhaps be tempted to bid for the cheaper slaves as well. However, his plan had backfired a little. The auction was almost complete and most of the wealthier and most important citizens had only recently arrived. Even so, all the chairs at the front were occupied and there were barely any places left on the benches behind them.

'I'll find you a chair,' Borax said, surveying the crowd.

'Don't worry, I'll find a space on the benches; there is no need to make a fuss.' To be truthful, Julia didn't want to sit at the front with Poppaea and her friends, or next to Gaius Cuspius and his cronies. She wasn't in the mood to listen to their cutting comments and facile remarks.

Borax led her to a bench. He didn't even have to ask the elderly man at the end to move along because, when the man saw the stepdaughter of Aulus Vettius approach, he immediately slid along the bench to make a place for her.

'Thank you,' Julia said with a polite smile as she sat down. It wouldn't be appropriate for Borax to sit on the bench beside his mistress, so he was forced to step to the side a few paces to prevent himself obstructing the view of those behind him.

Julia saw a tall well-built red-headed man being led on to the block. She had no interest in him, so she glanced around the room, wondering what price she would have to eventually pay to purchase Taranis. Most likely Poppaea was a prospective purchaser. She was a wealthy woman and very well connected: Emperor Nero's second wife had been her mother's older sister. However, unbeknown to her friends, Julia had inherited a very large amount of money and property from Sutoneus.

The bidding for the Briton started briskly, the price rising quite quickly. It soon became clear that the laniste, Decimus Valens, the trainer of the main gladiatorial troop in Pompeii, was interested in buying the slave. Julia had very little knowledge of the price paid for gladiators, but a good house slave might cost up to 3,000 denarii. However, even she was a little surprised when the bidding closed at over 15,000 denarii.

'Now that he has both Britons, do you think he'll pit them against each other in the next games?' the man seated next to Julia said to his companion.

As the Briton was led away, a palpable sense of excitement began to fill the courtyard. This was the moment most here had been waiting for – now it was the turn of the man from Gaul they had all heard so much about.

Maecenus was a canny businessman, and he didn't bring Taranis out straight away, as he wanted the tension to rise a little more, so he ordered the slaves to serve refreshments to those who wanted them. It was a sunny day and, with the large crowd and lack of any discernible breeze, the heat in the enclosed courtyard was almost unbearable. In order to provide some shade, Maecenus had ordered a fabric blind suspended above the heads of the audience, but it did little to disperse the heat of the sun's rays. Julia was very warm, and she was certain that her face was turning an unflattering pink in this heat. She was covered in perspiration and her crotch and underarms were damp and slippery with sweat.

As the minutes passed, the excitement increased, the crowd grew a little restless and the chatter grew louder and louder. Julia heard Poppaea's strident laugh emanating from the seats a few rows in front of her. Nervously, Julia clenched her hands; she had never bid for a slave before. Borax, as part of his household duties, purchased all the new household slaves, but she intended to bid herself this time around.

While she waited, rather apprehensively, she heard the man to her right say, 'Everyone is so curious about this slave. Did you hear what happened at the viewing last night?'

Julia leant closer to the man hoping to hear more.

However, she had no chance to hear anything else, as a cold male voice said, 'Curious about something, are you, daughter?'

'Stepfather?' She glanced nervously to her left as the tall imperious-looking man sat down beside her, even though there was not nearly enough room for him. She found herself uncomfortably pinned between her stepfather and the stranger on her right.

'Surely now that you are a wealthy widow you should feel able to address me by my given name?'

'Of course.' She smiled awkwardly. He still had the unerring ability to unsettle her and make her feel like a terrified child. The day he had become her stepfather he had also acquired absolute authority over her and every member of her family. The head of a Roman household had the power of life and death over his wife and children as well as his slaves. 'I'm surprised that you are not sitting at the front with your friends, Aulus?'

'I was for a time, but their inane chatter bores me,' he replied, sliding a companionable arm around her shoulders, which to others would look like a gesture of affection, even though she knew it was not. 'Poppaea and Gaius are bickering again and I wanted some peace and quiet, especially as the most important part of the auction is just about to start. I presume that you are here for that, daughter?'

'Yes,' she confessed. 'I was curious like everyone else.'

'My curiosity has already been assuaged,' he casually commented. 'I was at the pre-auction viewing.'

'Were you?' she replied, wondering what happened there. Then everything else vanished from her thoughts as Taranis was led into the room.

During the auction, the other slaves had just been wearing leg irons. However, Taranis's hands were manacled behind his back as well and there was a metal collar fastened around his neck, which had chains attached to either side. Obviously, Maecenus thought him a threat because these chains were held by a pair of muscular-looking guards, who dragged him into position and held him there. Clearly, this man was not cowed and browbeaten, as most slaves were, and he appeared to be a far from willing participant in this event. Perhaps this was a good sign, at least for her; many would balk at purchasing a slave who might rebel against his master at any time.

Julia's heart began to beat faster as she feasted her eyes on Taranis. He was beautiful, even though he was chained and at least temporarily subdued. He stood there, straight and tall, totally ignoring Maecenus and the guards who held him. His features were taut but his expression was proud, his manner dignified even in such a humiliating position. Her heart warmed to him almost as much as her body and she knew without a doubt that she had to purchase him.

Taranis was dressed in a plain knee-length tunic. His long blond hair was loose around his powerful shoulders and she thought that she had never seen a more handsome man in her entire life.

Maecenus gave the signal and the bidding started, slowly at first, with those who could afford to pay the highest holding back, allowing the price to rise a little before they even bothered to raise their hands. After last night, Maecenus had not thought it necessary to put a reserve price on the slave.

'Do you desire him?' Aulus whispered softly in her ear. 'I confess even I find him appealing and you will not be disappointed, I assure you.'

'What do you mean?'

'Just wait and see what Maecenus does next!' he added cryptically.

One of Maecenus's servants cautiously approached the slave on the block and unfastened the ties of Taranis's tunic. It fell to the floor, leaving him wearing just a short, full Greek-style skirt of white linen draped around his narrow waist. There was a gasp of admiration from those present. He was the epitome of male perfection that Romans admired so much. The thin strip of white contrasted perfectly with the slave's lightly tanned skin, which had been heavily oiled so that it had a slick sheen, putting even more emphasis on the well-developed muscles of his wide chest, strong arms and near-perfect legs. He was a magnificent-looking creature, and the bids began to come in hard and fast: twenty, forty, then eighty thousand denarii.

When an obviously very excited Gaius Cuspius bid a hundred thousand denarii, Maecenus held up his hand. 'Honoured guests – the true bidding is only just about to begin!'

He turned to look at Taranis and the slave stiffened anxiously, an entreating expression crossing his face for the briefest of moments before he regained full control of himself.

Julia held her breath as Maecenus stepped forwards and ripped off the brief linen skirt to reveal the slave in all his naked glory. It was as if someone had smeared red paint across the slave's high cheekbones as they turned suddenly scarlet. Clearly, he was ashamed, not only because he was naked, but also because his sexual organ was in an obvious state of arousal.

'He is magnificent, is he not?' Aulus said chillingly. 'I wager that even Poppaea would have trouble in accommodating a cock of that auspicious size.'

Julia was filled with a sudden sexual hunger that seemed to connect to every erogenous zone in her body as she stared at this gorgeous naked man with his engorged cock standing proudly out from his groin. But she also felt pity and acute embarrassment for Taranis, who was being so cruelly humiliated by his captors. 'How?' she muttered, not realising that she had spoken the thought aloud.

'Maecenus sent two slave girls to his cell. I watched them work on him only moments before they brought him to the block,' Aulus explained, seeming amused by what had happened to Taranis. 'Once his cock was fully erect, they fastened a silver ring tightly around the base of the shaft, to prevent it softening. The slave tried to fight them, hence the chains.' He squeezed her shoulder. 'Doesn't the sight of him like that excite you?'

'I pity him the indignity,' she retorted. 'No man, not even a barbarian, should be displayed in such a demeaning manner,' she added, trying to ignore the melting sensation in her pussy.

The bidding continued in a frenzied manner as Aulus said, 'You disappoint me, my dear.'

Aulus casually stroked her bare arm, as she suddenly heard someone shout, 'One hundred and sixty thousand denarii.' This topped Poppaea's last bid by a full ten thousand silver coins.

'One hundred and seventy,' Julia immediately yelled, raising her hand so that Maecenus could identify the new entrant to the bidding.

'You want him that much?' Aulus gave a coarse chuckle. 'Then you'll have to outbid Gaius. He wants to possess the slave,' he added in a low whisper, his lips just brushing her earlobe in a soft caress. 'He is determined to fuck him at all costs.'

By now, the sums were getting more and more outrageous, easily topping the one hundred and eighty thousand denarii, Gaius had paid for the young Greek boy some weeks earlier. Soon it was only Poppaea and Gaius bidding against each other and she heard Aulus give a grunt of surprise as the price reached two hundred and thirty thousand denarii.

Even now, the high colour hadn't faded from Taranis's cheeks, but he was managing to keep his expression impassive, as if this madness was beneath his dignity. Julia desired him desperately and admired his nobility, but she decided it might be prudent not to bid again until the unseemly feud between Poppaea and Gaius was at an end. One or other must give up and step down soon; this could not go on indefinitely. The most ever paid for a slave as far as she knew for certain was eight hundred thousand denarii, but that had been in Rome not here in the provinces.

'Gaius will never have him,' she said determinedly, turning her head to stare coldly at her stepfather. 'I couldn't bear to think what that creature would do to him.'

'Gaius is a respected citizen of Pompeii,' Aulus reminded her. 'You dare to speak of him in an offensive manner while planning to bid an outrageous sum for a slave just because he is attractive and has a big enough cock to satisfy your needs. Don't you think that rather hypocritical? Anyway, was my friend Sutoneus not man enough for you?'

'He was a loathsome old man, whose attentions disgusted me,' she hissed in a low voice, embarrassed to think that someone might overhear their conversation.

'Two hundred and sixty thousand denarii,' Maecenus announced with obvious glee, as he repeated Poppaea's last bid. 'Ladies and gentlemen, I should remind you that this slave, who goes by the barbarian name of Taranis, is a former Roman citizen and a powerful warrior. He is highly educated and can speak, read and write at least four languages with uncanny fluency. And of course,' he added, pointedly tapping the engorged cock, which had been heavily oiled and gleamed slickly in the diffused sunlight, 'he is well equipped to pleasure his new master or mistress in every conceivable fashion.'

As Maecenus touched his cock again, Taranis gave an angry growl and pulled desperately at his chains. He was clearly very strong, because the guards had to struggle with all their might to control him, nearly choking him in the process as the metal collar dug deep into his neck.

'He may need to be subjugated a little of course,' Maecenus admitted rather uncomfortably. He had stepped away from the slave during the brief altercation with the guards and he made no attempt to move closer to him again. 'I am certain, however, that many citizens would relish such a challenge.'

'The barbarian has spirit,' Aulus said softly, as he worked his tongue delicately into Julia's ear, while his hand slid down to press against the side of her full breasts. She was wedged so tightly she could not pull away. Unfortunately, not one person appeared to have noticed that her stepfather was behaving so inappropriately towards her. 'Just like you, my sweet daughter. Why bother paying all that money for a troublesome barbarian slave when I could just as easily satisfy you sexually myself?'

'No, never,' Julia muttered, unable to loosen his strong grip. There was heaviness between her thighs and her pussy was getting even wetter just at the thought of possessing Taranis and feeling that magnificent cock inside her. 'It is sinful to even suggest such a thing. The gods will strike you down.'

'Sinful?' He gave a cold laugh. 'I cannot even begin to count the sins I have committed, and no god would ever dare lay a hand on me.'

'Two hundred and ninety thousand denarii,' Gaius shouted excitedly, as he struggled to his feet, scarlet faced and sweating profusely.

'After paying so much for that Greek boy such a short time ago, he cannot afford to bid more without putting himself in severe financial difficulty,' Aulus said, still casually stroking the side of her breast over the fine fabric of her gown. 'His sexual desires have always overruled his common sense. Nevertheless, Poppaea is a rich and very determined woman, she will easily outbid him. And, if it comes to the crunch, I can outbid them both. Even you, my sweet Julia.'

She stiffened anxiously as his hand slid inside the loose armhole of her gown and brushed against the naked skin of her breast, which had suddenly become acutely sensitive to touch. 'I doubt that,' she retorted boldly. 'I'll bid four hundred thousand if needs be.'

'I have more than enough to treble that bid and not even notice it,' he told her, capturing her breast in his hand and squeezing it sensuously.

'I don't believe you,' she countered, embarrassed and appalled by what he was doing to her.

Gaius, meanwhile, was still on his feet, mopping nervously at his brow, having just entered a counter bid to Poppaea's latest of three hundred thousand.

'Sutoneus left you very well provided for,' Aulus said as he watched Poppaea raise the bid by twenty thousand. 'I know exactly how much he left you, and I should warn you that it is a mere drop in the ocean compared to my wealth and power.'

Desperately, she tried to struggle and loosen his hold on her but he held her fast, digging his fingers cruelly into the soft flesh of her breast. 'Three hundred and forty thousand,' she shouted defiantly.

For a brief moment, Taranis turned his head, staring into the crowd, trying to see what woman was also bidding for him. Julia wanted to stand up and let him see her, but Aulus was holding her so tightly she could barely move a muscle.

'Bid one more time, dear daughter, and I swear that I'll stand up and treble or even quadruple that sum and bring this auction to an abrupt end,' Aulus said coldly as he fingered her nipple. It stiffened, even though she knew she should be repulsed by his touch. 'I doubt even Poppaea would think it wise to bid against me.'

'Why do you object so much to the idea of me purchasing Taranis?' she asked, as she heard Poppaea raise her bid yet again.

'Because it would not be seemly for you to purchase this slave. Look at the sexual way Maecenus is displaying him. Now that the sums have become so outrageous it would be far too obvious to every decent law-abiding citizen that you want this slave for your bed.'

'I care not for reputation or convention,' she snapped, as she saw Maecenus look expectantly towards Gaius, who reluctantly shook his head and silently sat down, defeated at last.

'But *I* do, and I have decided that you shall not purchase that slave. Eventually, you'll marry again, and marry well. I want nothing to soil your reputation. Let my shrewish former mistress Poppaea have him, she has no reputation left to defend. The slave has a big enough cock to help satisfy her inexhaustible sexual appetite, at least for a time.'

'How can you claim to care what I do, when you are prepared to maul me, your own stepdaughter, in public?' she hissed, having no wish for him to know that her body was screaming out for sex, but not with him.

'I am powerful enough to defy convention, you are not. Do you wish to bring shame on your brother as well?'

Julia tensed as she heard Maecenus repeat Poppaea's bid for a second time. He was looking in her direction, waiting for her to bid again.

'Don't do it,' Aulus warned. 'Disobeying me will bring the wrath of Jupiter himself down on your head. I'll immediately stand up and bid enough to bring this auction to an abrupt end. I would relish taming the barbarian by any means necessary, even if I have to resort to gelding him myself. Then I'll fuck him, again and again before letting my friends like Gaius use him as well.'

Her heart sank and the colour drained from her face. Maecenus was still waiting for her to make another bid but Julia knew that she was defeated. It was far better to let Poppaea have him than for her cruel stepfather to become his master. She'd seen him beat a slave to death and enjoy every minute of it. Poppaea was a sexual predator but she wasn't an evil woman. She was unlikely to do any lasting harm to Taranis, and on the whole she treated her slaves very well.

'I'll not bid again,' she promised regretfully. Aulus smiled then raised his hand, turning his thumb down to inform Maecenus there were no further bids coming from this direction. 'As long as you take your hands off me right now, Stepfather,' she added threateningly. 'And promise never to touch me ever again.'

'You drive a hard bargain.' Aulus removed his hand from her breast, slid it out of her dress and laid it loosely across her shoulder again.

Just then Maecenus announced that he had accepted the final bid and that the slave now belonged to Poppaea for the princely sum of three hundred and sixty thousand denarii.

4

Sirona hurried through the atrium of the villa carrying a jug of the senator's best Falernian wine. She didn't even pause to glance at the huge painting of the god Priapus which had surprised her so much when she had first laid eyes on it. She could not understand why a large picture of a man with an enormous erect phallus, way out of proportion to the rest of his body, should take pride of place in the entrance hall of an eminent citizen's house. The Romans were a strange people; apparently, they found this and other sexually explicit paintings, quite appropriate decoration for their homes. According to Tiro, pictures of Priapus could be seen all over Pompeii; he was a symbol of sexual fertility and served to ward off evil influences from the house.

The first day she had arrived Tiro had taken her on a tour of the large villa, showing her just about everywhere apart from the senator and his wife's private quarters. Sirona couldn't help being impressed by its size and opulence. Tiro had told her that the senator had paid a vast sum to lure an important painter from Rome to do most of the beautiful paintings which decorated the walls of just about every room.

Sirona made her way into the bigger of the two dining rooms. It faced the large peristyle, which was flanked by high stone columns and surrounded by a covered portico where one could relax when the weather was inclement or the sun too hot. Even under the portico, just about every available wall was covered in amazing paintings.

Usually, as the name triculanium suggested, there were only three large couches in this room, but the servants were moving in more couches to accommodate the guests. At least twenty people were expected to dine with the senator.

The walls of the dining room were even more impressive than those in the rest of the villa. Sirona had crept in here earlier to look again at the gold-painted panels surrounded by elaborate borders of deep ochre red. In the centre of each panel was a picture depicting scenes from Greek and Roman mythology: baby Hercules strangling the serpents; the death of Ixion; Ariadne being awakened by Dionysis; all stories that Taranis had told her in the past. Just looking at them reminded her of her lost love.

'There you are, Sirona.' Tiro strode into the room. 'I wondered where you were.' He turned to watch the slaves positioning the low tables, which would soon be covered in platters of cold food, appetisers to be served before the main meal began.

Sirona had discovered that the household ate much like she had in Brittania. They consumed bread, cheese, roasted meats and plain vegetables. However, the menu planned for tonight contained the strangest of dishes, such as a stew of nightingale livers, cooked mice rolled in honey and poppy seeds and sautéed tongues of stork and flamingo. The elaborately expensive dishes were to be served purely to impress the guests and further display the wealth of their host.

She placed the jug of wine on a table next to a number of exquisite crystal goblets. 'I was trying to help. Everyone looked so busy,' she said with an awkward shrug of her shoulders. 'And I've been assigned no particular duties.' Tiro had been kind to her since she had arrived here and oddly enough he appeared to be trying his best to keep her well away from the senator at all times.

'Yes, I understand.' Not surprisingly, he seemed distracted. Entertaining on such a scale needed a lot of organisation and Tiro ran this household very efficiently. Of course, Sirona did not know the extent of the other more personal and intimate duties that he was expected to perform for the senator and there was no way she dared question him about such matters. 'But remember,' he added, 'the guests should arrive any time now.'

'You would wish me to return to the servants' quarters straight away?'

'Yes,' he confirmed. 'You know the senator's orders.'

For some reason, she knew not what, Aulus Vettius had no wish for anyone, apart from members of the household, to know of her existence.

'I'll go at once.' She turned and made her way back along the corridor to the atrium. Sirona was just passing the stairs leading to the upper floor when she sensed that someone was behind her, even though she had not heard any footsteps. Thinking it must be one of the servants, she didn't pause to look back. Then she felt a firm hand grab her shoulder and she stiffened anxiously somehow sensing that it was Aulus Vettius.

He swung her round to face him. 'In such a hurry, slave?' he said coldly, as his long fingers dug into her flesh. 'Quite amazing. Now that you are cleaned up, you are startlingly beautiful,' he continued as he stroked her pale cheek.

Sirona fought the bone-chilling fear that this man managed to arouse in her. Sensibly, she made no attempt to pull away. She just lowered her eyes submissively, as any slave would do in the circumstances, hoping that this encounter would be brief because of the imminent arrival of his guests. That was if they were on time of course.

His fingers slid down her neck to her breastbone, but at that precise moment there was a loud knocking on the street door. Sirona thanked the gods for her salvation and Aulus cursed under his breath, as the doorkeeper hurried through the atrium to greet the first arrivals.

She expected Aulus to release his hold on her, but he didn't, he just pushed her through an open doorway into the room he used as his office. He slammed the door shut and shoved her against a long carved table that was covered in papyrus scrolls.

'Tiro has kept you well out of my sight, my beautiful barbarian.' He fingered the long silken strands of her hair. 'I've no idea why. After all, at present I am still your master.'

At present? Strange words, she thought. Was he planning to sell her to someone else?

His hands were all over her, tracing the curves of her body through the thin fabric of her ankle-length gown. Sirona shuddered and turned her head away from him, fixing her gaze on the opposite wall. She found herself looking at a painting of a naked man lying on a couch, a nude woman astride his hips, obviously copulating with him.

'So you dare not even look at your master?' Aulus grated, pulling painfully at her hair as he forced her to turn her head and look up into his cold grey eyes. 'Or perchance you are admiring my paintings?' He gave a coarse chuckle. 'Perhaps they arouse you, barbarian?'

He dragged her over to the wall and made her stare at the picture. It was more crudely executed than most of the other paintings in the house, but that somehow only served to make it even more erotic. 'Which do you prefer?' He jerked her round to look at the picture on the adjoining wall. It showed a woman sucking on a man's cock. 'Not that one, I wager, judging by your useless attempts when we first met,' he jibed sarcastically. 'Perhaps you prefer this?' He thrust her towards one showing a woman crouched on all fours with a man about to enter her from the rear. Sirona didn't want to look at the picture but somehow she couldn't resist the temptation. Despite her fears about what Aulus might do to her, she still found the sight of it oddly arousing.

The senator pulled her round to face him again. 'Now you know exactly what is required of you, barbarian. Pictures tell everything, don't they?'

Even if she hadn't been able to understand Latin, the meaning of his words would have been uncomfortably clear. She froze in terror, as he pulled off her loosely fastened girdle and grabbed hold of her gown, jerking it off over her head. Slaves in his household were not afforded the protection of any undergarments, so she was left totally naked.

She knew she dare not fight him as he roughly fondled her breasts. If she did, she was certain that he would call for some of his male slaves to hold her down, while he did whatever crude thing he wanted to her. She stumbled and only just managed to regain her footing as he pushed her back until her bare buttocks were pressed against the carved side of the table.

Sirona grabbed hold of the edge so tightly that her knuckles turned white as he bent his head and fastened his lips on one of her nipples, while running his hands over the rest of her body. He sucked so hard on her teat that she gave a faint groan, half from discomfort, half from a perverse kind of arousal.

'So,' he murmured, as his fingers started to explore her pussy, 'Tiro did not think to have your body hair removed. Perhaps he translated my instructions concerning the masque a shade too literally. No matter . . .'

His teeth nipped cruelly at her soft flesh, while his finger slid intrusively inside her. Sirona could not contain her gasp of horrified surprise, as to her consternation her sex started to moisten almost immediately. Oh how she despised her body's unwanted reaction to the attentions of this man.

Aulus gave a lustful grunt as he thrust his fingers deeper. Her legs trembled and she leant back against the table, still gripping it tightly while through strength of will trying to prevent herself from responding to him. He pulled away from her and she thought that she might be saved from further indignities, but it was only so that he could brush his hand across the tabletop to clear a space. The scrolls scattered unheeded in all directions, many falling to the floor as he spun her round and pushed her upper body down on to the hard polished surface. He held her there, the flat of his hand pressing down hard on the small of her back as he fondled her buttock cheeks.

Sirona suddenly heard the sound of the door opening, followed by a soft gasp of surprise.

'Husband?' The lady of the house, Livia, had a high-pitched, rather childish voice. 'I've been looking for you.'

Sirona slumped against the tabletop, filled with relief. It was common enough for the head of the household to use his slaves for his own sexual pleasure, but surely not in full sight of his wife?

'Livia, my dear.' Aulus's voice was tense with fury.

'I'm sorry, I should not have disturbed you.' She sounded nervous, frightened even. 'I will leave –'

'No. Wait!' Aulus jerked Sirona upright and swung her round to face Livia. Judging by the lady's expression, she was scared witless of her husband. Sirona could not even bear to look at the poor woman so she fastened her gaze on the floor at her feet. 'I was just making the acquaintance of the new slave from Brittania,' Aulus said in a voice dripping with sarcasm. 'Would you deny me that pleasure, wife?'

'No, of course not.' Livia stared at Sirona in puzzled confusion. 'But, Aulus, in the circumstances,' she stuttered, 'should you not leave this girl –'

'You question *my* actions?' he interjected furiously.

'In normal circumstances, you know that I would not do so. But if Lucius were to discover. You know how close he is to Titus.' She spoke in an agitated rush as if forcing the words out, even though she really didn't want to say them.

'Your beloved son,' Aulus said through gritted teeth. 'Sometimes I wish –' He paused as he heard a loud voice coming from the atrium. 'It appears that our most honoured guest, Cnaius, is here, my dear.' His anger had not decreased but he appeared a little more in control of it as he roughly pushed Sirona away from him. 'We had better go and greet him, Livia,' he continued, then turned to look at Sirona who was just reaching down for her tunic. 'Put that on at once, girl, then remain here until you can leave without bringing yourself to the attention of my guests. Go to your room. I've no wish to lay eyes on you again tonight.'

Taranis paced the small room that he'd been confined in since his arrival at Poppaea Abeto's house. In the past, being locked up like this for three days might well have sent him insane with boredom, but since his capture he had become accustomed to inactivity in far worse conditions than this. At least he was being fed plentiful nourishing food and he could move about freely.

He had tried hard to forget the humiliations he'd endured on the block, thankful at least that he had been purchased by a woman and not by that foul creature Gaius Cuspius. Poppaea was probably a good few years older than him, and she was a little too skinny for his taste, but he didn't find her unattractive even though she would not be considered conventionally beautiful.

Only a few hours after he'd arrived here, she had strode majestically into this room accompanied by a couple of burly slaves. They'd held him down and she had watched them brand him; not on his arm like other slaves, but on his upper inner thigh, close to his sex. Purely, she had told him, so that he would be constantly reminded of why she had paid so much money for him.

The following morning, she had visited him again and handed him a small jar of sweet-smelling ointment. He was to put it on the burnt flesh to help it heal, she told him. He'd smiled, shaken his head and returned the jar to her as he pointed out that it was better not to try and numb the discomfort. After all, it served as a permanent painful reminder of the reason she had purchased him.

She'd been angry but he had also detected a glimmer of something like admiration in her eyes, as she had tossed the jar on to his low cot and told him curtly that he could please himself if he used it as it didn't matter either way to her. Then she had turned and stalked out of the room.

Later, he had decided to try the ointment. It was soothing and had a numbing effect that took away the sting of the burn. It would heal in a few days but whatever happened in the future he knew that it would always be there to remind him of Poppaea.

That morning, he'd been taken to her small but adequate bathhouse, and afterwards he had been given a fresh tunic to wear, which was much softer and of a far finer material than the one provided by Maecenus. Was today the day she would send for him? he wondered. Frankly, he was surprised that it had taken so long, as he'd seen the desire in her eyes every time she'd looked at him. He suspected that Poppaea Abeto was not only very highly sexed, but also a strong and very independent woman.

He ceased his pacing and turned, as the door to his cell opened and a man, one of those who'd been present at his branding, beckoned to him. 'Come, slave, the mistress wants to see you.'

'My name is Taranis,' he said to the man, as he accompanied him from the room.

He received no reply as he was led up a wide staircase to the first floor. Dusk was fast approaching. Through a window, Taranis caught sight of the blue sky, streaked with long ribbons of red and gold, as the sun slowly set.

'In here.' The man paused by an elaborately carved door.

Guarding the door was another of Poppaea's burly servants, who knocked, then cautiously pushed the door open. 'My lady, the barbarian slave is here.'

Bracing himself, Taranis strode in the room, not entirely sure how best to deal with his new mistress. Her bedchamber was huge with furniture and decorations fit for an empress. The last rays of sunlight filtered through the curtains and a pleasant breeze filled the room.

'Taranis, come closer.' Poppaea lay on her wide bed,

lounging on a pile of richly embroidered pillows. 'Salvo, you may leave now.'

'But, mistress?' The man looked with suspicion at Taranis.

'You and Clovis may remain outside. If I have need of you, I have only to call you.' She seemed amused by his concern.

Taranis didn't wait for the slave to depart as he walked boldly towards her bed. He looked down at Poppaea. Her hair was elaborately dressed and she was made up as if going out, yet she was stark naked apart from a large filmy scarf arranged artfully over her slim body. He presumed this was carefully staged, almost as if she wanted to try and seduce him. There was no need: if she desired sex she only had to order him to pleasure her and, if he wanted to escape punishment, he would do as he was told. However, if she wanted an illusion then he would give it to her.

'My lady.' His words were polite, but his eyes roved her partially concealed body in a frankly sexual manner.

'Your brand, is it healing well?'

'Any discomfort is of no importance,' he said dismissively. 'I've endured far worse in the past.'

'Battle wounds,' she said thoughtfully. 'Have you fought many battles, Taranis?'

'Enough,' he replied, knowing that the most challenging was yet to come. 'But surely we digress. It is not my life history you want, is it?' He pulled off his tunic and dropped it on the floor.

'I did not order you to strip.' She rose on one elbow and the covering slid down to reveal one pert breast. Her body was obviously untouched by childbirth and her breast was small and firm.

'No, you did not,' he said. 'But is it not what you want

of me? I have no desire to disappoint you. Surely you wish to discover whether I'm worth the exorbitant sum you paid for me?'

'Slaves are supposed to be submissive,' she said, looking him up and down. She stared pointedly at his groin and he felt his cock stir unconsciously as the lust of battle suddenly surged through his veins.

'If you want submission, you can get that from your other slaves.'

He strode to the end of the bed and pulled off the filmy scarf that was covering her. Ignoring her gasp of surprise, he grabbed hold of her legs and jerked them apart. She tried to resist but he dug his fingers into her flesh as he held her there, staring at her naked mound. Her breathing quickened; she was angry it appeared but also highly aroused. Sliding his hands upwards, he forced her thighs further apart as he knelt on the bed. Like most high-class Roman women, her pussy had been plucked and her lips were plump and a little pink as if she had already been touching herself there. Taranis could imagine her lying there waiting for him, sliding her finger into the slit and rubbing it hungrily against her clitoris.

Did she expect him to be gentle with her, submissively trying to gauge what excited her, as he slavishly gave in to all her sexual demands. Somehow, he thought not. She'd known that he was a warrior when she'd purchased him, so he'd give her what she expected and far, far more.

He peeled apart her swollen lips and slid his fingers inside her. She was sopping wet and as soft as silk, her flesh hungrily embracing him as he thrust deeper. Poppaea gave a soft, almost submissive whimper, writhing helplessly on the bed, as his fingers plunged in and out

87

of her cunt. A deep-seated need flooded his veins. Damaged pride and resentment were, it appeared, as powerful an aphrodisiac as love at times.

After removing his fingers, he replaced them with his mouth, his tongue delicately circling her clit until she wriggled and writhed beneath him like a woman possessed.

'Touch it,' she begged.

As he flicked his tongue across the small bud, it seemed to swell in size, until it was as firm and hard as a small sweet grape. Taranis clamped his lips around it and began to suck on it until she gave a pleading whimper of pleasure. He eased the tip of his tongue into her soft moist cunt while his hands reached for her small breasts. They were amazingly firm, and he kneaded them roughly. Then he touched her nipples, pulling and squeezing them with his fingertips, while his mouth went to work on her clit again. In seconds, her body was trembling beneath him and she gave a short sharp scream as she climaxed.

Taranis was nowhere near finished with her yet; she was no longer his mistress and, at least for a short time, he was the master. Without any more preamble, he covered her body and thrust his cock deep inside her. He started to move, hammering into her as if he were part of an invading army, taking possession of the first woman he came across in a captured city. It felt good, so good; the blood sang in his ears as the bitterness and lust he felt magnified into something far stronger. Then it exploded in a climax of such intensity that it surprised even him. Beneath him, he felt her body buck and tremble as she came again with a low keening moan of bliss.

Taranis stayed inside her, his groin still melded to hers, looking down at Poppaea as he supported most of the weight of his body on his arms. There was a contented expression on her face, but he waited, wondering if her satisfaction would soon turn to anger. He had treated her brutally and there was the distinct possibility that he had read this woman quite wrongly.

'Worth every denarius,' she murmured as she curled her arm around his neck and pulled his face close to hers, then she kissed him passionately on the lips.

Taranis returned the kiss, knowing without a doubt that this could turn out to be a very long night. Maybe it was a good thing that he had been resting for the last couple of days, he thought, as he rolled on to his side and pulled her close. Employing a tenderness he did not feel, he caressed her breasts then ran his hands possessively over her slim body.

As she kissed him, thrusting her tongue deep into his mouth, he heard a faint sound followed by the click of the door closing. Poppaea's passionate moans must have sounded like a call for help to Salvo. Now he'd seen that Taranis was in her bed, pleasuring his mistress, and she was obviously enjoying every intimate minute of the experience.

'This is all wrong,' Sirona complained to Tiro, as the slaves finished dressing her. 'My aunt would never have worn something like this.'

'I know,' Tiro agreed with a wry smile and a shrug of his shoulders. 'But you cannot disagree with the master. You are to wear this when you perform tonight.'

Nearly two weeks had passed since the dinner party and to her relief she had not laid eyes on Aulus again as he had been in Rome. The senate had been recalled when Emperor Vespasian had died after a short illness. Aulus had returned today, just in time for the celebration that he had been planning for some time. It was being held to honour the senator's stepson. He was a legate, the Roman equivalent of a general, who had just returned to Pompeii after spending almost a year in Judea. Now, of course, it would also serve to celebrate the ascension of the new emperor, Vespasian's son, Titus Flavius Vespasianus.

The Romans loved spectacles, especially those celebrating the power of the Empire, so Aulus had decided to organise a masque, which would show the defeat and capture of the rebel queen Boudicca by the Roman army.

Sirona was to play the part of her late aunt, Boudicca, the woman who had defied Rome and fought to drive the invaders from the shores of Brittania. Of course, the events Aulus planned to show were far from the truth, as her aunt had never been captured. Her father had told her that, after the terrible defeat and the death of almost eighty thousand of her followers, Boudicca had fled. Victory or death had been her battle-cry and, knowing that all was lost, she had taken a massive dose of poison then died in her brother's arms. With the Romans hunting the last of the Icene down, Borus, his wife and baby Sirona had fled further north and taken refuge with a tribe of Brigante.

Sirona was wearing a gold metal breastplate that was artfully moulded to her body and designed to cup and lift her bosom, but it was cut so low that it did not even cover her nipples. Her lower torso and thighs were barely concealed by a gathered skirt made of muslin. On her feet were delicate sandals held on by gold ribbons that criss-crossed her legs up to her knees.

'I hate it.' Sirona stared at herself in the mirror made of highly polished silver. Like all mirrors it distorted her image somewhat, but she could still see how sexually provocative the costume was. 'This is totally inappropriate and more suited to the goddess Athena than a Celtic warrior.'

'It is what the senator wanted,' Tiro reminded her. 'Now, do you know what you have to do?' He'd gone over her part with her a number of times, although there had been no actual rehearsal of the event.

'Of course, it is simple enough.' She touched the wooden sword at her hip, which looked convincingly real. 'My followers and I fight the men dressed as Roman soldiers. We lose, all my men are slaughtered and I am captured and taken before the general. He condemns me to death. End of story,' she repeated a shade irritably.

'Good.' Tiro didn't take offence, and he just smiled encouragingly. 'I am sure your performance will be convincing.'

'Just like the real thing,' she replied, trying not to sound sarcastic; after all, this was none of his doing. 'Except, of course, that I don't get put to death,' she added, feeling nervous and apprehensive.

'Of course you don't get put to death. This is a celebration not a Greek tragedy.' Tiro patted her arm. 'You worry too much, Sirona. Your situation is not as bad as you believe it to be.'

'What do you mean?'

'You will find out soon enough,' he said cryptically. 'Now let's put on your helmet. You will need to be ready soon.'

Sirona's hair was pinned lightly atop her head. Tiro gently eased on the surprisingly heavy and far too ornate helmet, which was just as silly as the rest of her costume. It was topped by a large plume of white feathers that would make her a prime target on any battlefield.

'Everything will be fine,' he assured her, before leaving to check if the celebrations were running smoothly.

Sirona picked up the filmy scarf that had been included with the rest of her costume and wound it around the top of the breastplate, so that it covered both her nipples and the upper part of her breasts. Suddenly, one of the slave girls, who had helped her dress, noticed what she was doing. As the girl went to grab hold of the scarf and pull it off, Sirona slapped her sharply on her arm. Nervously, the girl stepped back and made no attempt to touch Sirona again.

Moments later, the door opened and a male slave appeared and beckoned to Sirona. She followed him along a corridor and into the stables where her chariot was waiting for her. It was less than half the size of a real chariot and was pulled by a pair of pretty white ponies. Trying to control her anxiety, Sirona jumped on to the footplate, grabbed hold of the reins and drew her sword.

She waited, hearing the distant sound of the guests laughing and talking, probably eager for the entertainment to begin. The sudden loud trumpet blast made her ponies dance skittishly and she pulled at the reins, holding them back. Her followers, who looked nothing like true Celtic warriors, were assembled behind her. They were a dirty-looking bunch of men, clad in rags and animal skins and smeared with mud and grime.

She heard another trumpet blast and the faint clatter of iron-shod sandals on the stone paving, as the small cohort of fake Roman soldiers marched into place. Perhaps she might have found this at least mildly entertaining if she had been in the audience watching and hadn't been forced to take part in this travesty.

At the third trumpet blast, just as she had been instructed, she began to move, guiding her chariot out of the stable, into the narrow road at the back of the villa. The wide doorway at the rear of the peristyle had been left open and, as she drove through it, she flicked the reins.

The soldiers looked a little nervous as her chariot thundered towards them, while Sirona yelled a Celtic battle-cry and waved her sword. She was skilful enough not to plough into them and the barbarians surging round her chariot to protect her, as one of the soldiers lunged forwards to grab hold of her lead pony's bridle. The fight was reasonably convincing but very brief; wooden swords clashing on wooden swords, her followers screaming futile insults at their attackers. Sirona was barely aware of the audience's shouts of encouragement as, in no time at all, the last barbarian was beaten to the ground and she was pulled from her chariot.

She was dragged over to the man portraying the commander of the soldiers. They were supposed to be acting, yet she felt that these men were being unnecessarily brutal as they divested her of her fake sword and pulled off her helmet. Her glorious hair tumbled down her back as she was forced to her knees. Then she felt rough hands pull away the flimsy scarf covering her breasts. Angrily, she tried to fight them off but yet more hands moved to hold her down. One of the men produced a dagger, which had a frighteningly real, highly polished blade. He sawed through the straps of her breastplate and jerked it off, leaving her naked to the waist. Surely this wasn't part of the planned masque? she thought, struggling furiously, as one of them reached for her skirt. She caught sight of Aulus sitting on his thronelike chair, smiling in amusement. The bastard, he had planned this all along, she thought, screaming in futile fury, as the thin muslin was ripped from her body, leaving her totally naked apart from her sandals.

A hand was shoved between her thighs to roughly

finger her pussy. Sirona was terrified that they were about to rape her, but first it appeared she had another humiliation to contend with, as she saw a soldier walking towards her holding a small knotted whip.

Fear made her act instinctively to protect herself. Her skin had been oiled so that it gleamed in the lamplight and it was relatively easy now for her to wriggle out of the soldiers' grasp. She punched one man in the solar plexus and he fell back, gasping for breath, just as another received a hard kick in the groin from her sandalled foot. Having rolled over, she sprang swiftly to her feet, just as another man tried to grab her. Instead of backing away, she lunged towards him, wrong-footing him completely. He half-stumbled, as she jerked the dagger from his belt and darted away before he could recover his balance.

Holding the dagger in a defensive position, she stood there in the flickering light, staring menacingly at the small group of fake soldiers, who clearly did not know what to do next, while the audience was shouting and cheering, thinking that this was all a planned part of the masque. Aulus, however, was frowning angrily and talking agitatedly to the tall man standing beside him, who was dressed as a Roman general in full ceremonial regalia.

Sirona was so furious at what had occurred that she could barely contain herself. Judging by the way the solders were milling helplessly around, they were as yet no real threat to her, so she had to decide what to do next.

'Don't stand there,' Aulus shouted. 'Grab her.'

'No,' his companion said angrily. 'Leave her be!'

Sirona focused on the one man she hated above all else, the one who had planned this humiliation especially for her. She moved menacingly towards the senator, dagger in hand, not realising how beautiful she looked: a stark-naked barbarian, her pale skin gleaming and her long auburn hair streaming down her back. She desperately wanted to plunge the dagger in Aulus's chest. But could she get close enough to him? Probably not. Damn the Romans, damn the senator, she thought, as she aimed, then threw the dagger towards her target.

5

Aulus shuddered in fearful surprise as the dagger grazed his forearm and landed with a thump in the arm of his chair. The blade had pierced his toga, pinning him to his seat. He looked too terrified even to move as a scarlet stain spread slowly over the fine white woollen folds covering his arm.

Total mayhem ensued. Now that she was without a weapon, the fake soldiers, who a few moments ago had been too nervous to touch Sirona, surged forwards. She backed away, fighting her automatic instinct to run, because, when she had glanced behind her, she had seen the senator's servants trying to creep up on her from the rear. She looked around helplessly, searching for her friend Tiro, but he was nowhere to be seen. Yet she knew that it was impossible for even him to help her now.

Many hands grabbed hold of her and she made no attempt to fight – what point was there in doing so? Judging by the senator's angry expression, she had forfeited all rights to mercy. She had humiliated him in front of his friends and now she would be punished for her transgressions.

'Aulus, thank the gods you are still alive,' Gaius Cuspius said agitatedly, as he waddled towards the senator, mopping the sweat from his brow. 'That barbarian bitch is a wildcat, is she not?'

'So it seems.' The senator's voice was shaky, but he appeared to be making an effort to recover some semblance of composure.

He looked questioningly at the man by his side. Lucius seemed untroubled by his stepfather's close brush with death, as he calmly removed the dagger from the arm of the chair and tucked it in his sword-belt. With a trembling hand, Aulus pulled back the bloodstained folds to look at his wound.

'It's only a scratch, nothing to be concerned about,' Lucius said dismissively.

'Maybe to a soldier it is nothing, Lucius ... er ... general,' Gaius, who was by nature an abject coward, said very agitatedly, not entirely sure how he should address this stern young man who was so very close to the new Emperor. 'The girl clearly intended to kill your father. You must have her executed immediately.'

'No,' Lucius replied loudly. 'I will not.' He raised his hand and from the shadows surrounding the peristyle marched a small group of obviously very real soldiers. 'Bring the girl here now, centurion.'

The excited chatter of the audience ceased. They stared in amazement, as the soldiers marched forwards with military precision. As they shoved aside the men surrounding Sirona and took hold of her, none dared to even try and oppose them. The servants had bruised her arms and dug their fingers into her flesh, but the soldiers held her lightly and she knew that their grip would only tighten if she tried to pull away from them. She still felt very scared as they led her forwards until she was standing directly in front of the senator and their commander.

'She obviously intended to kill me,' Aulus said, his voice still shaking slightly. 'It was only by the will of the gods that I was saved.'

'So you blame only her?' Lucius asked coldly, keeping his voice low pitched. 'Were you not about to have her whipped, then raped?'

'Matters got out of hand, the men got overexcited and carried away in the heat of the moment. I ordered no such thing.'

'Really?' Lucius said with cutting sarcasm. 'Unfortunately, I cannot bring myself to believe you. No one who serves you would dare take matters into their own hands.'

Sirona listened to their conversation in confusion. Aulus appeared to be a little scared and rather in awe of this man. If he was indeed the senator's stepson, why was he acting so disrespectfully?

'None of that concerns me now. We must deal with the matter in hand.' Aulus took a damp cloth from a kneeling slave and dabbed awkwardly at his wound. Once the blood was cleaned away it was obvious it was little more than a deep scratch. 'She still must be punished for trying to kill me.'

'The girl wasn't trying to kill you,' Lucius said with derision. 'If she planned to do that, the knife would be buried in your heart right now. Celtic women are warriors; they fight on the battlefield alongside their men. They are skilled in the use of weapons – the girl wanted to frighten you, nothing more.'

'Even so she must still be punished. If we allow one slave to get away with such a crime.' Aulus lowered his voice. 'They outnumber us five to one, remember the other rebellions, Lucius.' He winced as a slave placed a clean cloth soaked in a herbal healing compound over the wound. 'She is beautiful, so I won't do anything to mar that beauty. Once she has been suitably punished, you can take her away. I'll be pleased never to have to lay eyes on her again.'

'You have no right to do anything to her.' This time Lucius spoke loudly so that all around could hear him. 'Agricola sent this Icene princess as a gift to me –' He paused. 'Do you really want these noble citizens to see us arguing over the transgressions of a barbarian?'

'No,' Aulus was obliged to concede, as he saw his stepson's face tighten in grim determination.

'I should remind you that your slaves, all of them, are no match for my men.' Lucius looked pointedly at the soldiers who had recently returned with him from Judea. They had gathered so protectively around Sirona that only Aulus, their commander, Lucius, and the people just behind him could see her at all.

Sirona was still totally confused by this conversation. She didn't know whether she should thank this man or fear him. Nevertheless, she was grateful to him for trying to protect her from the senator.

'As you say, Lucius my dear boy,' Aulus conceded unhappily. 'She belongs to you and you alone decide her punishment.'

Lucius nodded at his stepfather then stepped towards Sirona. 'Lucius Brutus Flavius, Legate of the Fifteenth Legion of Apollo,' he announced to her. Then, to her amazement, he added in her own language, 'You have no reason to fear me, Sirona.'

He took off his long cloak and draped it around her shoulders, pulling it close so that her naked body was hidden from view. His men retreated a couple of paces, as Lucius placed a protective arm around her shoulders. Then he turned to address his stepfather again. 'I thank you for your hospitality. It is a pity, but it appears that circumstances have forced me to depart earlier than planned.'

Taranis strode along the corridor towards Poppaea's bedchamber. It was odd to think how much his life had changed recently and strangely enough he didn't dislike his new situation half as much as he thought he would.

He found Poppaea a challenge and the sex was certainly stimulating. Now that he was firmly ensconced in her bed, his position in the household had changed dramatically.

To be truthful, he did not mix much with the other household slaves. Mostly he spent his days with Poppaea. His room wasn't even in the slave quarters, it was close to her bedchamber so that she could call on him day or night. And call for him she did, often! She had a voracious sexual appetite.

She was expecting him, so he didn't bother to knock as he entered her room.

'Taranis, where have you been?' she demanded to know, just as she always did when he didn't appear seconds after she had sent for him.

'I was outside, exercising,' he explained, as he walked towards her. She was seated at her dressing table and a maid was combing her long hair. 'I had to wash, then put on a clean tunic.' He had many fine garments to choose from now, all provided by his mistress.

'Fetch me my blue gown, the one with the gold embroidery at the hem,' Poppaea told the maid. 'It was being mended by one of the seamstresses as the binding was loose.' As the girl hurried off, Poppaea turned her head to smile warmly at Taranis. 'There was no need to wash and change first, you know.'

'I stank – do you like a man covered in sweat?' Taranis was careful only to address her so personally when none of the other slaves was present.

'When it is dripping off a body such as yours, yes,' she said huskily, as he pulled aside her hair to kiss her neck. 'Perhaps I should arrange a regular exercise routine for you. I don't want those glorious muscles turning soft. Speak to my procurator, Eros. He can arrange for you to do exercises and weapons training with my personal guard.'

'I need to keep *very* fit to pleasure you, my lady,' Taranis said, pleased to be allowed this privilege.

He gently massaged her shoulders. 'That feels good,' she said with a soft sigh.

Taranis slid his hand down her body to cup her breast. 'And you look especially lovely this morning.' His words were genuine. Poppaea did look far more attractive without heavy make-up and with her hair loose around her shoulders.

'Surely not,' she protested. 'My hair is not dressed properly and my face is devoid of cosmetics.'

'You have no need of such artifices.' He drew her gently to her feet and pulled her round to face him. This was the first time he had dared to act in quite such a bold and intimately familiar manner towards her when they weren't having sex. Bed slaves were not expected to form proper personal relationships with their owners.

'But it is fashionable to have a pale complexion and my eyes are nothing without cosmetics.'

'In public, of course, if you wish it. But surely you can have no need of such things in the privacy of your bedchamber, alone with me?'

Her olive cheeks flushed and for the first time Taranis felt a genuine liking for this woman who had bid so much money for him and rescued him from the perverted clutches of Gaius Cuspius. He kissed her, gently at first, then with increasing passion. His cock stiffened, a good fuck was the perfect end to heavy exercise and at this moment he desperately wanted Poppaea.

She returned his kiss with equal passion but, when he went to draw the loose robe from her shoulders, she pushed him away. 'No, Taranis. I have matters to attend to. I am expecting a guest.' She frowned. 'Sometimes I let myself forget that you are a slave and that's dangerous.'

'Why?' he asked, hiding the sudden resentment that flared up inside him.

'Because I might come to genuinely care for you, thus making it much more difficult for me to control you.' She turned away from him and started sorting through her jewellery box. She pulled out a heavy gold necklace decorated with dark-blue stones. 'This will go well with the blue gown.'

'Surely a few moments –' he started to say as he reached out to touch her.

'I said no,' she snapped, slapping his hand away. 'I've no time for sex right now.'

Despite her words, he knew that she was aroused. Her breathing had quickened and through her filmy gown he could see that her nipples had stiffened into firm peaks. Yet she was casually dismissing him, just when he had thought he was getting a little closer to the real Poppaea. 'As you say, *mistress*.' Taranis strode towards the door.

'Wait!' she said curtly. 'I haven't dismissed you, yet.'

'Then I'll not leave.' He determinedly slid the door bolt in place.

Poppaea's colour heightened. 'Draw the bolt back, *now*, Taranis,' she said angrily. 'And get out of my sight.'

'Leave, stay,' he repeated, walking towards her. 'Which is it?' He grabbed hold of her robe and ripped it from her body. 'Sometimes I let myself forget that I am a slave, and that's dangerous.'

'How dare you!' She slapped him hard across the face.

He gave a cold laugh, as he grabbed hold of her wrist to stop her hitting him again. 'I dare because I want you to get down on your knees and suck my cock.' Poppaea stared at him in disbelief, breathing heavily. He placed his hands on her shoulders. 'Kneel,' he said pushing down hard until she sank submissively to her knees in front of him. Then he jerked off his tunic and flung it aside. When she didn't move, he meshed his hands in her hair and forced her face closer to his groin. 'Do it, Poppaea.'

Taranis knew he was taking an insane chance here, but he had suppressed his own need to be in control of his life for far too long. He'd willingly take whatever punishment she dreamt up for him, he wanted this moment for himself.

It appeared that he knew Poppaea far better than she knew herself, because she didn't protest or try to rise to her feet. She seemed aroused by his brutality as she took hold of his penis and guided it into her mouth. He drew in his breath sharply as her lips closed around the top of his glans. Her hot moist mouth hungrily swallowed more of his thick shaft, while she cupped his heavy balls in her hand. She used the pressure of her lips to caress his rod, while her tongue stimulated the helmet.

He found it highly arousing to exert such control over his mistress, and Taranis shuddered as she sucked harder, while one of her hands stole between his muscular thighs to gently stroke the strip of sensitive skin between his balls and anus. The sweet pulling sensation and the soft feel of her lips made him gasp with pleasure. When the tip of her finger wriggled its way into his backside, it became almost too much to bear. He felt the pleasure gather inside him, as his climax moved closer, but he was not finished with Poppaea just yet.

'I don't want to come in your mouth,' he growled, forcing her head back away from his sex.

She stared up at him in surprise, saying nothing, still trapped in the servile sexuality of the moment.

Taranis lifted her into his arms and carried her to the bed, then flung her face down on the mattress. He grabbed a pillow, stuffing it under her stomach, raising her firm little bottom in the air. Then he slapped each cheek hard until her olive skin turned scarlet and she was squirming with pain and pleasure. Digging his fingers into her inflamed skin, he thrust his cock into her, pulling her body towards him until he'd penetrated her as deep as he possibly could. He began to thrust hard and fast, using her in the most brutal fashion, while she begged him for more, her body shuddering submissively beneath him.

Sirona followed the servant girl through any number of fine rooms, most bereft of any furnishings. They walked past a large peristyle surrounded by high Doric columns, then through a couple of small courtyard gardens, the last of which led into an imposing atrium. They emerged on to a wide veranda, which led on to terraced gardens laid out in a formal style with low hedges, flowering plants and small Cyprus trees. They faced a narrow road and in the distance she could see Pompeii. She had been amazed at the size of the senator's house but this was at least three times bigger. Lucius had brought her here last night but she'd taken little notice of her surroundings. The legate must be a very important man to own such a beautiful property. The magnificence of the villa contributed to her confusion. What did this man, Lucius, want with her? she wondered, as she stepped forwards a few paces into the bright sunlight. The villa was built on the side of a hill, and in the distance, directly behind the house, she could see the high mountain she had first caught sight of in the harbour. Now she knew that it was called Vesuvius.

'Sirona.' He called her name as he appeared from the side of the building. Lucius was wearing just a plain white tunic slashed at the neck to reveal a portion of well-honed chest, and short enough to show the lower half of his muscular thighs. It was the sort of clothing a house slave might wear, apart from the elaborately tooled leather belt around his lean hips.

Sirona smiled awkwardly, not knowing how to greet him as he strode athletically towards her. 'You slept well, I hope?' he asked, as he reached her.

His tunic was a little grubby in places, as though he'd been doing some sort of manual work, which was surely unlikely. Lucius looked far less threatening, now that he was no longer wearing his impressive uniform but she was still overcome by the powerful aura of masculinity he projected.

'Yes, I did sleep well all night and most of the day it seems.' Judging by the position of the sun, she figured out that it must be late afternoon.

Lucius was a handsome man with olive skin, patrician features, short cropped black hair and deep-brown eyes. His good looks and muscular body unsettled her even more than her first impressions of this magnificent villa.

'Not surprising really. I ordered the maid to give you a sleeping draft.' He smiled warmly at her. 'It seemed wise in the circumstances, after all that had happened.'

So that was why the drink they'd given her had such a bitter aftertaste. Also the wide bed had been so comfortable it was like floating on air, in comparison to the hard pallet in the tiny room she had shared with two others in the senator's house. She suddenly realised that they were conversing quite happily in her own language. 'I am surprised that you speak my language so fluently,' she said shyly.

'Perhaps not the exact same dialect as yours, and my recollection is rusty in places,' he cheerfully conceded. 'My mother warned me that you did not understand Latin.'

Sirona didn't trust him enough to tell him the truth. In fact, she shouldn't trust him at all, but she felt drawn to him in a strange way that she just could not explain. 'You are very kind,' she said awkwardly. 'About last night – you must be angry with me for harming the senator, your stepfather?'

'I might not approve, but I can appreciate why you acted like that in the heat of the moment.' He shrugged his wide shoulders. 'He had no right to treat you that way.'

'Because I am your slave, not his?'

'You are not my slave.' He put a hand on her arm and led her back into the atrium. 'Let's get out of the sun and relax. It's well past cenna and I'm hungry.' He escorted her through one of the smaller gardens and into a dining room. 'Consider yourself my guest, Sirona. My friend Agricola asked that I care for you. He thought that I would appreciate your beauty as much as he admired your courage. That is why he sent you here to me.'

'And not to Rome to be executed like my father,' she said sadly, as he guided her to a couch.

'Be seated,' he said, as he slipped off his sandals. Lucius plonked himself down on the opposite couch to hers and lounged back on the cushions.

Sirona sat down, primly perched on the long dining couch, unable to relax herself. She had always found the idea of half-lying down to eat strange and rather uncomfortable. A number of slaves entered the room and placed tasty-looking, but relatively plain dishes of various foods on the table between them.

Once the servants had departed, she followed her host's lead and dipped her fingers in the bowls of water provided, then dried her hands. 'As yet I have no news of your father's fate,' Lucius said. 'Things are a little chaotic in Rome after Vespasian's unexpected death. Titus will soon have full control of everything. Then I'll contact him and find out if your father is still alive. If he is, I can probably persuade Titus to spare him. The new Emperor is a fair-minded and noble man.'

'So you have some influence in Rome?' Sirona paused awkwardly. 'I'm sorry – it is not my concern. I spoke out of turn.'

'I told you, Sirona.' He cut a hunk of fresh white bread. 'You are not my slave. Ask what you will.'

He began to eat as if he hadn't seen a decent meal for days, while Sirona just picked at the food on offer. Normally, she had a good appetite but she wasn't feeling very hungry today.

After he'd eaten what seemed to her a huge amount, Lucius paused. He wiped his hands on a cloth and took a large gulp of his wine. 'Forgive me. I have been eating soldiers' fare for far too long. I'm not being a proper host. Why not try the wine?'

She did as he suggested and tasted the wine, finding it sweet and refreshing. 'I would have thought that a commanding officer, such as you, would have servants to cook and care for him.'

'I don't hide myself away in my own tent and expect a life of luxury as most other commanders do. I eat what my men eat, and share their hardships and discomforts. They respect me more for doing so and would follow me into Hades itself if needs be.'

'Could I ask you how you learnt to speak my language so fluently?' She was curious about this man, who in many ways appeared very different from the other Romans she had known.

'I served in Brittania for a number of years when I was younger. For a time, I had a mistress who was of your tribe. It was she who taught me.' He paused, then added, 'She was not my slave, Sirona, and she is now married to a rich merchant and is a very happy woman.'

'Is that where you came to know Agricola? I presume that you and he are friends – why else would he have sent me here?' she asked curiously.

'He was my commanding officer when I served in Thrace.' He smiled in a boyish fashion. 'I admired him so much and in time got to know him well. I am honoured that he considers me a friend.'

'Then I also should be happy that he is your friend. Otherwise, what would have happened to me?' She found herself drawn to Lucius, perhaps she would come to like, maybe even trust him in time. It was likely that he was telling the truth and she was not his slave. However, she was still in a very strange situation: far from home in a strange land, a supposed guest in the home of a very attractive man and totally dependent on him for everything.

'Perhaps you should,' he agreed, as he hungrily devoured a large piece of almond cake doused in a sticky honey glaze.

She watched him finish the cake, as she drank the rest of her wine. It was certainly making her feel more at ease. She'd only tried wine a couple of times before and she didn't recall it tasting as pleasant as this. Wine was imported into Brittania, for the Romanised Britons and their conquerors, not for the barbarian hordes of the north.

'And the new Emperor, you speak as if you know him quite well?'

'I've known Titus since I was a small child. We are second cousins on my late father's side. Titus is a good ten years older than me, so when we served together he took it upon himself to watch over me, and we became close friends. He's a good man, Sirona. He'll be good for Rome, perhaps even for Brittania.' He smiled at her. 'Perhaps he'll even bring peace to your land. After all, a large number of your people already live peacefully beside us, enjoying the luxuries we are able to provide.' He leant forwards, picked up a jug of wine and refilled her silver goblet. 'Perhaps it is better we do not discuss matters that may lead to dissension between us.'

The divide between her and Lucius was wider than the sea between Brittania and Gaul, she thought, but she dare not say so. 'As you wish.'

It seemed impolite not to drink more wine since he had refilled her goblet, so she took a couple of large swallows.

'Have you finished eating? You ate very little.'

'Enough.' She smiled at Lucius. The warmth of the wine hitting her almost empty stomach somehow made her respond more warmly to him. 'I wasn't hungry. This wine is very good.'

'The best Falernian, from the lower slopes where the sweetest grapes grow.' He dabbled his sticky fingers in the bowl of water. 'I've come to prefer some of the Phoenician wines. They are stronger, and a little less sweet.'

'I've never had this, let alone Phone–cian wine before,' she said, stumbling over the pronunciation. Sirona suddenly wanted to giggle. She had no idea why. Perhaps it was the wine or perhaps it was this bizarre situation she found herself in. Yesterday, she had been a slave, now she was lying on a couch conversing with an important Roman commander about the benefits of various wines. She frowned, her thoughts were becoming a little muddled. 'I think this wine is affecting me. I feel most strange,' she said carefully.

'You should have eaten more before drinking. Mostly we drink wine watered down, but this is not and is a lot stronger than the bitter beer your people brew,' he said with a teasing grin, as he rose to his feet and slipped on his sandals. 'Come. I'll show you around the villa. The walk will help clear your head.'

He held out his hand and she had no choice but to take it as she stood up. When her skin made contact with his, she felt a flicker of sexual arousal. Lucius was a very attractive man, but he was also a Roman general, she reminded herself.

'Your villa is very large,' she said, feeling that she had to keep the conversation going, as he led her out of the dining room. By now, she was experiencing a strange light-headedness and her nipples began to tingle as he tightened his grip on her hand.

'Yes. My stepfather heard a rumour that it would soon be up for sale, just before I left for Judea. So I sent him the necessary funds and had him purchase it for me. I wanted a place of my own to return to. I prefer to avoid the political atmosphere of Rome when I can, and both my mother and sister live here in Pompeii.'

Sirona wondered if the attraction she felt for him was mutual, as he led her across the large peristyle, which was still in a state of some disrepair. 'This looks as if it needs a lot of work.' Unable to think straight with him touching her, she pulled away from Lucius and walked to the centre of the garden. The water in the fountain had dried up, the basin was cracked and it was filled with rotting matter.

'The villa had been empty for some time. The builders had only just finished the renovations when I sent a message to my mother telling her when to expect me. She arranged for a few basic furnishings but nothing more.' He hurried towards her as she almost stumbled over some loose stones. 'Careful, Sirona,' he said, as he slipped a supporting arm around her waist.

'Silly of me,' she said awkwardly, trying to ignore the sudden surge of sexual desire she experienced when he touched her again. Even though they'd been forced apart, she still loved Taranis, and she had no wish to be attracted to this man when she was feeling so alone and vulnerable.

'I have many plans for this garden,' he said, as he guided her under the covered portico. 'But the house –' he smiled and looked down at her '– I think that needs a woman's touch.'

Ever since she had first purchased Taranis, Poppaea had been planning this small gathering to show him off to her most important and well-respected friends, the majority of whom hadn't attended the auction. Dressed and ready to greet her guests, she glanced admiringly at her slave as he accompanied her into the garden.

She knew that he wasn't happy with the costume she had made him wear, which was modelled on a picture she had once seen of the half-man, half-god Hercules. Taranis was wearing just a brief linen skirt in the Greek style with a narrow gilded belt at his waist. The goldsmith had charged her an exorbitant sum for the two thick gold bracelets, which girded his upper arms and helped emphasise the size and strength of his glorious muscles. She'd given him an expensive perfumed oil to rub into his skin so that it gleamed attractively in the bright sunlight, and his long hair had been trimmed so that it just brushed his shoulders. Taranis had wanted it cropped in the Roman style but she preferred it longer.

She had decided to hold the gathering in her garden because she had just imported six life-size statues from Greece and had them placed decoratively around her pool. They were male nudes, but it was rather a pity that the sculptor had given them all such miserably small sexual organs. Poppaea glanced over at Taranis. Why be concerned about that when she had a deliciously large cock ready and eager to pleasure her whenever she wanted.

She sat down on one of the chairs that had been placed beneath the shade of a small row of Cyprus trees. As she had instructed, Taranis stood protectively by her side. She wanted her guests to catch sight of him as soon as they arrived.

'They should be here soon,' she said, as she irritatedly brushed aside a small flying insect that was buzzing around her head.

'Yes, my lady,' he obediently acknowledged.

She had warned Taranis that he must be on his best behaviour today. Sometimes she wondered if she was being too indulgent with him. Often she treated him more like a lover than a slave. However, she knew that she would never have enjoyed having sex with the pathetically servile bed slaves some women owned; they were too submissive for her specialised tastes. Sex with Taranis was stimulating and unpredictable. Sometimes he was loving and tender, other times rough and brutal. It was always different, always exhilarating.

Many years earlier, Poppaea had discovered that she could be aroused by a measure of violence and even mild pain. Taranis somehow sensed, then fulfilled her fantasies, although she had yet to push their involvement to the furthest extremes of her sexual desires, but she would, given time. Taranis was everything she had hoped for and more, although it wasn't easy having a warrior to serve her, as, on occasions, he totally overstepped the boundaries between mistress and slave.

Poppaea glanced back at Taranis, thinking how truly amazing he looked dressed like this. Yes, he had a great body, was very good looking and had one of the biggest cocks she had come across in a long time. However, he had something else that attracted her just as much – pure animal magnetism. The first time she'd laid eyes on Taranis he had been naked and chained, and her pussy had grown sopping wet just by looking at him. But she'd also sensed a dangerous air about him that would never be entirely contained. Of course he overstepped the boundaries at times, because she knew that he was a warrior in every sense of the word and would never truly be tamed. If she were honest with herself, she would not have wanted him any other way.

As she continued to stare at him, she fought the urge to slip her hand briefly under his skirt and stroke his sex. Just touching the magnificent cock excited her. It was strange, she mused, she'd never felt so highly attracted to a man before; sometimes she found Taranis just too tempting to resist.

'It appears that your guests are arriving.' His voice interrupted her train of thought.

She looked towards the tablinum to see a pale-faced Livia and Corelia, the rather straight-laced wife of Cnaius Nigidus, strolling along the side of the pool.

She greeted them cheerfully, finding it highly amusing when they both cast brief, covetous glances in Taranis's direction. Did the sight of him arouse them as much as it did her? she wondered. More guests arrived, all of them members of the most important families in Pompeii. The last to appear was the pleasant-natured

Julia Felix, the woman she considered her most trustworthy and closest friend.

Julia went a little pink when she first laid eyes on Taranis standing beside Poppaea. Julia had bid for him at the slave auction, but obviously couldn't afford his inflated price. Poppaea wondered what on earth Julia would have done with a slave like Taranis, as she'd never struck her as a highly sexed woman. It would have been a total waste.

Poppaea's slaves served chilled wine and fruit juices flavoured with honey, accompanied by dishes of eggs seasoned with chopped anchovies, small beef pastries, juicy olives and oysters from Brundisium. As the women drank and nibbled on the snacks, they discussed the local gossip. Pompeii was a hot-bed of intrigue and there was also much interesting news from Rome. Of course, now and then all of the women looked furtively at her new slave, most probably wondering what he was like in bed. Poppaea delighted in each covetous glance, finding pleasure in their envy of her new possession. She was certain that every red-blooded woman in Pompeii would want Taranis in her bed, thrusting his cock between her trembling thighs.

'My, it's warm today.' She looked pointedly at Taranis and he immediately picked up a peacock feather fan and waved it obligingly above her head. His expression betrayed nothing, but she knew he was hating all this – the women's stares, the way she had dressed him up to show him off and the fawning way she was expecting him to behave towards her. He had not looked very happy when she told him that, if she had dared, she would have been tempted to display him nude. However, in a situation such as this, with a number of very respectable women as her guests, that would have been considered too outrageous even for her.

'Very warm,' agreed Livia. She was looking decidedly pink, probably not from the heat, judging by the way she kept glancing hungrily at Taranis. The slave standing behind Livia began to wave his fan more vigorously.

Poppaea had never understood why Aulus had married Livia; it wasn't as if she was even remotely attractive. However, she had been a very rich widow, who was closely connected to the late Emperor Vespasian and his family. Of course, that was the only reason why Lucius had been made a legate at such an early age.

'The pool does look very tempting,' Corelia said. 'Perhaps we could have a swim?'

Poppaea knew that Corelia was having building work done, and her pool was out of commission at present. If Corelia hadn't suggested a swim, she had intended to do so herself. 'Yes, why not?' Poppaea agreed. 'Ladies, if you are not wearing suitable undergarments, go inside and my maids will provide you with something to swim in.'

Poppaea smiled as some of the women rose to their feet and hurried inside. Most likely they needed help even to undress. Many of them would have slaves who did absolutely everything for them, even apply the sponge on a stick to cleanse them after they had relieved themselves.

'I'll not bother,' Julia said, moving to Livia's side. 'You know that my mother doesn't like to swim, as she's scared of water. I'll take her inside for a while instead.'

'Of course.' Livia was such a pathetic woman, Poppaea thought, as she rose to her feet. 'Taranis, help me with my gown.'

He stepped forwards to unfasten the gold and sapphire fibulas that held her gown together at the shoulders. Just the feel of his warm fingers on her flesh made her shudder with pleasure. The gown slid to the ground and, as she stepped out of it, he bent to retrieve it and laid it neatly on her chair. 'Is there anything else, my lady?' he asked in his cultured Latin. It was far from the bastardised Latin most barbarian slaves used.

The fabric of her only undergarment was almost transparent, and it was so short it only just brushed her thighs. She felt his eyes upon her semi-naked body as she said, 'Yes, you can accompany me to the pool and help me down the steps. Yesterday, I noticed that they were quite slippery.'

His blue eyes narrowed as he accompanied her towards the water. Did he suspect her motives? Or was he just squinting because of the strength of the sun? When the thin linen of his scanty garment got wet, it would cling revealingly to the bulge of his sex. Poppaea was determined to let all her friends see just how magnificent he truly was.

They reached the pool and Taranis walked down the first two steps, then took her hand and helped her descend. 'Lower,' she instructed. 'I don't want to fall.'

Solicitously, he helped her, even though the steps were not slippery at all.

When the water lapped at the hem of his garment, he looked questioningly at her. 'Perhaps I should stay here and help the other ladies as well?' he suggested, as Corelia and the others appeared, now appropriately dressed for swimming.

'No,' Poppaea said curtly. 'Help me down further.'

His mouth tightened but he said nothing, as he helped her further down the steps until she reached the floor of the pool and he was standing waist deep in the water.

'You can go back to the top of the steps and help the others now,' she said.

She turned and waded away from Taranis, then she began to swim slowly towards the deep end. Taranis, however, did not move, but just stood there watching Poppaea. Meanwhile, her friends were managing to navigate the steps quite easily without any help. They waded past Taranis, glancing admiringly at the bare-chested handsome slave. Then they began to splash around in the water, laughing and giggling together, and making no attempt to join Poppaea in the deeper water.

Poppaea swam to the end of the pool and turned around. She was surprised to see Taranis still standing there looking at her. Why was he being so obstreperous? she wondered irritably. 'Move,' she shouted, feeling a little awkward as she waved agitatedly at him. 'Leave the water now, Taranis.'

Move he did, but not up the steps as she had ordered; he dived under the water and swam towards her, while her friends stared at him in total amazement.

'How dare you!' she hissed, as he reached her.

'I dare.' He gave a bitter laugh, then ducked under the water. He didn't surface again immediately because he'd dived between her legs. Poppaea tensed, her eyes growing wide with surprise, as she felt his fingers on her pussy. Lust and desire lanced through her body as his mouth fastened like a leech on to her sex, while his tongue flicked teasingly against her clit.

Poppaea tried to muffle her gasp of pleasure, all too conscious of her friends still staring at her, obviously wondering what was happening. Then, to her relief, he surfaced beside her again and took a deep breath as he pushed damp strands of hair away from his face.

'Damn you to Hades,' she cursed. 'What do you think you're doing?'

'This,' he said softly, as his bunched fingers slid smoothly into her cunt.

Poppaea gave a loud squeak of surprise. The sensation

was so delicious that she wanted to tell him to push them even deeper inside her. He began to move them slowly and sensuously. She had never realised before how wonderful sex could be when surrounded by water. If she'd known she would have fucked Taranis in the pool before this, but not in front of all her friends.

'You must stop.' She was begging now, not ordering. Yet she really wanted him to continue, the sensations of his cold fingers thrusting inside her and the water swirling round her pussy was exquisite.

'I want to fuck you,' he growled softly. She was so very tempted to say yes, even though the idea was totally insane. He pressed his hard body against hers, his fingers still working their magic inside her, while his thumb rubbed her clit. Her insides were melting and she barely felt the rough concrete against her back; all she was conscious of was the delicious feel of his thrusting fingers and his engorged cock rubbing sensually against her stomach. 'Do you want me to push it inside you right now?' he whispered.

'Yes,' she gasped, forgetting everything but her desperate desire for this man.

'In front of your guests?' Taranis asked caustically, removing his fingers and backing away from her.

'No, of course not.' She felt empty without him inside her, but she was also furious with herself for succumbing so easily. 'Get out of the pool, now,' she ordered, her face turning scarlet with embarrassment. 'Go to my bedroom, wait for me there.'

Taranis smiled, then grabbed hold of the side of the pool. Using his powerful arms, he heaved his body from the water. Then he stood by the side of the pool for a moment, looking down at her. The sopping-wet fabric clung to his body, fully revealing the size of his erection to all her friends.

He picked up one of the towels left for the guests, wrapped it around his waist and strode towards the house.

Taranis understood Poppaea's anger. He should never have given into the temptation of paying her back for parading him in this skimpy costume, in front of all her most respectable friends. It had just reminded him, much too harshly, of the fact that he was nothing more than a slave. That was something he had been hiding from himself of late. When they were in her bedroom and he was in full sexual control, he could almost forget the humiliations life had heaped upon him.

He walked into the tablinum, passing the wall covered with funeral masks of Poppaea's ancestors. Red ribbons were strung tightly between them, linking father to child, wife to husband, acting as an eternal reminder of how much the present was connected to the past.

The interior of the villa was quite dark in contrast to the bright sunlight outside. It took him a moment for his eyes to adjust and in that moment he almost cannoned into Julia.

'Oh!' she exclaimed, as she paused in surprise.

'Forgive me, my lady.' He stepped back a pace.

'It's nothing,' she said distractedly, as a pink flush spread quickly across her pale cheeks.

'I do not like to speak out of turn,' he said politely. 'And forgive me for doing so, but when I first saw you in the garden your features seemed so familiar. I could not place you at the time. Now I know where I have seen you before.'

She appeared to find it difficult to look at him at all. Then she lifted her eyes and stared straight ahead, but she was far shorter than Taranis and she found herself facing his bare still damp chest. 'The baths,' she said shyly.

'Yes,' he confirmed, well aware that he should not be talking to her like this. 'I did not know that there were ladies bathing at the same time.'

'There were no ladies bathing. It's just that I own the Venus Baths,' she admitted. Her breathing quickened as she at last looked at his face. 'I came upon you quite by chance.' She blushed an even deeper shade of pink. 'I did not mean to spy –'

'I should not have mentioned it, my lady.' He felt sorry that he had embarrassed her. She had obviously seen the slave pleasuring him and had most probably disapproved. 'Please do not blame the girl.'

'I did not.' She smiled awkwardly. 'To be honest I had completely forgotten the incident until you mentioned it,' she said hurriedly. 'Poppaea, she's not a bad mistress, is she?'

A strange question to ask of a slave. It was almost as if she was concerned for his welfare. 'No. She is very demanding and she expects my attention at all times.' He paused. Julia did not seem the type of woman who knew much about the intimate duties he was expected to perform, and he didn't want to upset her by being too frank. 'Mostly she is a good mistress. It is not my place to complain. I just felt a little uncomfortable when she dressed me up in this ridiculous outfit and paraded me in front of her friends.'

'It must be difficult,' she agreed. 'Poppaea does like to show off her possessions, but you don't look ridiculous at all, just very handsome.' She gave an uneasy laugh. 'I confess even I was relieved when Poppaea managed to purchase you at the auctions. It would have been terrible if Gaius had won. I do not like him, he has strange tastes.'

Their conversation was getting weirder by the moment. 'I thank the gods that they spared me.' Taranis frowned thoughtfully. 'You were there, I think. Your voice sounds familiar.'

'Yes,' she shyly confessed. 'After I'd seen you at the bathhouse I thought – I just decided to try and buy you, that's all.'

For once, Taranis didn't know what to say. Julia didn't strike him as a woman who would purchase a pleasure slave.

When he didn't reply, she added, 'There was just something about you, Taranis. I felt drawn to you.' She sighed. 'And you are a very striking-looking man.'

'It is a pity you lost,' he said without thinking. He liked Julia, she seemed a kind and thoughtful woman. She would most probably be a far easier mistress to please than Poppaea.

'I did not lose. My stepfather prevented me from bidding more, even though I could easily afford it,' she confessed, then hurried away from him.

6

Taranis sat on the floor by one of the windows in Poppaea's bedchamber, after deciding that it would not be wise to just strip and lounge on her bed as he usually did. He wondered how she had explained away his outrageous behaviour to her friends. She was proud of him and had wanted to show him off to them. In some ways, she was very insecure and she needed their envy, as it made her feel superior, and every inch the niece of a former Empress. He didn't like being thought of as her possession but, if he was brutally honest with himself, he was just that and he had behaved totally inappropriately in front of some of the most influential members of the nobility in Pompeii. He had lost it completely and acted without thinking.

He was becoming rather uncomfortable, sitting on the hard floor, and his crumpled garment was all but dry by the time she stormed angrily into the room. 'May Poseidon pierce your entrails with his trident,' she hissed as she caught sight of him. 'And stand up when I'm talking to you. After all, you are a slave, although you seem to forget that far too easily of late.'

'On the contrary,' he replied, as he rose to his feet. 'I remember it every moment of the day and night. Nevertheless, I should not have acted as I did. I'm sorry.'

'Sorry is not good enough, Taranis,' she shouted, as she ripped off her dress and threw it at him.

'I don't expect it is,' he agreed, as he stepped over the dress and walked towards her. 'I embarrassed you in front of your friends, even more than you embarrassed me it seems.'

'Embarrassed!' she repeated furiously. 'Slaves aren't allowed to feel embarrassed. If I order you to walk around the city stark naked, your cock strung with jewels, you do it. That's what slaves do, they follow orders.'

Acting purely out of instinct, Taranis pulled Poppaea into his arms and held her close. Still shaking with fury, she pressed her cheek against his broad chest as angry tears flowed from her eyes.

'Everyone in the city will be talking about this tomorrow. Corelia is a terrible gossip. They will all laugh at me for being far too indulgent with a slave. I'll have to hide myself away from polite society for weeks.'

'Send me to the forum to be whipped. Then they'll all see that you are punishing me,' he said, as he gently pushed her damp hair away from her face.

'If I do that, your beautiful back will be torn to ribbons.' She sniffed. 'You're worth too much money for that, Taranis. I have to protect my investment.'

'So lash marks would lower my value?'

'You know they would,' she responded, as he tenderly ran his hands over her bare back. 'Jupiter defend me.' She thumped his chest with her clenched fists. 'I'll find a way to punish you, Taranis.'

He nibbled teasingly at her earlobe. 'And in the meantime?'

'Finish what you started in the pool.'

He lifted her into his arms and carried her to the bed, laying her gently down among the scattered pillows. She lounged there watching him, angry tearmarks staining her cheeks and smearing her eye make-up. She didn't look much like the niece of a Roman Empress now, but Taranis didn't care, he would give her exactly what she wanted.

He removed the crumpled garment he hated so much and flung it away from him, hoping he would never have to wear it again. Then he moved to the foot of the bed. Poppaea immediately spread her legs for him and he could see her swollen pussy lips guarding the pink slit of her sex. Just looking at her lying there waiting for him aroused him. He felt his erection grow stronger, as he remembered the intense invigoration he had experienced when he'd touched her in the pool. The same angry fire filled his veins, but this time it was tempered by a strange mixture of affection and pity for his mistress.

'I want you so much,' Poppaea said, her eyes fastened on his cock, which was now standing provocatively out from his groin.

She sighed as he leant towards her and pressed hot kisses on the insides of her thighs, nibbling teasingly at her soft flesh. All his pent-up feelings came into perfect focus, as he smelt the sexual heat emanating from her pussy. He wondered what her important friends would think of her now, lying there legs spread like a whore waiting for her next customer. Taranis was filled with the sudden urgent need to treat her exactly like that. To jump on top of her and shove his cock inside her, using her brutally as a master would his slave. Nevertheless, he couldn't do that; he had humiliated Poppaea and, if he wanted to retain his position in her household, he had to play the submissive penitent tonight.

Poppaea moaned hungrily, as he parted her swollen pussy lips and ran his tongue up and down her rosy slit, flicking it against her clitoris, before sliding it down to delicately probe her vagina. The interior was moist and as smooth as silk and he felt her body tremble with pleasure as his tongue slid deeper. Poppaea's anger had made her incredibly horny and, when he touched her clitoris again, sucking on it gently, she climaxed almost immediately.

Taranis knew that he was far from finished yet as he eased himself upwards until he was lying across the lower half of her body. He tweaked her nipples between his thumbs and forefingers, pulling and squeezing until she started to moan, aroused by sensations that were on a knife-edge between pleasure and pain. Then he sucked on the dark tips, one by one.

'Please,' she begged. 'Fuck me. I want to feel your cock inside me right now.'

Taranis was only too happy to oblige. The tension was already building inside him and, when he slid into her moist, slippery warmth, the combination of sensation was so powerful that he almost climaxed immediately. Fighting to control himself, he gently lowered his body on to hers, pressing her down upon the pillows. He lay there for a moment, not moving a muscle, breathing deeply until he'd gained full control of his lust again.

'No one has every filled my cunt like you do,' Poppaea groaned, wantonly pushing her hips up towards him. 'Screw me hard.'

Taranis slid his hands round her narrow hips and dug his fingers into her buttock cheeks. His mouth moved to her breasts again and he sucked hard on her already abused nipples until they were both hugely distended. She gave a small whimper as he began to move his hips, fucking her hard and deep. Soon he was hammering into her like a man possessed. Putting all his weight behind each thrust, as if this would somehow excise both the demons inside him and the hurt he had caused her.

'Yes,' she screamed, as she twined her legs around his lean flanks.

Their bodies moved as one, the bed ropes groaning beneath their combined weights. The blood sang in his ears as his body released its load in a deep and prolonged climax, hearing Poppaea gasp and tremble beneath him as she too came.

They were dining late this evening, a celebration of sorts, Lucius had said. He had been working hard putting the villa to rights and Sirona had been helping him where she could. She had chosen materials: thick heavily embroidered fabrics to cover door openings and light sheer muslins to hang at the windows to help reduce the glare of the sunlight. Lucius had picked out most of the furniture, as Sirona wasn't that well acquainted with Roman tastes. Mostly he had selected his purchases from drawings and these items were now being made by artisans in Pompeii, while all of the more elaborate pieces were being shipped from Rome. It appeared that money was no object where Lucius was concerned.

Sirona had arrived here with nothing but Lucius's cloak wrapped around her naked body. Now she had a plethora of new garments to choose from: dresses made of fine linen, embroidered muslin and brilliantly coloured silk. Also, Lucius had given her a carved box containing cosmetics but she hadn't yet tried any of these on her face. She knew what each of the many pots contained. There were powders made with white lead or chalk to lighten sallow complexions and black antimony to outline eyes and dye lashes. Also there were tiny boxes containing various shades of pink and red powder to colour cheeks and lips. Lucius had also purchased scented oils for her and perfumes either made from rose petals or a heady mixture of myrrh and other spices.

Last but definitely not least, he had given her jewellery. A number of beautiful necklaces and bracelets made of gold and semi-precious stones, along with matching sets of delicately crafted fibulas.

Sirona was confused by Lucius. She had come to like, even admire the man, and the sexual attraction was still there, even though she did her best to ignore it. Yet to her amazement he'd not made the slightest attempt to seduce her. He had just been polite and respectful, as he would be with any guest. Nevertheless, after all the gifts and the kind way he had treated her, she had decided that she could not deceive him any longer. A few days earlier, before they had dined, she had admitted, rather awkwardly, that she could speak Latin perfectly well.

She had expected him to be angry with her, but he had just laughed and called her a devious minx. In fact, he seemed to find it amusing that she had managed to deceive his stepfather all the time she had lived in his house. By now, she had discovered that Lucius did not like Aulus Vettius very much, because of the thoughtless and often cruel way he treated Lucius's mother and sister.

Sirona had a personal maid, a sweet girl from Sicily called Amyria, who was just helping her into one of her new gowns. It was a long silk peplos, the exact same shade of green as her eyes. The long, full tunic had a folded hem at the top, which when it was fastened together at the shoulders draped delicately down over her full bosom.

'Now we need this,' Amyria said, as she wound a wide gold ribbon around Sirona's slim waist, criss-crossing it round her body, before fastening it tightly under her breasts. 'That's better. Do you like it?' Amyria asked, as Sirona stared at herself in the mirror.

The ribbon made the loose garment far more flattering as it held the silk tightly to her upper body, then it flowed gently out from her waist, moulding lightly to her hips and legs as she moved.

'It looks lovely.' Sirona smiled at her reflection. She felt strange dressed in such fine clothes and with her hair piled atop her head in the very latest style from Rome. Even the bone pins keeping her hair in place were beautiful, each one having a different, cleverly carved head in the shapes of animals and flowers.

'Now this.' Amyria fastened a necklace around her neck. It was a delicate ring of twisted gold, set with small green stones.

'It doesn't look like me at all.'

Sirona might have been a princess but it had always been in name only. She had never lived a life of luxury; most of the time she and her father had been on the run moving from place to place. That was apart from the five years she had spent in Colchester, living with a Romanised family who was sympathetic to her father's cause. It was there that she had learnt to speak Latin fluently as well as read and write the language.

'It just complements your beauty,' Amyria said with a warm, very genuine smile.

'If only Taranis could see me like this.'

'My lady?'

Sirona blushed, for a moment she had not realised that she had spoken her thoughts aloud. 'I was thinking of a friend – we arrived here together.'

Amyria probably knew all about her past life. Most household slaves gossiped incessantly about their masters and mistresses.

'I fear that all of those who came with me could well

have been sold as slaves,' she admitted sadly. 'Taranis, he was one of the leaders of the rebellion in Brittania. I never learnt of his fate.'

Amyria frowned, then glanced around to make sure no one could hear them. 'I'm not sure I should tell you this. The master has forbidden us to speak of what happened before you came here. I think he fears that it might upset you.'

'I need to know,' Sirona said. 'If you can tell me anything at all, please do.'

'There were stories circulating the city about a magnificent slave. He was said to be tall, blond and very good looking, but he came from Gaul, not Brittania.'

'That's him.' Sirona felt her chest suddenly tighten and she could not breathe properly. 'You know what happened to him?'

'Apparently, he was purchased by Poppaea Abeto, a very rich lady, and a relative of a former Empress, for three hundred and sixty thousand denarii. The highest sum ever paid for a slave in Pompeii –' Amyria hesitated, clearly not sure if she should continue.

'Go on, tell me all,' Sirona begged.

'It is said that the slave was very well endowed and the lady in question wanted him for her bed.'

Sirona knew that she should be relieved that he was safe, but she was filled with a sudden surge of jealousy and pain. She couldn't imagine the warrior she had known and loved as a pleasure slave, forced to bed his new mistress whenever she desired it.

'Thank you, Amyria,' she said. 'I'm pleased to know that he is safe.'

'Do you want to know about the other Britons?' Amyria asked. 'I'm sure I could find out if you want me to.'

'No,' Sirona replied decisively. 'I have no wish to upset

your master. Perhaps it is best that I leave the past where it is – dead and gone.'

'I'm sure that would be wise.' Amyria gently patted her arm. 'What is to be is to be. Our fate is in the hands of the gods. The master is a good man and he cares for you.'

'Yes.' Sirona swallowed hard, forcing her thoughts of Taranis to the back of her mind, at least for the time being. 'I must go, Lucius is expecting me.'

They were eating for the first time tonight in the newly refurbished main dining room. She hurried through the villa, her leather-soled sandals making no sound on the elaborate mosaic floors. The main peristyle was completed now. She had watched this afternoon, as a bare-chested Lucius had helped a number of slaves move the last statue into position. She had to admit that she had been rather excited by the sight of his naked flesh and the muscles of his back rippling, as he helped lift the heavy marble figure into place.

He really was a very good-looking man, she thought, as she caught sight of him waiting for her in the triculanium. He was lying on a couch, but when she entered he politely rose to his feet.

'Sirona.' His dark eyes slid admiringly over her shapely form. 'You look so beautiful.'

'Like a princess?' she replied with a wry smile.

She felt unsettled, just as she always did when she saw him again. She found it difficult to ignore the fact that she was very attracted to him. Yet her emotions were tempered with guilt because she felt that she was betraying Taranis. However, now she knew that her former lover spent his days pleasuring another woman, maybe willingly, maybe not, and it was highly likely she would never lay eyes on him again.

'Sit down,' Lucius said. 'Now that you look like a

Roman lady, you must dine like one,' he added teasingly, as he grinned at her. 'Lie down as I do, don't sit there looking as if you are going to run away at any moment.'

They ate together every evening and so far she'd not even tried to recline on her couch. 'As you wish.' She positioned herself properly, propped up on her left elbow, so that she could eat with her right hand.

She looked at Lucius relaxing on the couch opposite hers. Tonight, for the first time, he wore a toga to dine in, but he wore no undertunic. The fine white fabric was draped over one shoulder, so that half his chest and one muscular arm were on view to her. For a moment she could not tear her eyes from the expanse of bare tanned flesh.

'Here, try the wine.' He pointed to her goblet. Instead of a pale-straw colour, the contents were a rich ruby red. 'It arrived in port this morning.'

'Phoenician wine?'

'Yes, try it but be careful. It would be ruined if I had it watered down, so it is very strong.'

Sirona had fortunately suffered no ill effects from the first occasions that she had imbibed a little too much and she was now quite accustomed to drinking wine. However, when she tried this, she discovered that it was far richer with a strong fruity taste. 'It's delicious.'

A gentle breeze drifted in through the opening facing the peristyle. The torches flickered briefly and Sirona felt the cool air brush her flesh. She could hear the cicadas singing outside in the greenery. She felt as if she were trapped in some strange dream, living a life that did not truly belong to her.

She watched Lucius eating as he usually did, like the military man he was: consuming his food quickly and efficiently as if he wasn't expecting to eat again for some time. He suddenly paused. 'You're not eating?'

'Of course I am.' She put down her goblet and picked up a slice of rolled beef stuffed with chopped eggs and olives. 'I was just thinking of your life as a soldier. Do you find it hard to always be on the move, Lucius?'

'Easier for a man like me than you, Sirona. You are far too beautiful to live life as a warrior. Beauty such as yours needs to be cherished not wasted on the battlefield.'

For a moment she was overcome by the sensual way he was looking at her and her heart gave an uneasy somersault. 'Women in Brittania are not pampered as they are here,' she replied, unsettled by the intensity of his stare. 'We are simple people. We fight as we live in a wild rather uncontrolled fashion.' She bit into the beef, chewed it and swallowed it quickly. It slid down to her stomach as though it were made of lead.

'Is that why your father employed a mercenary from Gaul to lead his army.'

Sirona forced herself to eat more of the beef, even though she now did not have the slightest desire for food. She was filled with desire for something far more powerful, as she stared at Lucius's handsome face. 'My father was no fool.' She took a large gulp of wine to help force down the food. 'The mercenary was a Roman citizen,' she said, somehow not wanting to speak Taranis's name to Lucius. 'He was well versed in your ways and in your methods of fighting.'

'Agricola wrote to me. He said that, if your father had managed to find more men like that mercenary, his legions might well have been defeated.'

'It is too late to think of that now.' She had no wish to speak of the past with Lucius; she needed to concentrate on the present. She had to accept the fact that Taranis was lost to her and make the best of her new life. 'Tell me about Rome. What is the city really like?'

Sirona managed to force down a little more of the varied dishes on offer, but it was mostly the rich red wine she consumed as she listened to Lucius talk. Not surprisingly, he was far more eloquent when speaking his own language. He told her of the beauty and size of the eternal city and the power and strength of the two Emperors he knew so well. Vespasian had spent most of his short reign constructing the coliseum. The magnificent structure had been erected on the site of the Nero's Golden House. Now Titus was planning one hundred days of games, during which the coliseum would be flooded for a day so that a sea battle could be fought. It would be the most amazing spectacle ever seen in Rome.

'I should like to see that,' Sirona said, not realising that the battle would be fought in earnest and many of the participants would be killed.

'Perhaps you will,' Lucius replied. 'I can take you there, Sirona.' He smiled indulgently as he saw her conceal a yawn behind her hand. 'You look weary. Let's walk a while in the garden. It will help your meal go down before you retire.'

She was filled with a warm languid sensuality and yet she still felt confused by her conflicting emotions as Lucius rose to his feet and stepped towards her. She had expected the same pleasant tingling sensations she'd experienced before when their hands had touched, not this strong surge of sexual desire that almost took her breath away as he helped her up.

She had to hide her sudden arousal from Lucius, as he slipped a possessive arm around her waist and led her into the newly completed garden. The fountain was working now and the sound of the water was soothing. Somehow she couldn't seem to help herself as she leant against Lucius, feeling the powerful strength of his body, smelling the sweet-scented oil that clung to his warm flesh. The sensations were so overwhelming that she gave an unconscious sigh as she looked up at the night sky.

'Are you sad?' he asked.

'No, I was just thinking that the sky is very beautiful. There seem to be more stars here than at home.'

'I think it is just that the skies are cloudier in Brittania. When I was there, I used to miss the sun of my homeland so much.' His hand slid upwards, until it was just beneath her breasts.

'Sometimes I miss the grey skies.' She turned to look at him, knowing that as she did so she was stepping over a precipice and there was nothing that would stop her from falling. She lifted her hand and tenderly caressed his lean cheek as she pressed her body close to his.

'I don't want to force you,' he said softly. 'Do you feel as I do?'

'Yes,' she found herself murmuring.

His lips covered hers, his kiss deep and probing. Sirona returned it eagerly, wanting it to become as strong and violent as the desires that were suddenly flooding her body.

She felt a little dizzy and the stars above seemed to spin of their own accord, as Lucius's tongue eagerly explored her mouth. Sirona let him take complete control of the situation, shivering with anticipation as he lifted her into his arms and carried her to his bedchamber. The lamps were all lit and, as he set her down on her feet, she saw the need he felt for her reflected in his dark eyes.

Awkwardly, he started to fumble with the gold ribbon encircling her waist. 'Tell me to stop if you don't want this,' he said, unaware of how desperate she suddenly was to see his naked body and feel his warm flesh pressed close to hers.

'I don't want you to stop,' she said, her legs now feeling a little wobbly.

She pulled the folds of the toga off his arm, exposing his entire chest. There was a small arrow of silky black hair leading down towards his groin. Leaning forwards, she brushed it with her lips and Lucius gave a soft groan.

'Let me.' Pushing his fingers away, Sirona untied the ribbon and dropped it on the floor. Lucius's hands reached for the ornate fibulas holding the flimsy silk together on her shoulders. This time he wasn't so clumsy as he unfastened them quickly and the soft fabric drifted down her body and fell in a pool at her feet.

Lucius cupped one full breast in his hand as he rubbed his rough fingertip against her erect and aching nipple. The sensation was delicious and her sex felt warm and all too ready for him, as she pulled at the ties holding the toga around his waist. The long length of fine white wool fell to the floor, totally enveloping the small green patch of discarded silk.

By now, Sirona was desperate to see him naked as she kicked off her flimsy sandals and tugged urgently at his brief loincloth. He helped her pull it away, releasing his cock, which was already stiffly erect. A hot uncontrollable need filled her body and her pussy grew wet, as he gently guided her towards his wide bed. They fell together on the coverlet, hungry hands reaching for each other.

Lucius looked down at Sirona as if his eyes couldn't get enough of her, while he explored every subtle curve of her naked body. His hands were those of a soldier, roughened by handling weapons and she shivered as his callused fingers stroked her breasts. He kissed her again, working his tongue into her mouth.

Sirona forgot any of the lingering doubts she once might have felt. All she knew was that she wanted Lucius, as his lips slid down her neck and over her collarbone. He captured one of her nipples with his mouth and the gentle pulling sensation sent shivers of pleasure through her entire body. He curved his tongue around the hard tip while his hands gently squeezed and caressed her breasts. Then his mouth slid downwards again, his teeth gently nibbling at her flat belly.

She wanted to touch him too, but when she reached for him he pushed her hands away. 'Not yet,' he pleaded, as he gently parted her thighs. Her heart raced out of control, as his fingers stroked her auburn bush of silky hair, not appearing to find it at all offensive as some Romans would.

Lucius eased his fingers between her swollen sex lips and groaned softly when he felt how wet she was there. Gently, he slid two fingers inside her, while his callused thumb rubbed her clit. The flesh was so swollen and tender that she could feel the pleasure rising swiftly inside her. She sighed, no longer feeling the faintest tinge of embarrassment or regret, as he eased her thighs wider and buried his face in her pussy. Sirona shuddered with delight as his tongue slid into the narrow crack, seeking out the firm bud of her clit. He brushed it, very tenderly at first and the touch was far too gentle to satisfy her. Lifting her hips, she made an imploring noise deep in her throat. His lips fastened around the small bud, teasing and titillating, while his fingers slid deeper inside her. Sirona's senses soared and she seemed to leave her body, looking down upon his dark head buried between her thighs as the sweet sensations enveloped her completely. In minutes, her body was shaken by a voluptuous shuddering climax that left her satisfied yet still wanting more.

'My sweet love,' Lucius murmured, holding her close, as her body trembled in the aftermath.

'Please, Lucius.' She was still hungry for him; she wanted to feel him inside her and her hand reached for his cock. Her fingers closed around it, feeling its swollen strength, as she began to masturbate him gently.

'No, don't,' he said shakily. 'Or I won't be capable of anything in a moment.'

She didn't want him to come just yet; she needed to feel his body thrusting inside her so she pulled her hand away. As he moved his body atop hers, she trembled in anticipation. Then he slid his cock deep into her pussy. It felt so good to have this man inside her, as she savoured the musky scent of his body and felt the heat of his skin seeping into her flesh, while the weight of him pressed down on her belly and hips.

He paused and looked down at her with such tenderness that she could barely breathe for a moment. For the very first time since she had left Brittania, she felt truly safe, locked in this man's embrace, his penis buried deep inside her.

She knew that he desired her desperately, but he was holding back, trying to be gentle with her. Yet she no longer wanted tenderness, she needed him thrusting into her hard and fast. She pushed her hips upwards and dug her fingers into his shoulders. 'Fuck me, now,' she pleaded.

He began to move, thrusting into her compliant body with deep powerful strokes. She moaned with pleasure, as he increased his pace, angling his body so that, with each sweet stroke, the shaft of his cock brushed her swollen clit. One sensation layered atop another, the build-up slow and exquisite. She felt the first waves spreading through her body, just as she felt his cock twitch. Lucius gave a loud groan followed by an all-encompassing shudder as he came, while at that very same moment a second voluptuous whirlwind of pleasure swept through Sirona as she climaxed once again.

Taranis thought that he heard Poppaea call his name, yet he believed it was all part of the muddled dream he was having, until fingers dug into his shoulders and shook him awake. Surfacing slowly, he forced his eyes open, but for a moment he could see nothing but a faint blur, as they refused to focus. Then he tried to move his arms down from above his head and he felt the hard uncomfortable jerk of chains pulling at his wrists.

He blinked, trying to clear his vision. His head was aching and his thoughts were in confusion. It was morning, judging by the light filtering through the curtains, but he still couldn't quite remember why his arms were restrained. All too soon, he realised that his legs were held down as well. 'What in Hades?' he mumbled thickly.

'You're chained hand and foot, Taranis.' Poppaea was speaking to him.

Painfully, he turned his head and saw her standing near the head of his bed. 'I don't –' His words trailed off, as she moved down the side of his bed and jerked off the thin blanket covering his naked body.

'I promised to punish you last night and *now* I am going to.' She stared down at him as he licked his dry lips uncomfortably. 'In case you're wondering, I had the wine that had been left for you, and that you drank so greedily last night, drugged. I wanted some time to decide exactly what I was going to do with you. You didn't think that you were going to get away with your outrageous behaviour in the pool, did you, slave?'

Taranis swallowed hard; his mouth felt as parched and gritty as the desert of Thebes. Experimentally, he tried to move; the chains were restrictive but not as tight as he had at first presumed them to be. 'I never really know what to expect with you,' he admitted in a cracked voice. He coughed as he strained his head back.

Behind his bed there had been a wall hanging but that had been stripped away to reveal two iron rings in the wall, each now holding one of his chains.

'Here.' She held a cup of water to his lips and he drank it greedily.

'Thank you,' he said, relieved that she was showing some feeling for him. Whatever his punishment was to be, it was likely to be carried out here in his bedchamber, fortunately far away from the sight of the other household slaves. 'I'm not to be whipped in the forum?'

'No,' she snapped. 'And don't be so facetious.'

He winced as he felt the sting of a cane hitting his belly and chest.

'As I told you before, Taranis, you're an investment. I'll punish you but I've no intention of marking you permanently.'

Sunlight suddenly streamed into the room, as the curtains were pulled open. Taranis blinked again as his eyes adjusted to the brightness and he saw a tall, quite dark-skinned stranger standing by the window. 'So you need help to punish me, do you?'

'Even now you dare to speak in a manner not befitting a slave,' she said coldly. 'But, as you ask, I'll tell you, Taranis. I may need help of one kind or another and Africanus is the only person I can trust with this.' She snapped the end of the cane against the side of his bed. 'As you know, my tastes run in varied directions and I have no wish for my house slaves to learn of this side of my nature. They gossip far too much for my liking, and I am too kind a mistress to try and force them to hold their tongues by making them fear for their lives.'

'Too kind by far,' he mumbled ironically, while wondering uneasily exactly what help this man was intended to provide.

'Which shall I use on you first? This?' She held up the cane. 'Or this?' She picked up a small whip with knotted strands of very soft leather. It looked as if it was designed to cause pain but not tear the skin.

'The choice is yours, not mine, my lady.' Taranis forced himself to stare at Poppaea with surprisingly untroubled blue eyes. Above all else, she wanted him to show fear and he refused to allow her that particular pleasure.

'Indeed it is.' She flicked the cane sharply across his chest a couple of times.

This time he was more prepared and he managed not to wince, even though the blows left scarlet weals on his bare flesh.

Using just the tip of the cane, she gently poked his flaccid cock. Taranis felt a flicker of fear slide insidiously up his spine, yet logic told him that Poppaea wouldn't dream of harming his manhood, because that was what she treasured at present above all else.

'I want to hear you beg for mercy, slave.' She tightened her lips, as she put down the cane and picked up the small whip. Expertly, she flicked it across his flat belly. It stung like hell but it didn't cut his skin.

Taranis clenched his fists. He didn't cry out and he barely flinched, as she hit him again and again, letting the cruel strands painfully caress his belly and chest. He even managed to hold back his gasp of agony, as the ends of the strands just caught the side of his cock, even though the discomfort was even more intense on this sensitive part of his anatomy.

Immediately, Poppaea paused and frowned. She bent forwards, appearing concerned, as she closely examined his penis. 'Perhaps it would be better if we turned him over now, Africanus.'

The man stepped forwards and grabbed hold of Taranis. With a grunt, he heaved him on to his side. With another loud grunt and a great deal of effort, Africanus managed to roll Taranis on to his stomach. It was then that Taranis realised why the chains had not been fixed too tight as he felt his arms and legs pulled taut as the chains crossed and shortened.

'Reaffix the chains holding his ankles. Make sure his legs are held apart,' Poppaea ordered sharply.

Taranis felt the chains loosen momentarily, as the man unfastened and uncrossed them, before the sharp jerk, as his legs were forced apart when Africanus repositioned them. He twisted his head but, held down like this on his stomach, he couldn't quite see Poppaea. He waited for the familiar stinging pain of the lash but it didn't come. Instead, Africanus forced a very thick pillow under his stomach, which kept his belly away from the bed and lifted his buttocks in the air. He felt all too vulnerable, as his flaccid cock fell limply forwards on to the rough linen sheet.

Anticipation like this was not to be favoured, as he had no idea what she was about to do next. He presumed the lash, but he didn't trust Poppaea; knowing her, it could be just about anything. He thought that he heard her say something to Africanus but he couldn't make out the whispered words. Then she stepped into his line of vision and he saw that she had removed her loose gown. She appeared unconcerned that she was stark naked in front of Africanus.

'Do you fuck him too?' Taranis asked with derision.

Poppaea gave a soft laugh. 'You're not jealous, are you, Taranis? I might perhaps if I could but poor Africanus lost his manhood in battle with the Syrians many years ago.' She looked back at the man. 'Show him.'

Africanus calmly removed his tunic. His once muscular soldier's body had softened and turned to fat in places. Taranis barely noticed that, as he stared at one mutilated testicle and nothing else. He'd seen many terrible battle wounds in his time, including missing limbs, but nothing unnerved him quite as much as this. It was every man's living nightmare. 'By the gods.'

'Africanus has adjusted quite well to his change of fortune.' Poppaea smiled rather indulgently at the stranger. 'He gets pleasure from watching others and from inflicting pain. Sometimes he even plays the woman's part.'

'Acting as a cinaedi,' Taranis muttered, unable to hide his disgust. 'He enjoys men fucking him?'

'He enjoys many things – just as I do.' Poppaea gently caressed Taranis's muscular buttocks. 'Don't decry what you've never tried. Think what would have happened if I'd let Gaius purchase you.'

'I'd have died rather than let him –' Taranis mumbled.

'I'd rather you lived,' she said, as she picked up the whip again, and started to use it on his back and buttocks. She hit him once, twice, any number of times. When the pain increased exponentially, he lost count.

Poppaea paused, she was breathing heavily and he knew that whipping him was arousing her. That he had expected, but what he had not expected was how the sting of the lash had made the blood pound through his veins. The pain had started to magnify, then moments earlier it had changed, becoming almost sexual in its intensity and he'd felt his cock stiffen just a shade.

Gently, she slipped her hand between his legs to caress his balls and stroke his cock very gently. 'So the pain doesn't excite you too much, yet?' she purred. 'It will, given time.'

He didn't reply, he didn't see the point. Taranis was frightened that, if she did continue, a deep dark part of his psyche might even come to welcome the agony. In the past, he'd known men who were aroused by pain and he didn't want to join that particular fraternity.

He shuddered in surprise, as Poppaea bent to kiss his rear end, caressing his inflamed skin with her lips. Slowly, she ran her tongue into the crack of his buttock cheek. She was still stroking his shaft and, as he felt the moist tip of her tongue circle his anus, his cock started to grow hard and a faint groan of pleasure escaped from his lips. Damn Poppaea to Hades, he thought, as she masturbated him, her hand moving very slowly and deliberately up and down his thick shaft. He wanted to beg her to pump it faster, to fondle his aching balls, and push that teasing little tongue deeper into his anus, but he did not. He just clenched his fists even harder, his muscles tensing, as he pulled against his chains, while he loathed and yet enjoyed the slow sensual movements of her fingers. Taranis was under no illusion here; to be sure, she was arousing him with every intention of exciting him as much as she could. But this was a punishment, so Poppaea wouldn't let him climax; she'd just tantalise him a while longer, then pull her hand away leaving him screaming for fulfilment.

Suspicions apart, this still felt good, and he closed his eyes, giving himself up to the pleasure, which was gradually overpowering the stinging ache of the skin on his buttock cheeks. He gasped in surprise, feeling the familiar agonising pain, as the lash started to once again caress his back and hips. Poppaea was still wanking him so it could only be that bastard Africanus wielding the whip. He was far stronger and each stroke became more unbearable than the last, yet all the time Poppaea was still working on his cock and his arousal was increasing.

'No,' Taranis heard himself gasp. He was experiencing a strange kind of exultation as the pleasure and pain mingled into one exquisite agony.

'That's enough,' Poppaea said sharply. She pulled her hand away, leaving him frustratingly close to orgasm. 'I told you, I didn't want his skin permanently marked.' She sounded angry, as she added, 'Those blows were way too hard.'

'I'm sorry, my lady.' The deep guttural voice came from Africanus, but it didn't seem to suit his mutilated body in Taranis's fevered mind.

His cock was aching for release. If only he could press it down against the rough sheet and somehow bring himself to a climax. Yet his chains were too tight, he literally could not move. Both his pain and his pleasure were totally in Poppaea's hands. He was certain that she was far from finished with him and he'd never felt more nervous and acutely vulnerable than he did right now.

He heard movement and hushed voices, but he was unable to strain his neck round to see what was happening. Then he felt a cold trickle of oil being dropped on to his inflamed buttock cheeks. It felt soothing. Even more so when Poppaea began to gently massage the oil into his abused flesh. The sensation became even more delicious when her fingers slid into the narrow crack of his buttocks and teasingly circled the small puckered opening.

'Does that feel good?' she asked, as her fingers eased the tight ring open and slid inside.

Taranis felt a strange fire fill his body, as her fingers crept insidiously inside a part of his anatomy that he'd never really associated with pleasure before. Just her touching him there so intimately was making his cock grow harder again. He was all too ready to give himself up to this strange unfamiliar delight, but at that precise moment Poppaea stepped into his line of vision again. Yet all the time those fingers were still continuing their deliciously intrusive invasion of his anus. Sweet Jupiter, it must be Africanus touching him there. Despite his sudden surge of revulsion at such a discovery, he was still finding it highly arousing, as the fingers slid deeper and deeper inside him. Poppaea, on the other hand, was wearing a strange contraption strapped to her hips.

'There's a large carved cock, almost as big as yours, Taranis. It fits snugly inside me, while this one –' She touched the polished ebony cock protruding from her pelvis, which was held on by wide leather straps '– it's smaller. I didn't think anything bigger would be suitable for your innocent little hole.'

Taranis couldn't think straight with those teasing fingers inside him. He'd heard tales in the past of the fake phalluses used by some whores. If he hadn't known what she planned to do with it, he might have found the sight of her and her fake cock quite arousing.

'Please, no,' he pleaded, knowing that all the begging in the world wouldn't make an iota of difference to what Poppaea had in store for him. Africanus had removed his fingers now, and he should have been relieved, but he wasn't because they were about to be replaced by this carved obscenity strapped to his mistress's hips.

Poppaea climbed astride his legs and, despite his fear and apprehension, a small part of him felt weirdly elated, even aroused by what she planned to do to him.

'You've fucked me enough times, Taranis,' she said softly, as he felt the cold hard tip of the fake cock press against his anus. 'Now I'm going to fuck *you*.'

Taranis struggled with his confused emotions. Tensing would only make this worse, he knew that, and he tried to force his body to relax. After all, he'd enjoyed the feel of Africanus's fingers sliding inside him, surely this could be no worse. It would be Poppaea fucking him, not a man. And the fake cock wasn't that large, he reassured himself, as she began to ease the oiled dildo inside him.

It wasn't exactly painful; the sensation was strange, yet oddly sensual as the carved ebony slid deeper into his back passage until it felt as if it filled him completely. Was this even close to what it was like for a woman to be fucked by a man, he found himself thinking insanely, as Poppaea dug her fingers into his sore hips and began to bugger him with slow smooth strokes. To his amazement, he began to enjoy the sensation of being impaled by the hard cock, as he was overcome by the fiery pleasure of absolute submission. He felt the urge to spread his legs wider, welcome it even deeper inside him as her hips pumped harder.

Firm fingers touched his penis; it couldn't be Poppaea but frankly he was beyond caring. He just gave into the myriad of sensations consuming his body, as the hand began to roughly pump his cock, while another fondled his balls. He was chained and he was helpless while Poppaea was thrusting inside him like a woman possessed and some man was wanking his cock. He was way above any of that now as he gave himself up to the hellish delights and the lewd sensations consuming his body.

His muscles bunched, the tendons of his neck tensed and he arched his back. The sensations were increasing with such intensity that he almost lost consciousness when his climax came and he reached the summit of a dark pleasure that he never knew existed before.

7

'I wish that you didn't have to go, Lucius,' Sirona said, as she watched her lover walk across their bedroom. He looked delicious stark naked and she couldn't help but admire the width of his muscular shoulders and the delightful curves of his tight buttocks.

'I have to see Admiral Pliny. As I told you before, he's staying for a few days with the former consul Pedius Cascus in Herculaneum and it's easier to see him there than go all the way to Misenum.'

It would be the first time he'd left her alone at the villa. Yet she wasn't truly alone, as she had a house full of slaves to take care of her.

'I promise that I'll be back by noon tomorrow, my sweet. And the next time I'll take you with me, but this isn't a pleasure trip, it's military business.'

'I know.' She didn't feel ready to meet his friends, let alone his military colleagues, just yet. When she did, she would have to socialise with people who in her past life she would have despised. Yet now she had to accept them because they were part of his life and she'd come to care for Lucius.

Sirona sat up and the thin sheet slid from her body. Lucius gave a soft groan and strode back to the bed. 'I'm a soldier, Sirona. I never thought I'd ever become so besotted with a woman that I'd want to forget my duty to the Empire.'

'Especially not with a woman you consider a barbarian,' she teased.

She squealed with surprise, as he flung himself down on the bed and grabbed hold of her. 'You look so delicious when you've just woken up,' he growled.

His mouth captured hers and he kissed her passionately. As his lips slid down to her full breasts, her hand reached for his cock. She wrapped her fingers firmly around the shaft, as his lips fastened on her nipple and began to suck on it gently. Shivers of pleasure darted through her body. Lucius smelt musky and so masculine, the odour of their last night's lovemaking still lingering on his flesh. Tenderly, she began to rub his shaft, feeling it swell in her hand, while his fingers caressed her belly and moved tantalisingly closer to her sex.

'Lie down – let me,' she insisted, pushing him back on to the mattress.

He smiled cheekily. 'What now?' I'm a slave to your demands, my lady.'

Sirona gave a soft laugh, then leant forwards. She ran her tongue around the tip of his cock, then slowly down the rigid stem. Lucius gasped as his cock twitched and grew harder. Lovingly, she slid her lips over the bulging head and pulled it into her mouth, while her fingers gently massaged the root. It was strangely empowering to take charge of their lovemaking and to see Lucius lying there, shuddering and sighing with pleasure, as she mouthed and stroked his cock.

'Is that good?' she asked demurely, still caressing the thick shaft, as she stared down at him. 'Do you still want to leave?'

'I never did, damn Pliny,' he murmured, as she straddled his hips and gently guided his cock towards the entrance to her pussy. Sirona sank slowly down on to him, letting Lucius enjoy the pleasure of sliding deeper into her warm, moist depths. 'Ah,' he groaned, as he stared up at her. 'That feels *so* good.'

She lifted her body, letting him slip nearly all the way out before impaling herself again. Then she began to fuck him, slowly at first then faster, all the while watching the expressions of lust and pleasure flicker across his handsome face.

Leaning forwards, she brushed her nipples against his firm chest. He reached out and grabbed hold of one full breast, kneading it roughly, while his other hands slid down to where their bodies were conjoined. The tips of his fingers brushed her clit and a dart of pure pleasure flowed through her body, so strong that she almost lost her rhythm for a moment.

With a hungry sigh, she moved her body faster, grinding her pussy hard against his pelvis until her pleasure peaked. Her breath came hot and fast as she climaxed, feeling his cock twitch excitedly inside her. As Lucius too reached orgasm, she pressed her lips to his and thrust her tongue deep into his mouth.

Taranis strolled along the Via dell'Abbondanza, just enjoying the feeling of freedom he experienced when wandering around the city alone. He was dressed, like many citizens, in a plain cream sleeveless tunic, decorated with two vertical blue stripes, and no one gave him a second glance – or so he thought. He was oblivious to the admiring looks he received from most of the women walking past him. Many might believe he was wealthy, judging by the thick gold bracelets he wore on his upper arms and the wide band of gold he wore around his neck. It was only if one looked closely at the decorative engraving on the necklet that it was possible to see the words carved into it which stated that he was slave to Poppaea Abeto. She'd had the goldsmith weld it around his neck so that he couldn't take it off. Then she'd told him that he was lucky, as most slaves only wore cheap iron rings on their fingers as a sign of their servility.

Taranis decided to take the longer route home, as Poppaea was out visiting friends and wasn't due back for some time yet. So he didn't turn left at the tavern, and just headed on down the main street, wrinkling his nose in disgust, as he caught the strong scent of stale urine emanating from the amphora outside the fullery.

He noticed a woman just ahead of him. She had her back to him, but he thought that there was something familiar about her. Then he saw her catch her foot on a stone that was raised slightly higher than the rest of the pavement. She stumbled and would have fallen if he hadn't darted forwards and grabbed hold of her arm.

'Thank you,' she said agitatedly. 'Taranis?' she exclaimed, as she looked up at him.

He smiled warmly at Julia, completely forgetting to let go of her arm. 'Are you all right? You look a little pale.'

'I met my stepfather quite by chance in the forum. He was on his way to see my brother,' she said a little breathlessly. 'Something he said upset me.'

'Then I should escort you home,' he replied, as she was looking troublingly pale and appeared to be trembling. 'Is it far?'

'No, just down the street a short way. But will Poppaea mind?'

'She trusts me with all her personal matters now.' He looked down at the wax tablet he was holding. On it, he had made a short list of all the work that needed to be done at Poppaea's other house near the Stabian Baths. She had asked him to inspect the place, as she was thinking of renting it out. 'So surely she will trust me with the welfare of her best friend. I'm certain she would think it my duty to escort you home.'

'Then your situation has improved?' she asked shyly.

'Yes,' he confirmed.

'Please don't,' she said, as he went to let go of her arm. 'I'd like to lean on you a little. I'm still feeling rather unsteady.'

'Of course.' It seemed wiser to step closer to her and hold her even more tightly. 'I'm acting as Poppaea's secretary now.'

Poppaea's former secretary had been taken ill a few days after the incident in the pool and she had surprisingly decided that the only person she could trust to replace him was Taranis. Now he spent his days dealing with her correspondence, her financial affairs, her personal paperwork and all the other duties she heaped upon him. It was a lot of responsibility, especially when she still expected him to spend his nights satisfying her. Yet it was still far preferable to just being her pleasure slave.

'That's good news,' Julia replied, clearly pleased by his new position. Secretaries, whether slaves or free men and women, were highly respected members of any household. As they began to walk slowly down the street, Julia added, 'My stepfather and I do not get on well.' She began to tell Taranis a little about her unhappy marriage to Sutoneus.

He was sorry to hear that her life had been so unpleasant, yet he was also rather confounded by the fact that she was being so open with him.

'Is this your house?' he asked, as they paused by a large wooden door, studded with bronze nails.

'Yes. I'm sorry I've been chattering on. It's nice to talk to someone who is so understanding.' She smiled shyly. 'It is very hot, so why not come inside and rest for a while ... if you can spare the time?'

'I am in no hurry,' Taranis told her. 'I'd like that.'

'Then come in,' she invited, as her porter pulled the door open.

Taranis didn't want to appear disrespectful in front of her house slaves and she seemed quite steady on her feet now, so he let go of her arm. He followed her through the villa and they entered a large garden, at the end of which, of course, would be the Venus Baths. He'd got to know the geography of the city quite well of late.

'Please sit, Taranis.' Julia pointed to a wide stone bench placed beneath the shade of a tree.

He sat and, to his surprise, she sat down companionably beside him. Taranis was equally surprised when two slaves appeared, one carrying a lightweight table and the other a tray with wine and two goblets. They positioned the table and tray in front of Julia and departed. She poured out the chilled wine diluted with water and flavoured with honey.

'Thank you,' Taranis said, as she handed him a goblet.

Julia was treating him like an honoured guest and he appreciated that immensely. By now, he was relieved to see that the colour had returned to her cheeks. She really was a very pretty woman, he thought, with her soft feminine features, full lips and sparkling hazel eyes.

'On the contrary, I should thank you for preventing me from falling, then escorting me home.'

'It was my pleasure.' He wasn't just being polite. He found her even more sweet and likeable now than he had the first time they met. 'I'm sorry your stepfather upset you.'

'Aulus thinks I should marry again, and soon.'

'And that troubles you?' Recognising the name, Taranis wondered if, by some strange coincidence, this was the same man who'd examined him so embarrassingly before he'd been sold. 'You're a widow, so surely you are free to marry whoever you wish?'

'No, he is determined to choose for me.' She sighed. 'Aulus Vettius is a senator and a very influential man. Or rather he was when Vespasian was alive.'

So it was him, Taranis realised. 'And now?'

'He has far less influence, fortunately. My brother Lucius is legate of the Fifteenth Legion of Apollo and a close friend of Emperor Titus. They're like brothers in many ways.'

Taranis respected the fact that she was speaking to him as she would a friend. It was a long time since he felt as free as he did now, sitting in this garden with Julia by his side. 'So will he help? Will your brother stop your stepfather forcing you into a marriage you do not want?'

'I'm certain that he will. Lucius is a good man.' She gave a sigh of frustration. 'It is not easy being a woman at times –' She paused and looked thoughtfully at Taranis, as she placed her hand on his arm. 'But it's far easier than being a slave. Especially for a man born and raised as a Roman citizen.'

'Poppaea's not that bad a mistress.' He gave a wry smile. They'd experimented with bondage on occasions, but to his relief she had never tried to use that fake cock on him again. He'd done his best to put that incident out of his mind, mainly because in a strange way he'd been aroused more than he cared to admit by what she had done to him. 'Often I overstep the boundaries and she doesn't punish me as she might.'

'Probably because you please her in other ways.' Julia blushed awkwardly, as if she didn't quite like to think of his true relationship with Poppaea. 'I was inside at the time, but later I heard about the incident in the pool. Was she very angry?'

'Angry? A little,' he replied evasively. She had kept

him imprisoned in his room for nearly three days, chained by his ankle to the bed, with not a stitch of clothing and no means to wash. Yet she had still visited him regularly for sex. 'It was my fault, I embarrassed her in front of her friends.'

The longer he stayed here, the more he decided that he liked Julia. She was so different from Poppaea and he wondered how much better his life would have been if she had managed to purchase him. Truthfully, he would have been happy to spend his nights in her bed; he might even have come to care for her, given time. He liked her and she seemed to like him. It was then he decided to ask for her help. 'I was wondering . . .'

'What is it?' She moved even closer to him.

'I came here on a ship, with others captured during the uprising in Brittania. Among them was a young woman, Sirona, the daughter of King Borus of the Icene.'

'And you want to know what happened to her,' Julia said with understanding. 'Fear no longer, Taranis. I know that she is safe.'

'You know?' He struggled to control his sudden surge of emotion.

'Yes. The Governor of Brittania charged my brother with her care. He and Lucius are friends.'

'I don't understand. She's your brother's slave?'

She stroked his arm reassuringly. 'Not a slave, Taranis. Lucius treats her as an honoured guest. As long as she remains in his household, she'll come to no harm.'

'And his wife does not mind?' He wanted to know all he could, but he dare not ask too much.

'Lucius is not married. He is a soldier; he has never been concerned about finding a wife.'

A sudden wave of acute jealousy consumed him. So a young, probably rich and very influential man was charged with caring for Sirona. She was beautiful and he was sure that Lucius was bound to be tempted to either force her or lure her into his bed.

'Don't look so concerned.' Julia smiled reassuringly at him. 'Lucius is a kind and noble man and he'll treat her well. My brother lives just outside the city, so I'll visit him and find a way to speak to this girl, Sirona. You feel responsible for her safety, I understand that.'

'The King charged me with her care.' It did not seem wise to tell Julia how involved they had actually been, and that Borus had given his consent to their marriage. He'd hoped to hold the ceremony after the battle had been won, but Agricola had destroyed those plans.

'I'll tell Sirona that you are safe and well. I can bring any messages she has back to you.' Then she added with an uneasy shrug of her shoulders, 'If one believes that being Poppaea's pleasure slave can be considered safe and well.'

'Be assured that I carry out my duties reasonably willingly,' he admitted. He found it rather unsettling that Julia was looking at him in a manner not quite befitting his status as a slave. 'Anyway, my fate does not matter. I'll survive, I know that, but Sirona ... I just want to know that she is safe and happy. Thank you so much for doing this for me, Julia.'

For a moment, he didn't realise that he'd inappropriately used her given name, neither was it appropriate for him to lean forwards to kiss her cheek, but he did it all the same. However, at that precise moment, Julia turned her head and their mouths made contact. She didn't pull away. She twined her arms around his neck and kissed him passionately. As a surge of unexpected desire flooded his body, Taranis kissed her back, finding the sweetness of her mouth compelling, as their tongues met and intertwined. His hand went to her breasts, stroking them gently through her thin dress.

Suddenly realising how wrong this was, he forced himself to pull away from her. 'If only you'd purchased me,' he found himself saying, as his heart beat loudly in his chest.

'If only.' She sounded breathless and she was trembling a little, as she shyly lowered her eyes. 'I wish it all the time.' Awkwardly, she pleated the fabric of her gown between her fingers. 'I should never have done that, Taranis, you belong to Poppaea.'

'My *body* belongs to her, Julia,' Taranis said softly, as he rose to his feet, wishing he could stay but knowing that he couldn't. 'But my heart and my soul are my own.' Then he turned and walked away from her.

Sirona sat up and punched her pillows, not wanting to try and go back to sleep for a moment. She'd been having strange, very unsettling dreams that still lingered on the fringes of her mind. She knew why she was feeling so unsettled – who wouldn't be when Aulus Vettius had turned up at the house unexpectedly only an hour or so after Lucius had departed? She had forced herself to greet him as she would any honoured guest, yet she had felt quite discomfited by his chilly derisive stares and curt almost rude response to her greeting. Perhaps it was just because she'd addressed him in perfect Latin and he'd realised how easily she'd deceived him.

From then on, she had kept out of his way, as he had walked around the villa giving instructions to the slaves and acting as if he owned the place. Sirona had avoided the senator but not his companion, Tiro. He had sought her out purely because he wanted to know if she was safe and happy. Of course, she had told him that she was fine, and she was certain that he had soon begun to suspect that she and Lucius were lovers. After all, she was wearing fine clothes and expensive jewellery and the slaves treated her more like a mistress than a guest.

She'd shown Tiro around the villa, while making every effort to ensure that they did not bump into the senator by mistake. Tiro had admired the Nile land-scapes in the Tuscan atrium and the tablinum with its newly restored Egyptian fresco. They'd ended up in the huge salon at the rear of the property. It was the only room that Lucius had chosen to leave untouched and she had no idea why. She liked the room because there were the most amazing life-size pictures on the walls. They appeared to tell a story of sorts but, because Lucius had made such a point of avoiding the room whenever he could, she'd never felt comfortable enough to ask him to explain them to her. Tiro told her that they depicted one of the rites of initiation into the Dionysiac mysteries. Not that long before, worship of the god Dionysis had been outlawed by the senate, because the rites included ritual sacrifice, flagellation and all kinds of wild sexual depravity.

Probably because of what Tiro had told her, Sirona's dreams had been filled with weird confusing visions of these bizarre rites and they all seemed to involve Aulus Vettius in some way or another. She couldn't seem to drive the frightening pictures from her mind as she reached for the goblet of water she kept by her bed, but it was empty. It must have been well after midnight, and there was no way she would disturb any of the slaves, so she would go to the kitchen and refill it herself.

She slipped on a loose robe and left her room. Fortu-nately, it wasn't pitch black, as there was a full moon. The moonlight bathed the peristyle in an eerie silvery glow, as she heard the soft clicking noise of the cicadas. Then she became aware of another noise that sounded suspiciously like music. She was supposed to be alone apart from the servants so where was the soft hypnotic music coming from?

She crept through the rear of the darkened villa, the marble mosaic floor feeling cold against her bare feet, her heart beating loudly in her chest. She reached the huge empty salon, and peered round the heavily embroidered curtain covering the doorway. Then she saw them. At least a dozen or so naked men and women clustered around a tall man wearing a strange mask. There was a dark-haired woman on her knees, her hands bound in front of her and the man was beating her with an ornate whip. It was just like the pictures of the rite of Dionysis that were painted on the walls of this room.

The music changed; there was a discordant clash of cymbals and a young, beautiful youth stepped forwards. He was naked and wore a wreath of laurel leaves on his long, curly dark-blond hair. In his hand was an ornate crystal goblet filled with a red liquid that could have been wine, or maybe even blood, she thought nervously. He offered the goblet to a male figure, who was half-hidden behind the others.

The woman who was being whipped appeared to be enjoying it immensely, moaning with pleasure and rubbing her bound hands agitatedly against her breasts. Around her, the others began to touch each other, men caressing men, women caressing women, gender didn't seem to matter. They started to move in a more frenzied fashion, squeezing bare breasts, rubbing cocks, thrusting between thighs or buttock cheeks. Moans and groans of pleasure punctuated the strange music, as they sank to the floor and began to copulate in every conceivable fashion.

Sirona's breathing quickened and she felt her nipples stiffen and her pussy grow wet. Who wouldn't be excited by this strange sexual ritual? There was an odd odour of what she presumed was incense permeating the night air, and it seemed to seep into the pores of her skin, making her think of anything and everything sensual and sexual. She could almost understand why they were doing this, as she saw a woman on all fours being penetrated by a man. Another man, with a stiffly erect oiled penis, knelt behind the couple and fed his cock slowly into the other man's bobbing anus.

Sirona couldn't believe this was happening. She felt as if she too was being consumed by this strange sexual excitement. She pressed her hand against her pussy, half-tempted to creep into the room and join in this frenzy of pure unadulterated lust. Yet it also frightened her a little and a small voice in her head was telling her to run away and not look back.

Ignoring the voice of reason, at least for the moment, she glanced again at the man wielding the whip. When she did, she realised that he looked disturbingly familiar, even though he was still masked. Of course, it was Aulus Vettius – why else would he have visited the villa yesterday afternoon? Presumably to check that Lucius had left, as planned, for Herculaneum. Had this room been decorated like this purely to facilitate this ceremony? It was, after all, Aulus who had suggested that Lucius buy this place.

She recalled that Amyria had been a little uneasy when she had bid her goodnight and she had seemed troubled that the key to the bedroom door had gone missing. Had she intended to lock her in, perhaps having discovered what was to happen tonight?

Sirona decided that it might be wise for her to leave

before someone saw her and she was perhaps pulled into the room and forced to take part in this wild sexual depravity. She'd speak to Lucius about this when he returned.

By all the gods, surely this could not be? Her chest tightened, her breath coming in nervous gasps, as she saw the other masked man, who had remained in the background until now, suddenly step forwards. He was fully aroused and he knelt, as if intending to penetrate the bound woman who had been whipped. Sirona put a hand to her mouth to muffle her gasp of anguish, the masked man looked uncannily like her lover Lucius.

Sirona didn't recall how she got back to her room, as she huddled beneath the covers, trying desperately to convince herself that she had been deceived and that under no circumstances could it have been Lucius. The man she knew and had grown very fond of would never have taken part in such a bizarre, illegal ceremony. Lucius worshipped the gods as all Romans did, but in the temples like everyone else. He was close to the Emperor, he was a loyal subject of the Empire and a leader of men; he would never have gone against the rules of the senate. Also, he was far away from here, and he wasn't due to return until at least noon.

She closed her eyes, but she was too upset and troubled to sleep. Eventually, she might have dozed for a while because, when she opened her eyes, disturbed by a faint noise, the sky had lightened a little. She heard the sound again, this time much louder, and she realised that someone was in her room. Filled with fear and apprehension, she froze.

She heard another sound and she wanted to hide under the covers, but she forced herself to lift her head and she saw a dark figure lurching towards her bed. Sirona opened her mouth to scream but her throat had tightened and all she managed was a muffled squeak.

'It's me,' a drunken voice grunted. Lucius fell heavily on to the bed. He was naked and he stank of stale wine. All the suspicions she'd tried to suppress rose to the surface again.

'What are you doing?' she asked nervously, as he struggled to climb under the covers.

He rolled closer to her, his hot sweaty skin pressed to hers.

'You said that you wouldn't be home until noon.'

'Sirona.' He chuckled. 'You sound like an angry wife.' The strong scent of stale wine almost made her gag as he gave her a slobbering, drunken kiss. 'Couldn't stay away from you a moment longer, my sweet.' He shoved a hand between her legs and roughly fingered her sex.

She didn't want this but she was aroused just by the familiar touch of his probing fingers. 'Lucius, please!' She tried to protest, but he silenced her with another drunken kiss, and this time she barely tasted the wine on his hot breath, as he devoured her with his mouth. Sirona tried to push him away, still full of suspicions. 'Leave me alone, you're drunk.'

He gave a husky laugh and rolled on top of her, nudging her thighs apart with his knee. 'Can't be drunk if I can do this,' he mumbled, as his hard cock pressed against her pussy lips. Then he thrust it inside her, even though she was nowhere near moist enough for penetration. 'So hot so tight,' he groaned, ignoring her gasps of discomfort, as began to pound into her.

'No, damn you.' She dug her nails into his muscular shoulders, and thumped him on the chest.

With a chuckle of amusement, he let his full weight fall on to her, pinning her down, as he grabbed hold of her flailing arms and forced them above her head. 'My sweet barbarian, I adore you,' he mumbled into her ear. 'When you fight me like this, it excites me even more.'

His mouth roved her breasts, licking and kissing at her nipples. He fastened his lips around one and sucked on it hard. The strong pulling sensation and the feel of his cock buried inside her increased her excitement, and she no longer had the strength or will to fight him. She gave a soft moan, as his body began to move, screwing her slowly and sensually.

She caressed his chest, her fingers reaching for his nipples. As she pulled at the firm paps, Lucius lifted himself on to his arms and began to pound into her. Sirona dug her fingers into his muscular flesh, no longer in resistance but purely to urge him onwards, as his movements became harder and rougher. The entire bed was shaking with the wild strength of his thrusts, while Sirona's mind was suddenly filled with the visions of numerous naked bodies, fucking and rutting in every conceivable way in the worship of Dionysis. It was as if the strange lecherous god had somehow worked his way inside her head. She began to enjoy even more the raw power of Lucius's body pounding into hers, consumed by a fever of carnal desire she'd never known before.

Her pleasure peaked and she climaxed, as she heard Lucius give a grunt of bliss, and he came, his cock pumping wildly inside her. Sirona lay there, too overcome and exhausted to move, as he rolled off her and slumped by her side. Within moments, he was fast asleep, snoring softly beside her. But her mind was still full of wild suspicions and no matter how hard she tried she could not sleep again that night.

Poppaea was holding one of her special dinner parties and she had invited all the most important men in the city. Apart from the female house slaves, the only women present were a few of Poppaea's less salubrious friends and a couple of Famosae – they were whores from well-off families who only sold their bodies to powerful, influential citizens.

It was the first time that Taranis had laid eyes on Aulus Vettius and Gaius Cuspius since that humiliating night before he'd been sold, and even looking at the two men made him feel very uncomfortable. Poppaea didn't like Gaius overmuch but he was an aedile, so she felt she had to include him, especially as the three other magistrates who ran the city had also accepted her invitations to be here.

Poppaea's honoured guest was the most important man in Pompeii, Cnaius Alleus Nigidus Maius, a former chief magistrate with censorial powers. Poppaea had told Taranis that Cnaius had many influential friends in Rome and was in some circles even more powerful than Aulus Vettius. He had personally funded numerous gladiatorial spectacles in the city and only just recently a statue of him had been erected in the forum.

Cnaius had been staring thoughtfully at Taranis for some time. Suddenly, he leant across the table separating Poppaea's couch from his. 'Your slave Taranis should be in the arena. He is a strong and seasoned warrior. A brilliant fighter, so I've heard. He'd be the perfect centrepiece for my next games.'

'A gladiator?' Poppaea exclaimed in horror. 'My beautiful Taranis in the arena – never!' She turned to look at Taranis who stood by her side dressed in a tunic of the most expensive and finest white wool, decorated with thick gold embroidery at the hem and sleeves.

'I could ask the slave what *he* thinks,' Cnaius said with a teasing smile. 'Perhaps he'd prefer the excitement of the games to this pampered servile existence.'

'I speak for him,' Poppaea said tersely. 'He has no wish to fight for his life, perhaps die in the arena. Is that not so, Taranis?' she said, looking up at him. He bent his head respectfully towards her, as she added, 'It is far more comfortable in my bed, is it not?'

Poppaea brushed her lips across his cheek and the tender gesture was not lost on Cnaius or Aulus, who was sitting next to her.

'Yes, my lady,' Taranis replied. 'I live only to serve you,' he added, thinking those fawning words would please her even more.

She smiled dotingly at him. 'I'm getting a little chilly. Fetch me a shawl.'

As Taranis walked away, he heard Aulus say coldly, 'You are far too indulgent with that slave. Look at him, he's dressed as finely as any leading citizen.'

Taranis did not hear what Poppaea said in reply. He hurried through the villa and climbed the stairs to her room. He found Aulus a very unpleasant individual. There was a cruelty hidden under the smooth senatorial veneer, and he could easily understand why Julia feared him so much. His thoughts lingered on Julia, as they often did these last few days. He'd not yet found the opportunity to see her again, even though he was desperate for news of Sirona.

After finding a suitable shawl, he made his way downstairs again. He was just walking towards the tablinum when, quite unexpectedly, a short fat man stepped out in front of him, barring his way. 'Taranis,' Gaius said thickly.

Taranis stared uncomfortably at the fat, sweaty red-faced man. He couldn't push rudely past one of Poppaea's guests, so he just stood there saying nothing.

'It's good to see you again and you look so well, so handsome.' Gaius lecherously licked his lips and stepped

165

closer to Taranis. 'Not as handsome as you did stark naked, with that glorious cock sticking out from your groin.' He grabbed hold of Taranis's arm. 'I was so happy when Poppaea invited me here. I've been hoping that tonight she might be persuaded to share you around a little.'

'I think not, my lord,' he said politely, doing his best to hide his disgust.

Taranis tensed as the fat slug stepped closer to him, shoved a clammy hand under the hem of his tunic and slid it up his leg.

'Please.' Taranis pulled away from Gaius, fighting the urge to hit him squarely on the jaw.

'Gaius, for Jupiter's sake, leave him alone.' Cnaius stepped between the two men. Fortunately for Taranis, he had just taken a short walk to aid his digestion. 'You've no chance. Why don't you just accept that?' he added with a grin of amusement. 'After Poppaea paid what she did for the slave, she's not going to share him with anyone – let alone you.'

'I don't see why not.' Gaius pouted petulantly.

'I do.' Cnaius winked conspiratorially at Taranis. 'I'm sure you are giving Poppaea her money's worth, young man.'

Taranis didn't think it right to join in this discussion so he stayed silent.

'You can speak, you know,' Cnaius said. 'I'm not averse to having a conversation with a slave.'

'When I've something to say,' Taranis replied. 'Unfortunately, I think it better to remain silent where the honourable aedile is concerned.' He shrugged his wide shoulders. 'Otherwise, I might be tempted to say what I really think.'

Cnaius threw back his head and laughed loudly. 'By all the gods, I should leave well alone if I were you,

Gaius.' He grinned at Taranis. 'Poppaea isn't one for sharing her possessions. Perhaps I should tell her that I found you propositioning her slave; you know how bitchy she gets when she's angry.'

Without saying a word, Gaius waddled nervously away from them, muttering frustratedly to himself.

Cnaius chuckled again. 'A man like you shouldn't be forced to dance attention on a woman like Poppaea. You're a warrior through and through.'

'I think that is exactly why she likes me so much,' Taranis confided. 'Precisely because I'm not like her other slaves.'

'Maybe so,' Cnaius said thoughtfully. 'But, if your situation changes, you have but to get word to me. I am rich enough to pay anything Poppaea wants. Remember, Taranis, if you fight half as well as I've heard you do, you could become rich, famous and adored by many.'

'If I didn't die first, of course,' Taranis pointed out. 'Before I was sold, I believed that becoming a gladiator was the only chance left to me – now I'm not so sure.'

'I am.' Cnaius punched his fist against Taranis's muscular upper arm in a manly gesture of comradeship. 'The two Britons are doing well in training. I'm sure they'll be heartened to know that you are safe.' Cnaius glanced down at the shawl in Taranis's hand. 'You'd better get back to your mistress before she complains about your tardiness.'

Taranis smiled at Cnaius; he felt that he was a man he would probably come to like if his situation were different. 'Thank you for helping me get rid of the honourable aedile.'

'Honourable, never!' Cnaius chuckled, as Taranis walked away from him.

Taranis returned to Poppaea's side and draped the shawl solicitously around her slim shoulders. She smiled at him but made no comment about the time that he'd taken, then she turned her attention back to Aulus, who was still sitting beside her on the couch. Taranis knew that she and the senator had once been lovers but he couldn't understand how she could even bear to be close to such a man. However, she was ruled by her sexual desires and Aulus could well be a good lay, or alternatively perhaps he enjoyed pandering to her more perverse sexual demands.

He stood there, watching Aulus openly fondling her breasts. Then his hand slid under her dress and, judging by Poppaea's expression, he was touching her sex. Perhaps he was even pushing those long cold fingers, which had once been very briefly inside Taranis's own anus, up inside her cunt.

Taranis found it uncomfortable to look at his mistress being fondled by a man he despised, so he glanced around the room. By now, all the guests had finished eating and were concentrating on more salacious matters. Soft music was playing, as a number of scantily dressed slave girls began a slow erotic dance. A couple of the female guests had their gowns pulled down to their waist to display their breasts. Others were laughing and lewdly fondling their companions. Gaius, meanwhile, was sitting on a couch with a skinny, weak-faced young man, who appeared to be enjoying all the slobbering attention he was receiving. Unfortunately, Gaius caught Taranis looking at him. He immediately shoved his willing companion aside and stood up.

'You like your slave far too much,' Taranis heard Aulus say to his mistress. Judging by the glazed expression on her face his fingers were still working inside her. 'But I'm prepared to go along with that. Why don't we go to your room and take him with us? Three is always better than two.'

'No.' Her full attention returned immediately. She straightened and put a restraining hand on his arm, which was still under her dress. She looked at Taranis, then she noticed a red-faced Gaius lumbering hungrily towards her pleasure slave. 'You're dismissed, Taranis. Go to your room. I have no more need of you tonight.' She glared at Gaius who turned away sheepishly and waddled back to his young male friend.

Aulus gave a cold laugh, pulling his former mistress close to him again, as Taranis turned to walk away. 'Too greedy to share him, Poppaea? You will, given time.'

Taranis was relieved that he wasn't expected to take part in all this, as he walked past a couple sitting on a couch, too intent on their conversation to take any notice of anything going on around them. He overheard the man say, 'The Icene girl, she's supposedly some kind of princess. The entire thing was quite unbelievable.'

Taranis paused. He edged along the wall just behind them, so that he could get close enough to eavesdrop on their conversation.

'She actually attacked him with a dagger, in front of all his guests?' the woman said in amazement.

'Everyone,' the man confirmed. 'She only grazed his arm, so it turned out. But I've never seen Aulus more angry. He threatened to have her killed.'

'He recovered quite quickly –' The woman paused, as another man approached their couch.

He started to speak to them about an entirely different matter and, realising he would learn no more, even though he was desperate to, Taranis hurried away. His heart beating out of control, concern for Sirona consuming his thoughts, he walked swiftly through the servants' quarters and ran out of the rear entrance of the house.

* * *

Julia peered out of her window, certain that she had heard a noise coming from somewhere down below. It must be the night watchman doing his rounds, she thought, as she saw the light of his torch at the far end of the garden.

She was only wearing a thin muslin robe but she still felt warm and uncomfortably sticky. The weather this August was hotter than it had ever been. Longing for the cooler days of autumn, she lifted her hair away from the damp nape of her neck. Perhaps it might be more comfortable if she tied it atop her head. She was looking around for a spare ribbon when she heard a strange scrabbling sound. Nervously, she turned towards the window. Hands grasped the wooden frame, and then a face came into view. 'Taranis?' she gasped in surprise.

'That wasn't easy,' he said breathlessly, as he leapt athletically into the room.

'What are you doing here?' She blushed shyly. Her nightgown was very thin and clung revealingly to her naked body.

Taranis seemed too concerned to care about her scanty clothing, as he strode forwards and grabbed hold of her shoulders. 'I had to see you.' He sounded short of breath, as if he had been running hard. 'At the party tonight,' he continued agitatedly, 'I overheard two people talking about Sirona. They said that she'd attacked your stepfather.'

'Oh that,' Julia said dismissively. 'You're concerned about nothing.'

'Nothing?' he repeated in disbelief.

'Yes.' She placed a gentle hand on his arm, drawing him towards the bed. 'Sit, I'll explain.'

Taranis was still on edge and didn't appear to want to sit but to please her he did. 'Tell me.'

'Sirona *did* attack Aulus, but that was some time ago,

the day Lucius returned to Pompeii. He prevented Aulus from punishing her and took her to his house.'

'In other words, Lucius rescued her?'

'She told me all about it when I spoke to her the other day.' Julia was relieved to see that he appeared a little less concerned now. She admired him so much because he still took his obligations to the defeated Icene king so seriously. 'Sirona is a charming young woman. Lucius treats her like a princess. He showers her with gifts. He adores her.'

'He cares for Sirona?' Taranis said, his jaw tightening.

'Deeply.' Julia smiled. 'It was nice to see my brother so happy. She cares for him too.'

Unknown to Julia, her words pierced his heart like a shard of ice. He had been holding out so much hope, now there was none, it seemed. 'She does?'

'Yes, isn't that wonderful?'

'Wonderful,' Taranis agreed.

Julia was a little confused, as he didn't really sound that pleased. He obviously needed to see Lucius and reassure himself that he was an honourable man. Perhaps she could arrange that somehow and, if Taranis could talk to Sirona and see how happy she was, that would be even better. Julia tenderly touched his taut cheek. 'You see, you shouldn't have been concerned. You've come all this way for nothing.'

'Not for nothing,' he said huskily, as he glanced down at her full breasts barely concealed by the thin muslin. 'You reassured me, didn't you?'

'I hope I always will be able to.' Julia had never felt this way before, elated yet vulnerable all at the same time. She was so aroused just by sitting close to this man. His raw masculinity, the sweet musky odour of his body and the sight of the taut skin on his muscular arms affected her in the most amazing way. Her entire body felt weak, as if it would melt if he touched her. At first, she had just wanted him but now she'd come to like him as well. Was it possible that she was falling in love?

'So do I.' He smiled. 'You have been kind to me, Julia. You've treated me like a man, not a slave.'

Just the sound of his deep voice made her shudder with pleasure. 'That's because I like you a lot, Taranis, and I respect you. But surely you took a chance coming here? Poppaea will wonder where you are.'

'No she won't, she's entertaining guests.' The way he said 'entertaining' told her everything. Julia knew that Poppaea was quite attached to Taranis, far more attached than she probably cared to admit. However, one man would never be enough for Poppaea, her friend would always want others as well.

'Poppaea is an unfathomable woman at times.' She shrugged her shoulders, very conscious that his eyes were still lingering on her breasts, and she felt her nipples start to harden.

'While you . . .' Taranis said softly. 'Somehow I seem to know what you are thinking, Julia.'

'How can you?' she asked, feeling weak with anticipation, wondering if he really knew just how much her body yearned for him.

'Because your feelings show on your face,' he said with a warm smile.

Julia started in surprise, as his mouth swooped down on hers. His kiss was deep, probing and utterly sensual, arousing thoughts and feelings inside Julia that she had barely known had existed before. Taranis eased her down on the bed, the kiss continuing, becoming passionate to the core. He meshed his fingers in her long brown hair, holding her face tenderly between his hands, kissing her until she was breathless with bliss. She shivered with excitement as his lips moved downwards, pressing hot kisses on her breasts, which were still partially covered by the thin muslin. His tongue delicately circled each nipple, the dampness making the fabric stick to the firm rosy peaks.

He seemed consumed by a wild need as he pulled up her gown to brush his lips over her belly, sliding them slowly downwards to her pudenda. She gave a soft, embarrassed groan of pleasure, as he dipped his fingers between her sex lips, smiling to himself as he discovered how moist she was there.

'So sweet, so soft,' he murmured, almost as if he were surprised that she desired him so much.

Taranis smiled lovingly at Julia and her heart beat loudly in her chest. She had dreamt of this moment but she had never believed it would come to fruition. Taranis moved away from her and she tensed in disappointment until she realised that it was only so that he could remove his tunic. As he turned back to her, she struggled with shaking fingers to pull her nightgown off over her head.

He gave a soft chuckle, as he helped her, his blue eyes tenderly roving her naked body. Then he was atop her, his knees parting her legs. There was no preamble, no more need for foreplay, just this desperate desire to feel him inside her. She was hot and moist and she gave a faint groan, as he plunged his cock into her molten core. She'd feared that he might be too big for her but, as he eased his cock deeper, their bodies fitted so neatly together it was beyond belief and she gave a loud sigh of pleasure.

Taranis paused and looked worriedly down at her. 'I'm not hurting you, am I?'

'No. Please.' She couldn't think of anything else to say, as she clutched his broad shoulders, feeling the amazing power of his muscles beneath her fingertips.

Taranis moved his hips, thrusting into her with smooth strokes. Soon she was lifting her hips to meet and complete each sweet movement. She even felt bold enough to twine her legs around his beautiful body, and as he thrust harder they began to move as one.

8

Sirona was feeling very uneasy, which was not surprising considering that she was about to attend her first social event with Lucius. It was a small party being held by his sister, whom she'd first met just over a week earlier. Julia had visited them quite unexpectedly and, when Lucius had left them alone for a brief moment, she had hurriedly told Sirona that her friend Taranis was safe and well. There had been no time for them to speak further on the subject but Sirona had been grateful for that small kernel of information. Perhaps, in time, she'd get the opportunity to learn more from Julia. Yet she knew that she had to be cautious and not reveal too much about her true relationship with Taranis; after all, the woman was her lover's sister.

Not surprisingly, since witnessing that strange ceremony she had become a little less trusting of Lucius. The following morning, he had been quite unwell and appeared to have forgotten how brutally he'd behaved towards her. Even his recollections of the evening appeared to be a little hazy. He told her that he had returned to Pompeii earlier than planned and had, quite by chance, met up with two of the men who had served with him in Judea. They'd gone to a tavern and drunk until the place had closed.

Surreptitiously, she had questioned the house slaves, but they all claimed to have seen and heard absolutely nothing. Even the night watchman had determinedly insisted that no one had come to the villa that night. So she'd eventually decided it might not be wise to even mention what she had seen to Lucius. She had tried to forget all about it, but forgetting that event wasn't so easy and she'd been having strange erotic dreams about the worship of the god Dionysis.

She looked anxiously at Lucius, as their litter stopped outside Julia's house. 'Are you sure this dress is suitable?' she asked him for the umpteenth time. The dress was one of her finest, made of heavy white silk embroidered with sparkling beads and real pearls.

'Of course,' Lucius confirmed, showing infinite patience. 'You look beautiful, Sirona. Everything will be fine; after all, you have already met my sister.'

He helped her out of the litter and took hold of her arm, as he guided her through the villa into Julia's garden. They walked towards the pool which looked wonderfully inviting. Sirona would have loved to be able to swim whenever she wanted, as she was finding the weather here unbearably hot at times. Lucius was planning to have a pool built at the villa but work hadn't started on it yet.

The dying rays of the sun glittered on the surface of the water, as Julia stepped forwards to greet them. She looked very pretty tonight, her face flushed with excitement.

'Lucius, Sirona.' Julia embraced Sirona as if she were part of the family and not just her brother's barbarian paramour.

'Julia.' Lucius affectionately kissed his sister's cheek. 'You look lovely this evening.'

'That's because I'm so happy,' she said brightly.

Even though dusk had not yet fallen, the lamps and torches decorating the garden were already lit. A number of guests had already arrived and they were sitting or standing around enjoying the cooler early-evening air.

'Come here, Poppaea. Say hello to Lucius.' Julia beckoned to a slimly built, attractive woman who had deep-red hair and wore a great deal of expensive jewellery.

Had she said Poppaea? Sirona stiffened. Hadn't the woman who'd purchased Taranis been called Poppaea? Of course, it could just be a strange coincidence. After all, there must be dozens of women with the same name in Pompeii. She glanced at Julia, wondering if she somehow might be able to let her know if this was indeed the woman who owned Taranis, but her expression betrayed nothing to Sirona.

'Lucius, how nice to see you after all this time,' the redheaded woman purred in a husky voice.

'Poppaea wants to ask your advice about a matter involving the Emperor. She feels that you can help, as you know Titus so well,' Julia explained.

'Of course.' Lucius politely inclined his head.

As Poppaea took hold of Lucius's arm and drew him aside, Sirona stood there feeling a little awkward. 'Why don't you take a walk?' Julia said. 'I know how strange and difficult this must be for you.' She smiled warmly at Sirona. 'If you just walk over the bridge and follow the path, you'll reach a part of the garden I know you will really like.'

It seemed only polite to do as her host suggested. It would be better than standing there like an idiot, waiting for Poppaea to stop monopolising Lucius. She smiled agreeably at Julia and made her way to the low wooden bridge, which spanned a narrow stream. After crossing the bridge, she followed the narrow path as it dipped behind some bushes and trees. By now, she was out of sight of the other guests and surrounded by greenery. It was a pleasant enough place but she was rather puzzled, as there was nothing of particular interest here.

Sirona paused; it was still light enough for her to see that she was quite alone. Yet she had a prickly feeling on the back of her neck, as if someone was watching her. She tensed, as she heard the rustle of leaves, then a hand grabbed hold of her arm. Another hand clamped across her mouth, as she was dragged behind some bushes into a small clearing. Her heart beat faster with fear, as she was held against a hard muscular body, then she felt a mouth pressed to her ear. 'It's me,' an achingly familiar voice said.

Sirona could barely comprehend what she was hearing and she was so overcome that she could only just manage to gasp, 'Taranis!'

'Yes, my love.' He turned her round and pulled her into his arms, staring at her as if he could hardly believe she was real. Sirona had never experienced such a powerful emotion in her entire life. Her heart swelled, feeling as if it might burst it was so full of joy. Never in all her wildest dreams had she truly believed she would see him again.

'How?' she asked shakily, amazed to see how well he looked. Taranis wore fine garments, gold jewellery and he was even more handsome than she remembered him to be.

'There's no time for explanations. We have Julia to thank for this.' His lips captured hers with a desperate sweet intensity, imparting all the love and passion he felt, as he kissed her long and deeply.

Sirona twined her arms around his neck, pressing her body against his hard muscular chest. 'I've missed you so much.'

Taranis stared deep into her eyes. 'You have a protector now, an important man, a legate – I thought that you and he –' He paused and shook his head, as if he couldn't even bear to ask if they were lovers.

'I care for Lucius,' Sirona admitted cautiously, remembering how confused she'd initially been about her feelings for Lucius. Yet she knew now that they were nothing in comparison to what she felt for Taranis. 'He's a kind man. He's been very good to me.' She lifted her hand and tenderly caressed his taut cheek. 'But it's you I love, Taranis. I always will.'

He smiled with relief, his hands moving to touch her body, tracing each gentle curve through her silk gown. 'Sweet Andrasta, I'd forgotten how beautiful you were. I love you so much, Sirona,' he murmured softly. 'That's what's kept me going all this time.'

'How much time have we?' she asked, knowing that she wanted him desperately, her pussy ached to feel him inside her again. They'd been given these few precious moments and she didn't want to waste them.

'Enough,' he said, kissing her again as he held her close. 'Tell me all that's happened to you.'

'Talk?' she murmured, her hand moving down to press against his groin. She shivered with anticipation, as she felt the hard line of his cock beneath his tunic. 'I want more than talk from you, Taranis.'

'But we shouldn't.' He glanced around the clearing. It was perfectly silent apart from the distant sound of birdsong; they could have been miles from civilisation. 'I don't want to put you in any danger.'

'I don't care, I want you,' she begged, rubbing his shaft through the thin fabric.

There was an urgency to his touch as he unfastened the fibulas holding her dress together at the shoulders. As the heavy silk slid down to her waist, Taranis gave a soft groan. Bending his head, he tenderly brushed his lips across her hard nipples and her body ached with need. The lust she felt for Lucius paled in comparison to this. Sirona clung on to Taranis, feeling she might swoon with the sheer pleasure of being close to him again. Swiftly, he removed his tunic and placed it on the ground. 'You mustn't damage your beautiful dress.'

Sirona was under no illusions. What he did not say was that she had to return to Lucius soon, looking serene and untouched, as if this blissful interlude had never happened.

Gently, he eased up her skirt, his breath coming faster, as he stared at her naked pussy. Sirona could not take her eyes off his handsome face so filled with love, the hard muscles of his chest and that glorious cock – she was getting wetter and wetter just looking at it. He was even more magnificent in the flesh than he was in her tortured dreams, as he knelt between her open thighs staring at her with such tenderness and desire it was almost more than she could bear.

Leaning forwards, he kissed her passionately again, then his lips slid down to her breasts, circling each hard peak with the tip of his tongue.

'No, let me feel you inside me,' she begged, knowing that Taranis was right and that every moment they spent together increased the danger they were in.

He covered her body and slid into her soft moist core. Tension and excitement surged through her body, as he started to sensuously move his hips, all the while staring into her face, as if he could somehow fix her features in his mind forever. Sirona's hands reached for his shoulders, her fingers digging into his hard muscles. She pulled him towards her, wanting to feel the entire weight of him pressing down on her as he thrust harder, knowing that never in a myriad lifetimes could any man ever replace Taranis in her heart.

Taranis fucked her with smooth hard strokes, angling

his body so that his shaft stimulated her clit at the same time. As she felt the weight of him powering against her pelvis, an intense erotic pleasure welled up inside her, becoming so strong she thought she might expire with bliss. The Elysian Fields moved closer and closer, as she heard his breath coming in short urgent gasps.

The sun was setting at last and darkness began to descend as the moon appeared in the sky. Its soft silvery rays bathed their bodies in an eerie almost magical light as their pleasure peaked. As Sirona climaxed, she heard Taranis whisper fevered words of love in her ear as he too came.

Aulus put a finger to his lips as one of the men accompanying him swore softly when he caught his foot on a small jagged stone. The men he'd employed for this mission were mostly former soldiers and all were well trained. There was the soft whispered swoosh of metal, as they drew their weapons, then crept forwards with military precision, skirting the rows of crops to enter the decorative part of the garden.

Dusk was descending fast but the moon was already visible in the sky and it was still easy enough to make out the two figures lying in the clearing, as they crept towards them. This was so utterly perfect, Aulus thought with glee, as he and his men just stood there and watched the man climax, hearing the woman give a soft keening moan of pleasure. The two lovers were so wrapped up in each other it was unlikely they would hear a herd of elephants bearing down on them.

Aulus almost envied the two slaves their mutual passion as they stayed there, still joined together, staring deeply into each other's eyes. He lifted his hand, gesturing to his men and they surged forwards. As they dragged the naked slave off Sirona, she gave a sharp scream of terrified surprise. The soldiers began pummelling Taranis, as he tried to fight them. He managed to throw a few punches and well-placed kicks but sheer strength of numbers enabled them to overpower him.

Sirona struggled to pull down her skirt with shaking hands, as two men grabbed hold of her and hauled her to her feet. Both looked lustfully down at her uncovered breasts as they dragged her in front of Aulus Vettius. By now, Taranis had been forced to his knees. Breathing heavily, he was held there by many hands, a dagger held threateningly across his throat.

'Good.' Aulus smiled, the self-satisfied smile of a man who had reached his objective.

He'd get his revenge on Lucius, and Poppaea would get her just desserts for becoming far too fond of her slave. Victory was sweet. He was pleased that he'd thought to place a spy in Julia's household just before that old reprobate Sutoneus had died. When he'd learnt that Julia had welcomed Taranis into her house like an honoured guest, he had been furious. He'd made a point of locating one of the slaves who'd been captured with the rebels in Brittania. Under intense questioning, the man had revealed that Taranis and Sirona had been betrothed. That, coupled with the fact that Julia had stupidly arranged for the two slaves to meet here tonight, had prompted this action. Then the two barbarians had played right into his hands, just as he had hoped they would, by being unable to keep their hands off each other.

'This way, men.' He moved up the garden followed by the soldiers dragging their captives with them.

Aulus smiled as he caught sight of Julia talking to Poppaea and Lucius. They were all together, that was even better, he thought, as they suddenly saw him walking towards them. Their polite smiles turned to expressions of anguished surprise, as they saw the naked man and the half-dressed woman he'd brought with him.

His thoughts in total turmoil, Taranis could do nothing to prevent the inevitable, as he was dragged up the garden. There were too many men even for him. Only the great Hercules himself could have overpowered all of them at the same time. He was certain that Julia would never have betrayed him. Why should she when he had led her to believe that he and Sirona were friends, nothing more?

As far as he could see, there was no way out of this mess. He'd been caught in flagrante delicto with the love of his life. Damn his stupidity to Hades! He should never have allowed his lustful desires for Sirona to overrule his responsibility for her safety.

Aulus had reached Poppaea, who was standing with Julia and a handsome dark-haired man who had to be Lucius, Sirona's protector. Taranis was forced to his knees in front of them and held there while all three of them stared at him in horrified surprise. He met Julia's tortured gaze for a brief moment and saw how upset and betrayed she felt.

'I told you not to trust him, Poppaea,' Aulus said with sickening satisfaction.

Oddly enough, Poppaea seemed just as upset as Julia did. Taranis had never seen her in quite such an agitated state before. It was almost as if it was her lover and not her slave that had betrayed her with another woman. Her face was as white as driven snow and her hand was shaking, as she lifted her peacock-feather fan in front of her face, moving it agitatedly, as if she were desperate to hide her true feelings from the senator.

The guards were still holding on to Sirona's arms,

preventing her from lifting up the front of her dress to cover her naked breasts. She stood there, head bowed, not daring to look at either Taranis or Lucius.

'Sirona, what happened?' Lucius's voice was filled with concern.

'What do you think happened?' Aulus said tersely. 'I found the two of them rutting at the end of the garden.'

Lucius shook his head. 'Sirona?' Judging by his haunted expression, it was obvious to Taranis that the Roman cared deeply for her.

She at last lifted her eyes and looked at him, tears trickling down her cheeks. 'Lucius, I –' She shook her head, unable to say anything more.

'Let go of her,' Lucius sharply ordered. When the men didn't immediately obey him, he stepped forwards and wrenched Sirona away from them. Tenderly he lifted the white silk folds so that they covered her breasts. Having nothing to fasten it with, he moved one of her hands, making her clutch on to it. 'It's all right, Sirona.' He spoke very gently to her, yet the muscles of his face were taut with anger.

'It was my fault,' Taranis said loudly. 'I forced myself on her.'

'Forced?' Poppaea repeated in disbelief. 'You came here together, you fought together. For all I know, you've always been lovers. Don't be insane, Taranis.'

'I did,' he insisted desperately.

One of the guards clipped him hard across the face, splitting his lip, and it started to bleed.

'She rejected me in Brittania. I desired her but she never wanted anything to do with me. Then, when I saw her in the garden, she looked so beautiful – I couldn't help myself.'

'The slave is lying,' Aulus said. 'I know that for a fact.'

Taranis gave a grunt of pain, as a guard punched him

hard in the stomach, but he didn't give up. 'I raped her.' He looked pleadingly at Sirona. 'Tell them.'

She clung on to her dress staring with anguish at Taranis, tears still sliding down her cheeks. 'How can I?' she whispered.

'Because it's true, isn't it?' Lucius put a protective arm around her shoulders and pulled her close.

Both Poppaea and Julia turned to look at Lucius, appearing surprised that he'd actually believed Taranis's desperate confession.

However, Aulus gave a snort of frustration. 'True!' he sneered derisively. 'You're insane with lust for that bitch, Lucius. They were lovers before they came here. That's why she betrayed you. The slave never forced himself on her.'

'No.' Lucius shook his head determinedly. 'He *did* force himself on Sirona,' he said quietly but very insistently, as he turned to look threateningly at his stepfather. 'She is not to blame.'

Aulus shrugged his shoulders, as if unwilling to defy Lucius. At least Lucius cares enough to protect her, Taranis thought with relief.

Poppaea was still fanning herself agitatedly, as if she were about to melt at any moment, while he dared not even look at Julia. She'd been so happy when he had made love to her and he suspected that she liked him far more than she cared to admit. She'd arranged for him to see Sirona again out of the kindness of her heart and he'd thrown it back in her face. Nevertheless, despite these feelings of guilt, he would never have given up those few precious moments he'd spent with Sirona.

'We are leaving,' Lucius said, as Taranis stared with increasing desperation at his beloved.

Sirona cast one brief anxious glance in his direction

that told him how much she feared for his safety, then she allowed Lucius to lead her away.

'What will you do to him?' Julia asked Poppaea.

For the first time since he'd known her, Poppaea appeared unsure of herself. When she turned to look with troubled eyes at Taranis, he grew more and more certain that she had no intention of punishing him severely for his transgressions, let alone order his death, as some slave owners might have. 'He must be punished,' Poppaea said hesitantly. 'Yet, despite what he says, I blame the girl as well. He would never have ravished her; Taranis must have believed she was willing.'

'Are you mad, woman?' Aulus said in total disbelief. 'You cannot even consider letting him get away with this. Lucius is a fool for protecting that bitch Sirona, but you, Poppaea. Are you so enamoured of his cock?' He stared penetratingly at her. 'Or is it something else?'

'I'll punish him. I've punished him before.' Poppaea continued to wave her fan agitatedly.

'A lot of good that did,' Aulus said in exasperation. He turned to glare at Taranis still held there by his soldiers. 'He's your pleasure slave and I found him fucking my stepson's personal whore!'

'So?' Poppaea snapped, the colour returning to her cheeks in a sudden rush. 'Slave or not, he's still a man. We all know that men are ruled by their cocks. The girl was just a passing distraction. I paid an enormous amount of money for him and I'll not have him harmed.'

'That's your excuse, protecting your investment?' His expression hardened. Stepping towards Poppaea, Aulus grabbed hold of her arms, as if he wanted to shake some sense into her. 'He needs to be punished,' he said through gritted teeth. 'You won't make a proper job of it, so I'll do it for you.'

Poppaea's reluctance to comply was obvious. 'But his worth will decrease if he's marked,' she protested weakly.

'There are many ways to punish a slave.' Aulus looked penetratingly at Taranis, who knew he could cope with just about any punishment Poppaea thought up for him, but the senator was an entirely different matter. 'You let me take charge of him and I'll return the slave properly chastised. Yet I promise I'll leave no visible marks on his body.'

Poppaea's shoulders slumped. It was as if she was forced to agree, even though she did not want to. 'Two days,' she said hesitantly. 'Three at the most.' She cast a concerned glance at Taranis then looked determinedly at Aulus. 'Then I want him back.'

'Agreed,' Aulus said with a self-satisfied smile that made Taranis's blood feel as though it had turned to ice.

The sun rose, flooding the peristyle of the senator's house with the soft light of morning. Taranis wearily lifted his head. He'd been left there, naked and chained, all night, with his arms stretched high above his head and his feet barely touching the ground. As the hours had passed, he'd lost all feeling in his arms, while his legs and back were aching from the unaccustomed strain. Living with Poppaea had made him soft, he thought, as he saw a slave girl hurrying across the paved garden. She paused to look curiously at him, but scurried away as a tall figure appeared and walked towards him.

'I trust that you are enjoying my hospitality, Taranis?' Aulus said coldly.

He stepped closer to his prisoner, running his cool fingers over his bare chest then down his flat belly to his sexual organs. Taranis couldn't help tensing, as those fingers touched his penis, then gently fondled his balls.

'No wonder Poppaea likes this cock so much. I'd forgotten how large it was.' Aulus grasped the flaccid shaft as he looked straight at Taranis. 'Are you frightened, slave? You should be.'

Ignoring the fluttering sensation in his belly, Taranis clenched his jaw and said nothing, determined to remain brave and steadfast for as long as he could. He saw one of the soldiers who'd captured him the previous night approaching. He was carrying a large whip with knotted strands. It looked far more threatening than the one Poppaea had used on him, but he'd been present at enough whippings in the past to know that this lash was designed to cause pain yet not slice into the skin too much. Once again he was grateful that Poppaea still had this obsessive need not to have him marked permanently in any way. He was certain that he could easily endure such a punishment, in fact, it was infinitely preferable to the cold feel of Aulus's fingers exploring his body.

'Poppaea told me how she had punished you after that unfortunate incident in her pool. I think it would be wise for me to proceed in a similar direction,' Aulus said with a cruel smile.

Taranis licked his dry lips. Did Aulus mean the lash or the more intimate facet of the punishment? He realised exactly what Aulus meant when the senator's hands reached round him and slid intrusively between his buttock cheeks. 'Eventually, you may even come to enjoy what I have in store for you,' Aulus promised threateningly. 'But first that rebellious nature of yours has to be crushed.' He stepped away from Taranis.

Taranis saw a large number of slaves filing into the peristyle, as the soldier moved behind him.

'I always insist that my slaves witness punishments.

It reminds them that they should be obedient at all times,' Aulus announced chillingly. 'Begin, soldier.'

Taranis prepared himself, gritting his teeth, as he felt the first stinging pain of the lash across his back. It hurt like hell but was not as bad as it could have been. Pain was only relative, he told himself, as he endured the whipping, trying to ignore the stinging agony that time and time again seared his back and buttocks. He would have clenched his hands but there was no feeling left in his arms, and his legs were becoming weaker by the moment. His body jerked forwards now with every lash stroke, as he struggled to draw breath into his lungs, determined not to cry out at all costs. There was no sign of any sympathy on the faces of the onlookers. Just a dull look of acceptance on some, while others were clearly enjoying, or were excited by the sight of him being whipped, just as Aulus Vettius was.

Agony turned his thoughts into a muddled blur, as the pain increased exponentially. Then, to his horror, it did what it had done before, turning into something almost sexual in its intensity, as he felt his cock stir and start to stiffen. Why in Hades was his body betraying him like this?

Aulus suddenly raised his hand, indicating that the whipping should stop. Filled with relief, Taranis immediately tried to straighten his legs but his knees were trembling so much he would have fallen if his arms were not chained. However, the strain on his arm sockets was nearly unbearable and he managed to force his legs taut as Aulus stepped behind him and examined the marks on his back.

Gently, his fingers touched the scarlet weals and Taranis shuddered. 'You've cut the skin in places,' Aulus tersely informed the soldier.

Taranis heard the man's stuttering apology. He sounded scared of the senator and looked relieved, as he hurried away after being curtly dismissed. Meanwhile, Aulus stepped back in front of Taranis, and he saw the scarlet blood staining the senator's fingertips.

'My mistress would be very upset if she saw that,' Taranis said in a cracked voice.

'It is of no concern,' Aulus said dismissively. 'I have a slave who is skilled in dealing with such wounds. He'll apply a salve which will ensure that you will heal with no obvious scarring.' Aulus wiped his finger across Taranis's flat stomach, leaving a smear of blood on his skin. Then his hand reached down to examine his cock, which was nowhere near as flaccid as Taranis wanted it to be. Aulus smiled. 'Poppaea has taught you something, it seems. Or have you always enjoyed pain, Taranis?'

Taranis just managed to gather up enough saliva in his mouth to spit on the senator's feet.

Aulus stepped back, his expression hardening. 'You'll be on your knees begging so very soon.'

'Never,' Taranis shouted as the senator walked away from him.

Sirona had no wish for morning to come; yet it did, as sunlight streamed through the thin curtains covering the window. She lay stiffly beside Lucius, surprised that he was sleeping so soundly, while she had barely slept a wink all night. She wearily closed her eyes and once again remembered what had happened the previous evening.

She hadn't known what to think, as they'd made their way home, because Lucius hadn't said a word and he had barely even looked at her. When they reached the villa, he had grabbed hold of her arm and marched her into their bedroom. Filled with fear for her lover's fate, Sirona had stared nervously at Lucius, as he had torn off his toga, then his tunic, and flung them on the floor. When she hadn't moved, he'd walked over to her, undressed her as if she were a recalcitrant child then roughly pushed her down on their bed.

Very coldly, he had told her that, if she wanted sex so much, she could have it, before he'd fucked her with a brutality he had only displayed that once before when he was drunk. Soon his anger had turned to a wild sensuality and, despite everything that had happened, she had been aroused by his lust and had climaxed only seconds before him. Then, with a muttered comment about still being able to smell that barbarian bastard's scent on her body, Lucius had rolled over and gone to sleep. She had known without a doubt that he had not believed Taranis's desperate claim that he had raped her. She'd lain there too emotionally drained to even cry, hardly daring to think of what might be happening to Taranis.

'Sirona.'

She heard him softly whisper her name and she apprehensively opened her eyes to find Lucius propped up on one elbow looking down at her. 'Lucius,' she said awkwardly, as their eyes met. She did not know what to say to him.

Sirona went to slide from the bed but he caught hold of her arm. 'I'm so sorry. I treated you so badly last night. Can you ever forgive me?'

'Forgive?' she stuttered. 'You were upset.'

'But I didn't consider your feelings at all. You were upset too.' He pulled her into his arms, cradling her close to his chest. 'I had no right to be so brutal. I care for you so much, Sirona.'

'I know.' In some ways, it had been easier to cope with his anger than it was his affection. She was consumed with guilt. He had been so good to her, yet she had betrayed him without a second thought. Nevertheless, she couldn't help still loving Taranis. 'Lucius, I have to tell you. Taranis didn't –'

He put a finger to her lips. 'I don't want to hear it,' he said softly. 'It's over. We'll try and forget it ever happened.'

Impossible, Sirona thought, as his mouth covered hers and he kissed her with a gentle passion that displayed how sorry he was and how strongly he cared for her.

Taranis had endured the curiosity of the senator's household slaves for some time. They all wanted to know if he was worth those thousands of denarii Poppaea had paid for him, as they poked and prodded his body, cruelly twisted his nipples and curiously examined his cock. He had remained stoically silent, as he tried to ignore them, along with the stinging agony of his back and the constant pain of being held in this unnatural position for hours at a time.

His thirst had now become almost unbearable. The sun had risen high in the sky, he was no longer in the shade and he could feel the burning heat of the rays on his skin. Still the slaves came, two or three at a time, their cruel interest heaping fiery coals on the pain of his punishment Two women were with him now, crudely fondling his cock while exchanging lewd comments about what it would be like to own such a pleasure slave themselves. Neither of them was remotely attractive; they stank of garlic and their clothes were badly stained, so they probably worked in the kitchen.

Suddenly, there was the sound of someone clapping their hands sharply and to his relief the women stepped nervously away from him.

'Return to your work,' a pleasant-looking young man

with short brown hair instructed. As the women hurried off, he turned to the two burly slaves accompanying him. 'Let him down.'

As they loosened his chains, Taranis's legs almost gave way. He would have fallen if the two slaves hadn't grabbed hold of him. His arms fell uselessly down and, as the blood surged into them, he almost screamed out with the intensity of the pain. They half-dragged, half-carried him into a small room and lowered him down on to a narrow cot. Too drained to care about anything, he slumped face down on to the thin mattress.

'Can you lift your head enough to drink this?' Surprisingly, the young man addressed him in Sirona's Celtic dialect. Because he couldn't bear to roll on to his back, Taranis managed to lever himself up on his aching arms as the young man put a cup to his lips. 'This will help with the pain.'

The lemon-flavoured drink had a sweet herbal taste and he swallowed it quickly. 'Thank you,' he managed to say. 'Who are you?'

'My name is Tiro. I need you to trust me,' the young man replied, glancing at the two slaves who appeared puzzled by the fact that he was speaking to the prisoner in a barbarian language. 'I'll do all I can to help you for Sirona's sake.'

'She's safe?' Taranis asked, still too exhausted for complex explanations, but somehow feeling that he could put his trust in Tiro.

'I don't know. Rest now,' Tiro said, as Taranis, his arms not yet strong enough to hold him up for any length of time, collapsed back down on the bed. 'I promise I'll try and find out what I can. In the meantime, we need to see to your back.'

The soothing feel of healing hands cleaning his abused

flesh, then applying a salve, coupled with whatever was in the drink, allowed Taranis to gradually fall asleep.

When he awoke, the small room, with its high barred window, was in darkness. The rest had eased his aching muscles and the pain in his back had dulled considerably. However, his brief moment of respite disappeared in an instant as the door was flung open and slaves brought a number of oil lamps into the room, flooding it with light. What now? Taranis wondered nervously, as he rolled on to his side and saw Aulus stride into the room, accompanied by two heavily armed soldiers.

'On your feet,' Aulus snapped. When he didn't obey immediately, the two men stepped forwards and hauled him to his feet. 'Chain him.'

They pushed Taranis towards the opposite wall, then clamped manacles around his wrists, which were attached to short lengths of chain fixed to the wall at waist height. Surely not another whipping, Taranis thought. At least they hadn't chained him to the bed – that would have been a far more ominous move. Nevertheless, he had not anticipated what happened next. The two men pushed a wooden table between him and the wall. One of them grabbed hold of his neck and forced his body downwards, while the other tightened the chains so that he was held face down, his belly and chest pressed against the rough wood. He had no chance to resist as his legs were pulled apart and his ankles chained to the legs of the table.

How vulnerable he felt. Was Aulus going to fuck him like Poppaea had? he wondered, filled with disgust at the very idea. His anxiety increased, his stomach churned and he felt bitter bile rise up in his throat, as he heard the door being pulled shut. At first, he presumed he was alone with Aulus as the senator bent his head and stared penetratingly at Taranis.

'Still so brave, slave? Somehow I think not.' Straightening, Aulus slipped off his tunic to reveal a naked, utterly hairless body. Taranis shuddered apprehensively, as he added, 'Poppaea told me how she had fucked you with her fake cock. It's about time you tried the real thing.'

Taranis's heart sank, as the horror of those words permeated his mind. He closed his eyes unable to even watch Aulus standing there reverently stroking his own penis, trying not to think about what the senator planned to do with it, especially as he knew that it was quite common in Roman society for owners to use their young male slaves for their own sexual pleasure.

Suddenly, he felt gentle hands on his buttock cheeks and he realised that there was someone else present. A thin trickle of cooling oil dripped into the crack, then soft fingers began to rub the oil round the rim of his anus, before gradually sliding inside him. Taranis tensed, briefly recalling the strange desires Poppaea had managed to arouse in him when she'd penetrated him with that fake penis. Nevertheless, the idea of Aulus doing that to him was horrifying. There was no way he could stand this, he thought, as the fear welled up inside him.

'Stroke his shaft as well, Zymeria,' Aulus instructed. 'I want him to associate penetration with pleasure. Eventually, he'll enthusiastically accommodate any number of my most important friends.'

Sweet Jupiter! Did Aulus have any intention of ever returning him to Poppaea? He'd rather be dead than forced to become a cinaedi, he thought, as Zymeria's fingers slid between his open thighs.

Taranis did not want to respond but his body betrayed him yet again, as the slave girl gently caressed the sensitive strip of skin between his balls and his anus. It felt so good; he should have hated it but he didn't. He drew in his breath sharply, as she stroked his balls, then curved her small fingers around his cock. As she began to wank him, he felt his arousal increasing, yet he was still consumed by the fear of what Aulus intended to do to him.

Suddenly, the girl's soft hands were pulled from his body to be replaced by long cold fingers tracing the lines of the lash marks on his buttock cheeks. Taranis shuddered, as they were pulled apart and he experienced the unnatural sensation of a hot, hard cock pressing against his anal opening. Gradually, the obscenity eased its way slowly into his back passage. Taranis's soft groan was laced with fear, yet also a wild uncontrollable longing, a primitive sensation he could not explain, as the cock slid deeper inside him. He knew he should feel only disgust, but truthfully there was a raw kind of pleasure at being impaled on living flesh that was far more erotic than the hard dildo that Poppaea had used on him.

Aulus's belly was pressed against Taranis's whip-marked skin, and he could swear that he could actually feel the senator's cock pulsing with life inside him. He wanted to beg him to desist, but perversely he wanted him to continue – he was too far along the road to turn back now.

Slowly and deliberately, Aulus began to shaft him, his balls slapping against Taranis's buttock cheeks, his thin fingers digging into his abused flesh. Taranis gave another troubled groan of anguish, as he pressed his face, turned scarlet with shame, against the rough wooden tabletop.

He tried to stop himself becoming even more aroused, but it proved impossible as the slave girl crawled under the table and began to mouth his cock. It was sheathed in her warm wet throat, while Aulus continued to thrust his cock deeper and deeper into his anus.

Taranis loathed Aulus almost as much as he did himself, as the senator led him across the river Styx into the molten core of Hades itself. His lust increased beyond all explanation, as the sharp combination of sensations sent him over the edge and down into the erotic darkness where redemption no longer existed. As he climaxed, pumping hard into the slave girl's willing mouth, he heard Aulus give a long drawn-out gasp of pleasure, and he felt that intrusive cock pulsing wildly deep inside him.

He lay there, breathing deeply and trembling with emotion, so abjectly humiliated that he could only wish he were dead. As Aulus withdrew, he shuddered, his body feeling as though it had peeled open and was now utterly exposed.

Seconds later, a hand grabbed hold of his sweat-stained hair and lifted his head. 'You enjoyed that, didn't you?' Aulus hissed in his ear.

Taranis couldn't even bring himself to look at Aulus, in case he caught sight of that cock which only moments earlier had been sheathed inside him. 'It was disgusting,' he managed to say in a strained voice.

Aulus gave a coarse chuckle. 'Somehow, Taranis, I can't bring myself to believe you. I wager that in less than a day you'll fall to your knees and beg me to fuck you.'

It seemed hours since the senator had left, every second stretching into a lifetime, as Taranis lay on his cot, his wrists manacled, his legs chained to the bed, feeling too exhausted and dispirited to even try and move. The lamps they'd left in the room were still burning but far less brightly now and he wished they'd expire and wreathe him in darkness, as shame overpowered his thoughts, while he tried not to remember how aroused he'd eventually become when Aulus had arse-fucked him. He had resented his servitude to Poppaea but he'd do anything now to be back in her bed.

Tiro came and went, bringing food, which Taranis rejected, and a strong wine, which he drank in the hope it might help numb his pain. Yet nothing could cloud those terrible memories. Two more days, he prayed, blessed Andrasta, let it be no more than that.

Still the oblivion of sleep eluded him as his mind was consumed with thoughts of what the senator might do next. Fear was the enemy, not Aulus Vettius, he told himself, as he heard the door of his room open again.

Taranis shuddered, trying to control his conflicting emotions, as Aulus Vettius strolled into the room holding a goblet of wine. The senator's long fingers played idly with a small key, which Taranis presumed must unlock his manacles.

Having placed the key pointedly on the table, across which Taranis had been so cruelly stretched not that long before, Aulus walked towards the low cot. Taranis automatically sat up, trying not to show how scared he was, as the senator sat beside him on the bed.

'Wine?' he asked with a cold smile, as he stared thoughtfully at his captive.

Taranis shook his head, as the senator's long fingers slid slowly up his thigh. He repressed an unconscious shiver, half of loathing, half of a bizarre kind of primitive excitement, as Aulus touched his sex.

Almost unbidden, his heart began to beat faster, forcing more blood into his groin, as Aulus gently stroked his penis. It started to stiffen and he coloured in embarrassment, wondering how those cold fingers could arouse anything in him but disgust. Taranis was at a loss to understand why his body responded like this. He sat there stiffly, enduring the humiliation and trying to ignore the lust he felt, as Aulus played teasingly with his cock and balls, while idly sipping his wine. After he had all but drained the contents, Aulus tipped the goblet and dripped the dregs over Taranis's belly and sex.

Suddenly, he paused and looked towards the door. 'There you are at last, come in.'

Taranis had thought that his situation was bad enough but it became far worse, as Gaius Cuspius lumbered into the room.

'Shut the door, we want some privacy,' Aulus said, as he dripped the last of the sticky liquid on to his victim's cock. 'Come here, Gaius, I think you might want to try something else to drink. It's a little tastier than my usual wine.'

As Aulus stood up, Gaius walked hungrily forwards and with some difficulty sank to his knees beside Taranis. He tried to pull away but Aulus grabbed hold of the chain holding his wrists together. The senator was stronger than he looked, as he jerked the chain, forcing Taranis back down on to the bed.

'What a vision of delight,' Gaius said with lustful excitement as he leant forwards and began to lick the droplets of wine off Taranis's belly.

Taranis shuddered, as the moist mouth slid inexorably down towards his sex. Aulus gave a soft laugh and tightened his hold on the chain.

Gaius made a hungry sound deep in his throat that made Taranis feel physically sick, as the loathsome toad's flabby tongue slid over his balls and cock. Before he knew it, Gaius was sliding his fat slobbery lips over the head of his penis. Taranis had been partially aroused by the feel of Aulus's hands on his body, but now his erection sank like a stone. The feel of that hot wet mouth trying to near swallow his shaft was disgusting and his repugnance was highly visibly to Aulus.

'Don't you enjoy my friend's attentions?' he said. 'Gaius so wants to fuck you, Taranis.' He gave a coarse laugh. 'He denies it, of course, but I know that he's fantasised about you fucking him. How do you feel about that, slave?'

Taranis didn't reply, as he endured the foul creature's slobbering attentions. Then, to his relief, Aulus grew tired of this game and he let go of the chain. Taranis immediately sat up and managed to jerk his body away from Gaius, not even wincing when the toad's teeth accidentally grazed the head of his penis.

Gaius seemed surprised that he had been denied what he wanted, as he raised his head and frowned, staring with frustration at Aulus. Taranis could see the sweat on Gaius's low forehead, and he smelt the over-powering scent of roses which clung to his flabby skin, while his fat lips gleamed with gobs of saliva. If there had been anything other than a little wine in his stomach, he would have thrown up all over Gaius, as the foul creature reached greedily for his cock again.

'No, leave him be for now,' Aulus said sharply. Grabbing hold of Gaius, he hauled him to his feet. 'Now, Taranis,' he said, as he watched his prisoner clamp his hands protectively over his sex. 'You have to choose.'

'Choose?' Taranis repeated.

'Between Gaius and I,' Aulus said with a cheerful grin. 'Either I call the guards in here and have them chain you down like you were earlier, then let Gaius play with you for as long as he likes.' He picked up the key to Taranis's chains. 'Or you get down on your knees and beg me to fuck you. Then you submit to me quite willingly.'

'There is no choice, is there?' Taranis stared with loathing at Gaius. 'I have to choose you, noble senator.'

'Just as I thought.' Aulus looked very pleased with himself.

'But you said I could have him,' Gaius complained, pouting petulantly.

'Sorry, old friend.' Aulus shrugged his shoulders. 'I let the slave decide and it appears that he wants to please me. I told you that this would happen, didn't I, Taranis?'

'The chains,' Taranis said at last, in a resigned unhappy voice. 'You will have to release my legs, my lord, if you wish me to fall to my knees and beg you to fuck me.'

Aulus chuckled, seeming very pleased with himself, as he undid the manacles fastening Taranis's ankles to the bed. He stepped back, still smiling, as Taranis rose to his feet. Taranis didn't trust the senator to keep his side of the bargain. Once he'd given himself to Aulus, it was highly likely he'd let Gaius have his way with him as well, just in order to make his humiliation complete.

Taranis stepped forwards, bending his knee as if intending to genuflect before the senator. He did no such thing, as he twisted slightly and headbutted Gaius hard in the stomach. The breath driven from his fat body, Gaius fell against the wall with a hard thump. Aulus turned towards the door intending to flee, but Taranis was quicker. He lunged forwards and hit the senator hard across the side of his head with his clenched fists. Half-stunned, Aulus made no attempt to fight, as Taranis looped his manacled hands around the senator's neck and pulled hard, forcing the length of chain deep into the senator's throat, nearly throttling him until he began to choke.

Gaius was still sprawled on the floor, legs akimbo, desperately gasping for breath, while Aulus was fast losing consciousness, as Taranis hissed in his ear, 'I'm going to chain you down, senator, then I'm going to fuck you, just like you fucked me.'

9

The amphitheatre in Pompeii served as a visible representation of the might of the Roman Empire and Cnaius Alleus Nigidus Maius was its most important benefactor. He had personally funded numerous games, including the current four-day event, which was being held to honour the new Emperor and also celebrate the festival of Vulcanalia. Each day of the games was more or less the same. First were the Venationes, the animal hunts, then criminals were executed by being thrown to wild beasts to be devoured in the arena. In the afternoons came the most popular events, the gladiatorial contests, with gladiators from the local troupes and sometimes from the famous gladiatorial school in Capua. On this occasion, during the last day of the celebration, there would also be a spectacular recreation of the battle of Troy.

This was only the first day of the proceedings, yet the crowd was even better than expected and almost all of the 24,000 seats in the arena were filled.

Julia glanced anxiously at Cnaius as he escorted her through the wide tunnel at the south end of the arena. 'It is all arranged,' Cnaius said. 'You may speak to him for a short while.' They stopped by a heavy wooden door, which had an armed guard posted outside. 'Not long, Julia. The Venatione will be finished soon.'

Julia could hear the excited shouts of the crowd as the beastfighters attempted to slay the two bears and three wild bulls that had been let loose in the arena.

'Thank you, Cnaius.' She knew that she could never have arranged this without his help.

'I just hope all goes to plan.' He walked away, not wanting to be present when she bribed the guard with twenty asses, a tidy sum when a whore could be purchased for just one.

Making sure that there was no one around to catch sight of him letting the woman in to see the prisoner, the guard opened the door and Julia slipped inside. There were no windows in the small chamber and it was only dimly lit by two flickering oil lamps. It was stiflingly hot and smelt rank, which wasn't surprising, as it was used to house prisoners and also dead gladiators were brought here to be stripped of their equipment before being taken away to be buried.

Taranis was seated on a low stone bench built into the wall. He was wearing only a brief grubby loincloth and to Julia's consternation he was chained hand and foot.

'Julia!' He sounded surprised to see her.

'I've been so worried,' she said, upset to see him like this.

Taranis smiled warmly at Julia, as she sat down beside him, trying to resist the temptation to embrace him and tell him how much she still cared for him. There were a number of half-healed cuts, and many bruises on his body, which he'd received in the final struggle before he had been captured. After Taranis had escaped from the senator's house, Aulus had despatched a number of his private soldiers to hunt him down. Taranis had eventually been spotted leaving the city by the Erculano Gate and the soldiers had waylaid him on the road leading to Lucius's villa. Julia could only presume that he had been desperately trying to reach Sirona.

'I didn't think you'd ever forgive me, let alone come to see me like this,' Taranis said haltingly. 'I'm sorry I had to deceive you.'

'I understand why you did.' When she had learnt of his capture and subsequent imprisonment, she had come to realise that she would always care for him no matter what. He had hurt her but she had willingly forgiven him, even more so when she had discovered, via her mother, that Taranis and Sirona had been betrothed in Brittania. If Taranis cared half as much for Sirona as she cared for him, then she could easily understand why he had wanted to see the woman he loved just one more time.

'Forgive me, but I have to ask,' Taranis said awkwardly. 'Sirona, is she safe?'

'Lucius loves her, and he was all too willing to forgive her. In fact, he's convinced himself that it was entirely your fault.'

She saw the relief etched on his face and for a moment she felt incredibly hurt, wishing that he might care for her that strongly.

'Thank you, Julia.' He sighed heavily. 'I know now that Sirona and I were never meant to be. At least I was captured before I reached her, so she wasn't somehow implicated in my escape. Now all I hope is that in time Sirona may find happiness with Lucius.' He looked tenderly at Julia and she saw the sadness and regret that clouded his blue eyes. 'You must not concern yourself for my fate.'

'I can't help it.'

'I didn't lie to you that time when I visited you in your bedroom. I do care for you,' he faltered. 'This is all such a mess.'

Taranis had been condemned to suffer the very worst fate that could be imposed on a criminal. He would be tied to a stake in the arena, to be torn to pieces and then consumed by wild beasts. His crimes had been compounded because not only had he attacked both the senator and the aedile, before trying to escape, but also he had humiliated them both in a most impressive fashion.

All Pompeii had been laughing when they had learnt that Aulus and Gaius had been found in a most embarrassing and compromising position. Taranis had stripped them both naked, then strapped Aulus across the table, just as he had been. Then, he had tied Gaius over him as if he were fucking the senator. What had made it even more entertaining was that when they had been found Gaius had been obviously aroused. According to the slave who had freed them, Gaius's engorged cock was trapped between the senator's buttock cheeks and he had been jerking up and down, as much as his bonds allowed, desperately trying to reach a climax.

'Of course, in the circumstances, my stepfather is livid and utterly humiliated.'

Taranis grinned. 'It was just too tempting to leave them like that.'

'We haven't much time,' she said, realising that she had digressed from her initial intentions here. 'There are things that I must tell you.'

'They can wait.' His chains were loose enough to enable him to slide an arm around her shoulders and pull her close. Taranis kissed her as passionately as he had on the night he'd made love to her. Determinedly, she forced herself to pull away from him. 'I thought that you had come to say goodbye,' Taranis said in confusion.

'Not goodbye,' she replied, amazed at how well he was managing to hide any fear he might be feeling.

'Surely Poppaea hasn't somehow managed to stop

this insanity?' He gave a wry smile. 'After all, I'm worth too much to her as an investment for her not to do something.'

'She tried, but it proved impossible. Aulus and Gaius have too much influence in the city and you humiliated them completely.'

'Then how can this not be goodbye? Lions, tigers, wolves, whatever beasts they choose, I'll have no chance against them. If I were left free in the arena, I might be able to defend myself, but tied to a stake –' he shook his head '– survival is just an impossible dream.'

'Not entirely impossible.' She lifted her skirt and removed the slim sharp dagger she had strapped to her leg. 'Cnaius has arranged for the ropes fastening you to the stake to be partially severed. Not enough for the cuts to be visible, but with luck you can break free. And with this –' she put the dagger in his hand '– at least you may have a chance.'

'A chance is all I need.' He pulled her to him and kissed her again.

Taranis, now free of his chains, was escorted by a number of armed guards along the tunnel towards the arena. Above the roar of the crowd, he could just hear the agonising screams of the first two criminals, as they were pulled to pieces by the wild creatures let loose in the arena.

His reunion with Julia had by necessity been brief but it had given him hope. A hope born of desperation but there nonetheless. Even if he did manage to break free of his bonds, one small dagger was less than adequate protection, but at least he'd die like a warrior and not a slave.

As they approached the barred gates, he heard loud roars, which could only have come from some large cat.

Lion, tiger or leopard, it really didn't matter, they were all lethal, even more so when they'd been specially trained to attack men like him. Taranis saw a number of slaves, protected by armed guards, drag the mutilated remains of two bloodied corpses out of the arena. Inside, he knew that animal handlers would be trying to force the big cats back into their cages before the next event, involving him, of course, began.

Taranis swallowed hard, choosing not to look too closely at the two half-eaten criminals, as the guards tightened their hold on him, fully expecting him to struggle and try to run away, but he had no intention of behaving in such a cowardly fashion. As was usual for such executions, a slave stepped forwards, carrying a small bucket of animal blood and a sponge. He dipped the sponge in the blood and went to dab it on Taranis's arms and chest, but a richly dressed man stepped forwards to stop him.

'No,' Cnaius said. 'The magistrates have deemed that this criminal is to die very slowly. Blood will encourage the beasts to attack in a more frenzied fashion and it will all be over far too quickly.'

The slave had no intention of disobeying their noble benefactor, so he hurried away, that part of his duties now complete.

'I've done what I can,' Cnaius said quietly to Taranis. 'Now it is up to you.'

Taranis had no chance to reply, as the barred doors were flung open and the guards marched him swiftly into the arena. He held his head high, determined not to struggle or beg for mercy like a common criminal, and the crowds were surprised by the sight of this man walking so calmly to his death. Only Christians were brave or foolish enough not to display fear, as they sacrificed themselves in the honour of their god. Yet this man was no follower of the Galilean, he was the barbarian who had set all Pompeii talking; the pleasure slave sold for an outrageous sum who had so humiliated both a senator and an aedile.

Strangely enough, there was no roar of excitement from the crowd, just an uneasy silence, as Taranis was bound securely to the thick wooden stake, still stained with the last criminal's blood. It was the 20th of August and the sun beat down unmercifully on the pale sand of the arena, while the crowd was grateful for the thick linen canopy stretched above them, which protected them from the intense heat.

Taranis wasn't even aware of exactly how hot it was; he was too intent on psyching himself up for the fight ahead, just as he had before every battle in the past. His arms were bound to his side, and it was impossible for him to reach the dagger concealed in his loincloth so he had no choice but to try and break the ropes. He just hoped that the man that Cnaius had bribed had done his job of cutting them properly. As the guards departed, he began to pull determinedly against his bonds, to his relief feeling them give just a shade. They were not going to be easy to snap, but with desperation came strength.

At last the crowd uttered a sound, a loud roar of surprise laced with disappointment, as one of the narrow barred doors was pulled open and three large wolves loped into the arena. Most had expected something rather more impressive; the last two criminals had faced two hungry leopards, which had pulled them to pieces in seconds. Taranis struggled with his bonds, warily watching the three wolves circling the arena. The creatures were unsettled by the unfamiliar territory and unaccustomed noise, as they hugged the inner wall of the amphitheatre. Just above them, most of the important citizens were seated in the ima cavea, which was divided off from the rest of the onlookers by a narrow waterless moat.

He felt the ropes give even more, and some of the strands started to snap, just as the crowd gave a second, even louder roar. Another creature was being driven into the arena, a massive lion with a thick golden-brown mane. It bounded forwards, blinked in the bright sunlight and promptly sat down on its haunches, looking around the arena as if assessing its size. Taranis knew that it had probably been confined in semi-darkness, in a small cramped cage for hours, maybe even days, so it wasn't surprising that it was a little disorientated.

His struggles became even more determined. The creature wouldn't take long to recover and he knew that it would have been starved for days. Taranis gritted his teeth, his muscles straining beyond endurance, as he pulled harder. The ropes dug deep into his flesh, then he felt them give even more, as his struggles forced the frayed strands to part. Meanwhile, a number of animal handlers had run into the arena. They prodded the lion with their long-handled spears, trying to drive the creature towards Taranis. With an angry roar, the lion turned on them, trying to claw at the men. All three, in a perfect display of cowardice turned and ran, while the lion loped after them. Just before they reached the refuge of the gate, one almost tripped and dropped his spear. Not pausing to pick it up, he darted into the tunnel after his companions and the door slammed shut just before the lion could reach them.

Was the spear Cnaius's doing or was it just a welcome gift from the gods? Taranis wondered, as he at last managed to free his hands and arms. The now rather angry lion suddenly spotted Taranis and, perhaps thinking he was an easier mark, padded towards him. Part way across the sand, the creature paused and sniffed the air, before turning its head to watch the three wolves still slinking round the edge of the arena, unwilling to try and attack Taranis now that an even larger predator was around.

Taranis slowly and cautiously moved his arm, feeling for the dagger concealed in the back of his loincloth. It felt comforting to hold even this small weapon in his hand. At least the wolves were creating a small diversion, he thought, as he bent to cut the ropes tying his ankles to the stake.

His movement attracted the beast's attention, and with a loud roar it bounded towards him. Tucking the dagger into the waistband of his loincloth, he bent and grabbed two handfuls of sand just as the lion sprang. It was as if time stopped for a moment: he saw the gaping jaws, the massive yellow teeth and smelt the foulness of its breath. Moving swiftly, he darted to one side and threw the sand in the creature's eyes.

The lion gave a strange wailing roar as it landed a little clumsily, shaking its head and pawing at its face trying to wipe the sand from its eyes. Taranis took the brief opportunity to sprint for the spear, still lying so tantalisingly on the ground. He flung himself down and in a smooth rolling motion grabbed the spear and sprang lightly to his feet.

The crowd had been taken totally by surprise, nothing like this had ever happened before during an execution. They roared their approval, this time not siding with the beasts but with the slave who was ready to fight for his life.

Taranis pulled out the dagger, holding both weapons in front of him, as the lion, now recovered, bounded furiously towards him. As the creature attacked, Taranis stepped forwards and plunged the tip of the spear in the thick yellow pelt of its chest. It veered aside, blood dripping from the wound. Taranis had been born to be a warrior – man or beast, it was all the same to him, now he felt he was on more level ground. Keeping one eye on the wolves still circling the arena, but gradually moving closer, attracted by the smell of fresh blood, he faced the lion again, as he and the king of the beasts fought each other for supremacy.

Every time the beast lunged towards him, Taranis jabbed at it with the spear, each time driving it back. The adrenaline rush of battle gave him extra speed and strength – fear was no longer an issue here, it was a fight to the death that he had to win at all costs. The lion went for him time and time again. Taranis countered with his spear, but, on the last attack, the beast just managed to catch his left thigh with the tip of its claws, but he didn't even feel the pain of the wound, as the blood dripped down his leg. He knew that the lion was tiring a little and this time, when it snarled furiously and pounced again, he managed to thrust his spear deep into the massive chest. It slid past the creature's breastbone, the tip of the spear piercing its heart, whereupon its front legs gave way and it fell to the ground panting heavily.

Taranis leapt astride its back and put an arm around the thick neck. He felt the springy hair of its ruff rub against his arm, as he swiftly slit its throat.

He barely heard the loud roar of approval from the crowd as the creature's life began to drain away on to the sand, because the wolves, attracted by the slaughter, suddenly attacked. Taranis didn't know if it was him or the dying lion that was their ultimate prey but it didn't really matter. If he wanted to get out of this arena and perhaps be allowed to live, he had to kill them all.

With a loud snarl, one wolf sprang towards the felled

lion and Taranis kicked it hard in the chest with his bare foot. It gave a yelp of pain, as it fell back. After springing away from the corpse of the lion, Taranis lunged forwards and managed to grab hold of another wolf by the scruff of its neck. Ignoring the snapping jaws, he dug his dagger deep into its side and it collapsed on the sand. Hearing a low menacing growl, he just managed to veer aside, as another of the creatures sprang. Jerking the spear from the lion's chest, he aimed and threw it in one smooth movement. As the second wolf fell dead to the ground, the spear buried deep in its body, the crowd gave another excited roar of approval.

The last wolf, the one he'd kicked and obviously hurt in some way, slunk nervously away from him. Blood still dripping from his wound, Taranis ran after it. Knowing it was cornered, the wolf turned to attack. Opening its jaws, it sprang for his arm. Before it could grab hold of him, Taranis punched it hard on the side of the head. Half-stunned, it fell with a yelping bark, whereupon he bent, grabbed hold of its neck and swiftly slit its throat.

Covered with his own, and the slaughtered creatures' blood, Taranis, now gasping for breath, straightened and turned to acknowledge the approval of the crowd. He stood there like some primeval blood-drenched hunter, as they roared their approval and stamped their feet.

They stood up, nearly all of them, and raised their right hands in the air, thumbs turned up towards the sky, and Taranis knew that the magistrates had no choice but to spare him now. Exhausted but elated, Taranis lifted his arms in a defiant gesture of acknowledgement, then he walked towards the wide barred gate of life that had been pulled open for him.

* * *

The gladiatorial barracks were located just behind the larger of the two theatres in Pompeii, as the original barracks, close to the arena, had been badly damaged in the catastrophic earthquake almost seventeen years earlier.

Julia went to the games like everyone else did in Pompeii, but she had never been inside this place before. The rectangular training ground was massive and it was surrounded by a colonnaded walkway on to which the individual cells opened. Each cell could accommodate up to six gladiators and there were at least twenty-five cells on the ground floor alone, as well as a guardroom, storage chambers, a kitchen and a communal dining hall.

'How many gladiators are there here?' Julia asked the guard who accompanied her.

'One hundred and eighty at present, although we can house up to two hundred at a time.'

Julia had never realised that so many men were housed here, spending their days training just to kill each other and now Taranis was one of them. Fortunately for her, it was quite common for rich women to take gladiators as their lovers, so it was easy enough for her to slip the guards a few coins in order to be allowed in to see Taranis.

She had covered her eyes half the time he was in the arena fighting the lion and wolves, fearing that he might be killed at any moment. However, her prayers had been answered and he had survived. She had been so proud when she had seen him standing there, drenched in blood, acknowledging the roars of approval from the crowd. The magistrates had been given no choice, as the crowd wanted them to spare Taranis. However, they'd refused to return him to Poppaea; instead, he had been sentenced to life as a gladiator.

'He's in here,' the guard said, unbolting a door.

Julia was nervous, not at all certain how badly hurt he might be. As she entered the room, she saw Taranis lying on a low bed covered by a thin linen sheet.

When he saw her, he smiled and sat up and, to her relief, he looked surprisingly well. 'Julia, I hoped you'd come.'

Taranis swung his feet to the floor, leaving only his lower torso concealed by the sheet, and she could just see the wide bandage covering the claw marks the lion had made on his thigh, but no other visible wounds.

'Taranis, you are all right?' she said haltingly, feeling a little unsettled at just seeing him again.

'Surprisingly well,' he confirmed, patting the narrow mattress. 'Come – sit beside me.'

Her skin began to tingle in anticipation, just at the mere thought that he was totally naked beneath the thin sheet draped across his groin. She forced herself to keep her eyes away from his wide chest, flat belly and the fine arrow of pale golden hairs leading tantalisingly down to his sex. 'You look so much better than I had expected.'

'Cnaius kindly arranged for Galen, a doctor from the Imperial gladiatorial barracks at Capua, to treat me,' he explained, as she sat down beside him. 'Galen has practised there for some time and appears able to work miracles. His knowledge of the human body is amazing, so I'm recovering quickly. I have to be fit, as Cnaius wants me to fight the day after tomorrow on the last day of the games.'

'So soon,' she said anxiously.

They were so close their legs were touching, with only the skirt of her stola between her body and his. Her skin tingled and she felt as weak as a kitten, as she thought of his delicious cock hiding under that thin linen sheet. Lust had once been unknown to Julia but now her life seemed to be controlled by it, as she stared at Taranis's handsome face and inhaled the clean masculine scent of his body.

'I have no choice,' he told her.

On the whole, gladiators did not fight all that often, and, when a new man joined the troupe, he underwent vigorous and extensive training before he was let loose in the arena. Nevertheless, Cnaius had a right to decide because in the eyes of the law he now owned Taranis. After the magistrates had transmuted his sentence, they'd made a special arrangement with Cnaius. He had immediately sent Poppaea the three hundred and sixty thousand denarii that she had initially paid for Taranis, and she had no choice in the circumstances but to agree to the sale.

'I could ask Cnaius to give you more time,' she suggested.

'Don't be concerned,' Taranis said confidently. 'After all, I spent a lot of time training with Poppaea's guards so I'm still reasonably fit. Don't forget, Julia,' he said with a self-assured grin, 'I've taken part in enough battles in the past to fully prepare me for a moment like this.' He tenderly kissed her cheek. 'I'll survive, never fear.'

She couldn't understand how he could appear so untroubled by all this. Most likely he would face one of the most experienced gladiators Pompeii had to offer. She just couldn't bear to think of him dying, when yesterday morning he had fought so hard to survive. 'I'll go to the temple of Apollo and pray to him to protect you.'

'Why waste time on talking and praying?' he said huskily. His lips covered hers and he kissed her passionately, as he gently pulled her back down on to the bed.

She didn't know how he achieved it, but moments later she was naked, her bare flesh pressed to his. Julia shivered as his hands stroked and kneaded her breasts, pulling at her nipples until they stiffened and ached with pleasure. Slowly, he ran his large hands over her body, tracing the line of her hip, the soft curves of her belly. His fingers brushed her groin; she'd given up the painful plucking and he buried his fingertips in the dark springy curls that had started to flourish again.

'Sweet Julia,' he murmured, kissing her again, pushing his tongue deep into her mouth. He pulled her even closer so that she could feel the hard line of his erect penis pressing against her body. She felt moisture fill her sex and, when his hands parted her thighs, his fingers slid smoothly inside her, just where they were meant to be. He moved them gently and she moaned aloud with bliss.

'I'm the one who's wounded,' he said teasingly, as he rolled on to his back, pulling her atop him. 'So you'll have to do all the hard work.'

Julia didn't want to wait a moment longer to feel that glorious cock inside her. Sliding her thighs astride his lean hips, she took hold of his shaft, which was already hard, and guided it slowly into her vagina. Then she sank down, sheathing herself on his body and it felt so wonderful to have this man inside her again.

'You're so big. The first time, I thought I'd never be able to accommodate your whole manhood,' she confessed, deliberately squeezing her internal muscles, clasping his cock even tighter and he gave a soft groan.

'You did and it feels so good,' he managed to gasp, as she started to move her hips.

She stared at his handsome face, desire etched on his features. Her legs trembled just at the sheer delight of making love to him again. Everything was so much simpler now that his blue eyes were no longer clouded by the secrets he'd hidden from her in the past. Tenderly, he held on to her hips as she lifted her body, then thrust down again, enjoying the sheer pleasure of being impaled to the hilt.

'Julia, faster,' he begged, working his body with hers, lifting his pelvis, trying to press his groin harder against her pussy.

He reached for her breasts, kneading them gently, pulling on her nipples as she fucked him slowly and deliberately, wanting to draw out this pleasure for as long as she could.

Taranis wasn't having any of that – grabbing hold of her waist, he rolled her over in one smooth movement. Then somehow he was on top, pounding into her with hard decisive strokes, grinding his hips against her soft willing body. His mouth closed over one full breast, evoking a tingling sensation that shot through her, deep into her sex, as his rhythm increased. As he thrust even harder, his lips pulling on her hard teat, she twined her arms around him, digging her fingers into his muscular back, which was still criss-crossed with faint weals from the whipping. She felt the amazing strength of his body powering into her until she thought she might expire from the sweet unmitigated pleasure.

Julia came in a sudden rush, climaxing so violently that she was barely aware of his cock pumping orgasmically deep inside her. Afterwards, he cradled her lovingly in his arms. There was no need for words and, for a short while at least, no fears for the future. Then, before she left, Taranis made love to her again.

Sirona had never been to an amphitheatre before, let alone witnessed the games where men were forced to fight each other to death in the arena. It seemed utterly barbaric to her for men to die in the name of entertainment, yet in the Romans' eyes *she* was the barbarian, not them. Sirona had not wanted to come here today, but Lucius had insisted. She had got ready, feeling very apprehensive, because she had no desire to sit there and watch slaves being forced to kill each other. Then, moments before they were due to leave, Lucius had told her in a matter-of-fact tone, as if the subject would be of little interest to her, that Taranis was fighting today.

How would she cope with watching Taranis fight and perhaps die in the arena? she wondered anxiously, as she saw the impressive building for the very first time. Many people were milling around the place, among them were the programme sellers and food and drink vendors. She heard people talking excitedly about the main events and which gladiators they might make wagers on. Most were not stopping; they were walking swiftly towards the outer staircases which led to the upper terraces where the general populace sat.

Lucius took hold of her arm and led her through a wide tunnel, under the outer part of the building. It was still very hot and there was a strange atmosphere in the air today. Sirona had the uneasy sensation that something momentous was about to happen, and she was certain that it wasn't just her fear for Taranis that made her feel this way. At home, she had somehow been able to sense when a storm or bad weather was coming; it was if she knew what Mother Earth was planning. Yet there was no sign of a storm on the horizon, and she knew that rain rarely fell at this time of the year, even though the parched countryside desperately needed water. Lucius had told her that public fountains in some of the nearby towns had all but dried up. It might be blockages or damage underground to the Aqua Augusta, which served many of the towns and cities in this area, yet the fountains in Pompeii flowed as freely as ever. Even so, Admiral Pliny was supposedly despatching an engineer from Misenum to investigate the problem.

They turned left into a corridor, which appeared to circle the inner part of the building. There were only a few richly dressed citizens walking this way now.

'Up here is our box,' Lucius said, guiding her up a flight of steep stone steps. They reached the ima cavae. Their seats, in a small private box, were close to where all the most important citizens were placed. Aulus Vettius was already here, sitting with four magistrates who ran the city and she hated them all, every single Roman citizen. Yet not Lucius, she thought, despite everything, he had been extraordinarily kind to her most of the time. Lucius led her into the privacy of their small box, a canopy covering the top so that they were shielded from the burning rays of the sun.

Sirona sat down on the carved, cushioned chair, and Lucius sat down beside her. The arena was huge, the bright sunlight reflecting off the pale sand. A mixed array of wild beasts, including a massive spotted creature with an incredibly long neck, and an elephant – an animal she'd only seen pictures of before – were being paraded around to entertain the crowd. Sirona knew that somewhere below her, in the bowels of the building, Taranis was imprisoned, waiting to fight.

Sirona had not known what had happened to him after they had been so cruelly torn apart at Julia's party. Lucius had told her nothing and had kept her confined to the villa. She had to let herself think that it was purely to spare her feelings that he had ordered the household slaves not to repeat any of the city gossip. It was only when Julia had briefly visited her brother, late the previous afternoon, that Sirona had at last discovered what terrible things had happened to Taranis.

She glanced at Lucius who didn't appear to be enjoying himself at all. His features were taut and he was irritably tapping his fingers on the arm of his chair. Not surprisingly, their relationship had become rather strained since the incident with Taranis, even more so when Lucius had discovered that in Brittania they had been betrothed. All their problems stemmed from the fact that Lucius was acutely jealous, despite the fact that, for the sake of their fragile relationship, she had determinedly denied that she still loved Taranis. However, she had never found it easy to hide her true feelings and he had not believed her lies. In many ways, she still cared for Lucius, but his jealousy had caused a barrier between them that she knew even Taranis's untimely death could not destroy.

All of a sudden there was a fanfare of trumpets and Sirona forced herself to look down into the arena. The first pair of gladiators entered, a heavily armed man called a murmillo who was pitted against a retarius, a man who fought with a net and trident.

Lucius consulted the papyrus programme he had purchased. 'Ten pairs of gladiators will be fighting,' he told her. 'Then they will be staging a recreation of the battle of Troy.' He didn't tell her in which part of the programme Taranis would fight and she felt it wiser not to ask him, as she would learn soon enough when she saw her beloved walking into the arena.

Time passed slowly for Sirona, as she stared straight ahead, but her eyes were not seeing the men fighting and dying on the sand, she was reliving in her mind all the precious moments she had spent with Taranis. It was said that the very last thing a dying person saw was their life spread out before them, maybe that was true but she was also seeing it right now.

'Sirona,' Lucius said softly. 'Are you unwell?'

'No. I'm watching the fighters.' Her green eyes were blank, nearly devoid of emotion, as she turned to look at him. 'Isn't that what you wanted me to do? Watch these poor creatures slaughter each other for the enjoyment of the crowd.'

'This is far more than an entertainment,' he said rather curtly. 'The power and might of the Roman Empire is on show here today.'

'Perhaps that is why this troubles me so much,' she replied scathingly. 'It displays nothing more than your Empire's cruelty. These men are slaves, they care not for your power and might, they have no choice but to fight.'

'Most of them are prisoners of war, slaves or criminals.' He didn't appear to like her questioning the morality of the games. 'If they'd been in Brittania, as prisoners of your people, they'd most likely be dead already by now. At least this way they have a chance of survival.'

'So we slaughter our captives, while you magnanimously force them to fight in the arena.' She shook her head, her eyes suddenly blinded by unshed tears.

'They are not your concern, *he* is! You're scared he'll die.'

'Taranis will not die,' she said defiantly. 'He's even more of a warrior than you are, Lucius. I've just no wish to watch him fight.'

'You'll stay, and you'll watch,' Lucius said determinedly.

Sirona forced herself to look down at the arena again. The recreation of the battle of Troy was just about to begin. If legends were to be believed more than fifty thousand Greeks besieged the city, but in this battle there were only about thirty or forty men on each side.

The Greeks wore Roman military-style outfits, while the Trojans were dressed more finely with tall winged helmets on their heads.

Where was Taranis? she wondered worriedly. Lucius would have told her if he were one of those helmeted men in the arena right now and she was certain she would have recognised him even if his handsome face wasn't visible to her. Yet her fingers still tightly gripped the narrow arms of her chair as she watched the fatal battle begin.

The Romans loved these elaborate forms of entertainment; it was like play-acting but the shouts and screams from the men fighting were all too real, as they cruelly cut and stabbed at each other. All fought bravely, and soon dead and wounded men littered the sand of the arena, while the battle appeared to have reached a stalemate of sorts and both sides drew back. A loud trumpet blast interrupted the proceedings and two men on white horses galloped into the arena. They had to be the two leaders of the opposing sides, King Agamemnon of Greece and King Priam of Troy.

Sirona couldn't quite make out what they were saying, as the acoustics were not as good as in a Roman theatre. She turned to look questioningly at Lucius.

'It has been decided that the battle will be settled by a champion from either side. Achilles for the Greeks and Prince Hector for the Trojans.' He smiled coldly, as he added, 'Your former lover is playing the role of Achilles.'

'Didn't Achilles win?' Sirona said nervously.

'Don't count on it this time, my sweet. Nothing is set in stone here, these men battle to the death. Taranis is pitted against Demeter, a renowned fighter and the most famous gladiator in Pompeii.'

Taranis will win, she told herself, ignoring the ice-cold fear eating away at her heart. She recalled how bravely he'd fought in the final battle with Agricola's legions. Then she had been convinced that her warrior lover could never die. However, she had also been convinced that they could not lose and here they were both prisoners of the Romans.

She glanced again at Lucius sitting beside her, his handsome face was set in a cold mask. Anxiously, she clenched her hands in her lap, determined not to show her fear for Taranis.

Sirona heard the roar of excitement from the crowd and saw her former lover, dressed in gladiatorial armour, but not wearing a helmet, stride on to the sun-drenched sands of the arena. He looked magnificent, his tanned skin gleaming, his blond hair loose around his shoulders. He wore a gold breastplate, thick gold bracelets around his muscular upper arms and the short Greek leather skirt left most of his muscular legs bare, apart from the golden greaves covering his shins. He was the epitome of perfection, Achilles himself reborn.

Sirona held her breath, as his opponent, also helmetless, entered from the other side. The muscular dark-haired man, almost a head shorter than Taranis, swaggered forwards. She heard the crowd yelling, some for Taranis, the majority for Demeter. Both men raised their swords in salute to the onlookers, but Taranis did not join Demeter in the gladiator oath – we who are about to die salute thee.

The battle between the two men began, the arena resounding to the metallic sound of sword clashing on sword, shields banging loudly together, as both men attacked. Sirona watched totally petrified and praying that Taranis would win, but she was expert enough in fighting to know that both men were equally strong and well matched, only the most skilled and the most cunning would survive.

She looked down on them battling it out on the bloodstained sand, hardly able to believe this was real. She saw Taranis thrust and parry, jumping aside nimbly, managing to dodge the cruel blows from his opponent as he lunged forwards and attacked time and time again. However, the last thrust from Demeter was frighteningly close to his side. They fought with the gladius, a Roman sword with a short double-edged blade designed more for thrusting and stabbing than elaborate swordplay. The polished iron blade was strong, but blunted quickly. She saw them swinging through the air, shining in the sunlight, as if this were all part of some terrible vivid nightmare she was having.

Both men attacked and retreated many times, driving forwards, being driven back, with both sword and shield being used in this determined onslaught. They fought long and hard, slashing at each other until both men were cut, only slightly, in a number of places. The iron blades swung through the air as they twisted and turned, swords clashing time and time again. She saw Taranis jump back, as Demeter's gladius caught his arm, this time cutting it quite deeply but the thick gold bracelet had taken part of the blow, preventing the flesh from being slashed to the bone.

With blood dripping down on to his right hand, Taranis backed away and wiped his slippery palm on his leather skirt seconds before Demeter lunged again. Taranis side-stepped and twisted the sword in his hand so that the blade faced away from Demeter, whereupon he hit the gladiator on the side of the head with the heavy hilt. Demeter staggered back, half-stunned, while Taranis circled him slowly.

Sirona's heart was beating so fast now she could barely draw breath, she was utterly caught up in the fevered excitement of the battle between these two men. She was so close to Lucius she could hear his laboured breathing, see his heightened colour, as the lust of battle poured through his veins. Suddenly, to her consternation, his hand clamped down on her knee and he began to pull up the folds of her skirt.

Trying to ignore his hand touching her, she kept her attention focused on the arena. Taranis had just managed to wound Demeter in the leg and he was hobbling a little, but by now the blood was flowing even more freely down Taranis's arm. Both men backed away from each other, chests heaving, gasping for breath, while the crowd in their lust for blood screamed for them to continue.

Taranis raised his sword to salute his opponent then, to the crowd's amazement, tossed aside his shield. He stood there looking infinitely weary, almost as if he could be beaten in an instant. With a low growl, Demeter lunged towards him, while Sirona felt Lucius's fingers slide under her gown and creep up her leg. Swapping his sword to his undamaged arm, Taranis parried Demeter's blows, edging back, never attacking, completely on the defensive.

'He is tiring,' Lucius muttered under his breath.

The scraping sound of sword upon sword set Sirona's already fragile nerves on edge, yet she was also filled with a wild elated excitement. She could now more easily understand battle lust and why men fought to the edge of insanity and beyond, while she felt Lucius's fingers caress her inner thigh then ease their way between her pussy lips. She was sopping wet and she gave a soft moan, as they slid inside her. How could she feel so aroused when Taranis was fighting for his life, especially as his strength appeared to be waning fast?

There was a loud gasp from the crowd as Demeter's attack became more frenzied and uncontrolled. The noise drowned out Sirona's loud gasp of sexual pleasure, as Lucius shifted in his seat so that he could thrust his fingers even deeper inside her, while his thumb pressed hard against her aching clit.

Consumed by wild, sensual sensations, Sirona saw Taranis turn and sprint to the edge of the arena until he was almost directly under the magistrates' box. She clenched the arms of her chair, drowning in sexual delight, as Lucius thrust hard into her pussy, while on the floor of the arena Taranis was losing his fight for life.

Demeter was taking his time now, walking slowly towards his near defeated enemy. Darting to his left, Taranis suddenly switched his sword to his right hand and quite literally sprinted towards his opponent. The intense orgasm ripped through Sirona's body, as Taranis leapt high in the air and, with a sharp downward stabbing motion, he thrust his sword deep into the juncture where Demeter's head and shoulder met.

Sirona sat there trembling in the final throes of her climax, as Taranis landed lightly on his feet and swung round, just in time to see Demeter fall face forwards on the sand. The crowd went wild as Taranis strode towards his dead opponent and raised his sword high in the air.

'So he lives to fight another day.' Lucius jerked Sirona to her feet, while the crowd still roared their support for Taranis. Lucius pushed her face forwards against the rough concrete wall of the box and lifted her skirt. Pushing aside his toga he pressed his belly to her buttocks and pushed his cock deep inside her vagina.

Taranis lives – the words formed an incantation in her mind, as Lucius thrust into her like a man possessed.

10

Julia awoke not long after dawn and just lay there watching Taranis sleeping, feeling happier than she had ever been. She had never known what it was like to fall asleep in her lover's arms and wake with him still beside her.

Cnaius had brought her to the barracks after the games had finished. Galen had already sewn up the deep gash on Taranis's arm and, apart from a few scratches and cuts, he was unharmed and surprisingly cheerful. Cnaius had congratulated him and then left to celebrate the success of the games with a few of his close friends. Cnaius had told the trainer that Julia could visit Taranis as often as she liked, so she had chosen to spend the night with her gladiator lover.

Taranis's near exhaustion in the arena had just been a ploy to goad Demeter into becoming more reckless in his attacks. He still appeared to have an infinite supply of energy and they had made love a number of times. Not only did Taranis have a magnificent cock, but also he knew how to use it and was an impressive and inventive lover. Eventually, she had fallen asleep, her body pressed close to his, feeling amazingly decadent and in many ways an entirely different woman.

Time passed and Taranis still slept, while Julia wondered what the future held for them. Cnaius recognised a great fighter when he saw one and now intended to take Taranis to Rome to fight in the coliseum. There, if the gods were kind, he might become a famous gladiator and eventually gain both wealth and his freedom. If Taranis was sent to Rome, she would go with him, she had decided that already.

She was so caught up with her daydreams about the future, that she had not even realised that Taranis was awake. He was propped up on one elbow looking thoughtfully down at her. Julia smiled. Their relationship was still young enough for her to worry that her hair was a mess and her eyes were probably still swollen from sleep.

'Awake so soon?' Taranis said softly, as he kissed her tenderly on the lips.

'Yes. I suppose I should leave.'

'There's no rush. Galen told me to rest and give training a miss for at least a week.'

'You call last night resting?' she teased with a cheeky smile, all her concerns for her looks deserting her mind. All she could think about when he was so close to her was sex. Her pussy grew moist at the mere thought of fucking him again.

'Maybe not resting exactly.' He played with her long brown curls splayed across the pillow. 'But I can't think of anything better to do, especially when you are around.'

All of a sudden, the bed started to tremble, as did the floor of the small whitewashed cell. Julia clutched nervously on to Taranis, until the shaking subsided only a few heartbeats later. Over the last few weeks there had been a number of very minor earth tremors in Pompeii. That wasn't unusual, the tremors had happened in the past, most often at this time of year. Yet, every time she experienced one, Julia was reminded of the last terrible destructive earthquake all those years earlier.

'It's all right,' Taranis reassured her. 'There will be no more massive earthquakes. Cnaius told me that he consulted a seer before the games. She assured him that Pompeii would still be standing many hundred years from now.'

'Do you believe that?' she asked him, sighing content-edly, as he stroked her breasts and played teasingly with her nipples. Julia felt the familiar lustful drawing sensation dart through her groin as her pussy became moister still.

'No.' He smiled wryly. 'I don't place my trust in seers or even the gods. Only in the strength of my sword arm and my will to survive. However –' his hand slid over her stomach and he ran his fingers through her dark springy pubic curls '– my strength elsewhere is also important to me – and perhaps to you as well?'

'So very important,' she murmured, her hand reaching for his cock.

Sirona was feeling almost as unsettled today as she had been before the games the previous afternoon. Yet she knew that logically there was nothing to be fearful of at present. Taranis was alive, he was well and she supposed safe at least for the time being. Perhaps it was just these strange unnatural earth tremors, she thought, as she strolled through the garden. The slaves had told her that they were not uncommon. Many believed it to be the earth resettling, as it dried out in the summer heat.

Lucius had left for Herculaneum that morning. He had wanted her to go with him, as Pedius Cascus's wife, Rectina, had expressed a wish to meet Sirona. Their home, the villa Calpurnia, overlooked the sea and Lucius was convinced that Sirona would love it there. But she had declined to go, claiming that she felt unwell. That was a lie, of course, but she couldn't forgive Lucius for forcing her to watch Taranis fight and she felt it better if she spent some time away from him. Their sex life was still passionate enough but the tension between them had not decreased.

One of the house slaves had recently returned from a shopping trip to the city. Apparently, a few hours earlier, the public fountains had dried up completely and even the supply to the villa had decreased considerably. The magistrates had distributed posters assuring the general populace that the necessary repairs would be completed before sunset, but there was still a sense of unease in the city. Some of the farmers working the fertile slopes of the mountain had come down to Pompeii, claiming that there had been some sort of explosion at first light and that many of their upper fields were now covered with a strange pale shroud of ash.

Sirona guessed that it was well past midday now, yet the sun appeared to be getting hotter. She stood in the shade of a tall plane tree as a sudden warm breeze rustled the plants and leaves, bringing with it a strange acrid smell.

She paused and shielded her eyes with her hand, as she looked towards the mountain. Suddenly the ground trembled beneath her feet with far more ferocity than it had done earlier in the day. There was a sharp gust of searingly hot air, which was tainted even more strongly with the strange acrid smell. Then she heard a loud booming sound. It was so incredibly loud that she crouched down and put her hands over her head. Her ears were still ringing from the noise, as she stood up and caught sight of the strange dark column exiting the tip of Vesuvius and streaming straight up into the sky. It was as if one of the gods had reached down and was pulling the centre of the mountain up towards him.

She could still feel the searing heat that had briefly brushed her skin, the weird smell sticking uncomfortably in her throat, as she ran into the house. 'Water,' she gasped, as Amyria hurried towards her.

'What is it, my lady?'

Somehow one of the slaves produced a goblet of water for Sirona. She grabbed it and drank it down greedily. 'I don't know.' The anxiety she had felt before had increased a thousandfold. 'The mountain – look.' She grabbed Amyria's hand and pulled her towards the portico, which surrounded one of the small peristyle gardens.

They both stared up at the mountain. The huge funnel was blossoming outwards like a flower, gradually forming a giant brown parasol high over the summit. It flowed slowly outwards in all directions, towards the sea, towards the villa and then Pompeii.

Gradually, the sky became darker and some of the slaves in the room behind them fell to their knees, praying to the gods to spare them. As the threatening cloud rolled closer to the villa, there were intermittent sharp bangs like claps of thunder. Sirona had no idea what was happening – had something like this occurred before in Pompeii? She watched in trepidation, as the dark cloud slowly enveloped everything in its path. Should she order the slaves to leave, or should they stay? She had no idea what to do – if only Lucius were here.

Suddenly, there was a loud clattering sound of hail-stones pouring down from the sky, and Sirona and Amyria ran back into the relative safety of the house. They had to be enormous hailstones to make such a terrible noise. Then a number of the smaller ones bounced under the covered portico and in through the open doorway. One of the slaves curiously picked one up, waiting for it to cool a little before he handed it to Sirona.

'I've never seen anything like this,' she said to the slave.

Hailstones in Brittania were small chips of ice but this looked more like stone. Although it wasn't stone exactly, it was much lighter and looked more like a greyish white hard piece of sponge.

The stones, or whatever they were, continued to pour down on the villa in a never-ending stream, while the sky grew darker until it was almost as black as night. Sirona didn't think it was wise to try and leave at present, but she really wasn't well informed enough to make such a decision. 'Order the servants to light the lamps, Amyria, and gather what food and water they can. We'll remain here for now.' She hid her own fear as she smiled reassuringly at her maid. 'As soon as this lessens or stops, we'll go to Pompeii and take refuge with Lucius's sister Julia.'

Taranis knew that Julia was very scared and he could understand why; he was feeling a little unsettled himself. It wasn't an earthquake but something equally strange was happening, a phenomenon he could not explain. He stood by the barred window of his cell, staring at the steady stream of greyish white rocks pouring down on to the quadrangle. It was late afternoon by his reckoning but it was so dark now it seemed to be night. Would this end soon and if so would something even more terrible come next?

Julia felt safer staying here with him and it would not have been wise to let her return home at present, as there would probably be panic on the streets. What frustrated Taranis most of all was that the guards had refused to let him and the other men out of their cells. If they had any sense, they would have released everyone before making a run for it themselves, preferably trying to reach the coast. Maybe it was just an instinctive reaction on his part, but that was what he would do if given the choice – just get the hell out of here as quickly as possible.

He was still trying to figure out how he could persuade, or force, the guards to release him, when the door of his cell was flung open and a ghostly white vision stepped inside. The door slammed shut, as the man, covered from head to foot in ash, threw back the hood of his cloak.

'Borax,' Julia gasped.

'My lady.' Borax gave a wheezing cough. 'Conditions are bad outside and I know that you might consider it wiser to stay under cover at present.' He paused and looked towards Taranis. 'I've no idea why this is happening, but my gut instinct tells me that this is a very bad omen and might be a precursor to something far worse. Perhaps a much stronger earthquake?'

'Earthquake?' Julia repeated nervously.

'Not necessarily an earthquake,' Borax amended. 'But I fear something terrible might happen and, in the circumstances, like many other citizens, I feel it wiser for us to leave the city and move further along the coast. I took it upon myself to send the slaves away. I've told them not to return until conditions here improve. Something tells me that the further away from the mountain we get the better, this is all coming from Vesuvius.'

'You should leave, Julia.' Taranis stepped over to her and gently pulled her to her feet. 'Please. I'd like to think you were safe.'

'I won't leave without you.' She clung on to him.

'The guards won't let me just walk out of here,' he told her. 'The Laniste left orders to keep us all locked in our cells.'

'What guards?' Borax said in a low voice, as he stepped over to Taranis. 'I only saw three or four at the most.' He shrugged his shoulders. 'I suspect that the others have already fled.'

'Three or four against almost two hundred,' Taranis repeated softly. 'No wonder they've kept us locked up.' He looked penetratingly at Borax. 'You know that we can't leave them imprisoned. If your worst fears should come to fruition, and there is another terrible earthquake, they'd most likely all perish.'

'It would be wiser to have armed men to accompany us, my lady.' Borax picked up Julia's cloak and placed it around her shoulders. 'There is chaos on the streets, a number of people have been hurt, trampled upon.' He glanced meaningfully at Taranis. 'Are you ready?'

'Yes.' Taranis positioned himself, as Borax stepped forwards and banged loudly on the door.

'We are ready to leave,' he shouted.

Taranis tensed, as he heard the bolt being drawn back. When the door was pulled open, he charged through it, shouldering the surprised guard aside, then swung round and punched the man squarely on the chin. His head snapped back and he crumpled to the ground.

'He'll only be out for a short while,' Taranis told Julia, as she and Borax joined him. 'When he awakes and finds everyone gone, perhaps he'll have sense enough to leave also.'

'What now?' Borax instinctively looked to Taranis for leadership.

So far there was no sign of the other guards. Above the soft thudding sound of the pumice falling to the ground could be heard shouting and swearing coming from the other cells.

'We'll release the men and give them a choice. They can come with us, or take their chances elsewhere. Once they are all free, I doubt the guards will have any objection to us leaving.' Taranis picked up the guard's sword along with the heavy bunch of keys he'd had clipped to his belt, and then turned to look at Julia. 'Sirona and your brother?'

'Don't worry. Lucius told me that he and Sirona were leaving early this morning to visits friends just outside Herculaneum.'

'One less thing to worry about,' he said with relief, handing the keys to Borax. 'Once we've released all the men, we'll go to the armoury.' Stepping out from the cover of the portico, he held out his arm. 'I don't think these stones can do that much damage but travelling still won't be pleasant. We'll wear amour and helmets to protect ourselves.'

Sirona had found a large amphora of sweet Falernian wine and ordered it distributed among the slaves. They were used to Posca, a vinegary wine diluted with water, so this was something to be enjoyed and with the stronger alcoholic contact came courage. The stones seemed to have been raining down on the villa for hours.

She hoped that, once Lucius realised what was happening in Pompeii, he would come for her; in the meantime, she had to be patient and stay calm. Suddenly, there was a loud knocking on the outer door. 'Lucius,' she gasped in relief.

The doorkeeper had fled along with at least half of the other slaves, so one of the house servants rushed to the door and pulled it open. Sirona was surprised to see a number of people, at least ten or more, crowd into the atrium. Their long cloaks were all thickly covered in white ash. She didn't know whether to laugh or cry, as the first man threw off his cloak and she saw it was Aulus Vettius. At least he had lived here most of his life so he might know more about these strange happenings, but she was also still very scared of him and Lucius wasn't here to protect her.

'Senator.' She stepped forwards to greet him. 'What brings you here on such a terrible day?'

'Lucius?' he questioned.

'In Herculaneum.'

'Good.' Aulus smiled not with relief but a strange kind of satisfaction. He paused then added, 'I'm pleased to hear that he is safe.' He glanced pointedly at her steward, who had chosen to remain with her. 'I wish to speak to your mistress in private.'

The steward frowned. 'But my lady Sirona said –'

'I am not to be questioned,' Aulus interjected furiously. 'When my stepson is not here, I am the master in this house. Order all the slaves to return to their quarters. They will be as safe there as they are here.'

Sirona had no wish to be left alone with this man, but Aulus was right, as Lucius's paramour she had no real control over the slaves. Yet she wasn't to be left totally alone with Aulus, because there were all the people that he had brought with him. She glanced at them and her heart sank. Now that they had removed their cloaks and washed the ash from their faces, she realised that she had seen them before but then they'd all been totally naked.

Her eyes widened nervously and she swallowed hard. Aulus did not know she had spied on their ceremony, so he had no cause to think she might be concerned by their presence in the villa. She looked nervously around, wondering if she could make a run for it. But where would she go?

'Not so fast, barbarian whore.' Aulus, sensing her intentions, grabbed hold of her, digging his long fingers into her arms. 'I have need of you.'

'Need of me?' she repeated nervously.

'The gods are angry, can you not see that?' Aulus hissed. 'They must be appeased.'

'Appeased, how?' she asked, her mouth dry with fear.

'Our god Dionysis requires a sacrifice.' Sirona saw the deranged look in the senator's eyes. 'A human sacrifice, Sirona. It is you and your barbarian lover who brought this curse to our land. I can't sacrifice him but I can you. As your blood drains into the ground, Dionysis will be appeased and this madness will end.'

The pumice was everywhere, covering both the road and the surrounding countryside as if Medusa had looked down upon the entire land turning it to stone. Taranis reckoned that by now night must have fallen, but there was no way to tell how many hours had passed – time had little meaning any more. They had decided to make for Stabiae, a town along the coast, where a friend of Julia's, Pomponianus, had a number of small vessels docked. If it hadn't been for one of the gladiators, they might well have wandered away from the road. The man had been born and raised in Stabiae so he could follow the road as easily as a blind man making his way round his own house.

The rock fall had lightened a little but the road was covered by pumice, which came more than halfway up their calves. It was like wading through a sea of grain. A journey that on a good day would only have taken an hour or so seemed to take forever. The pumice broke easily underfoot, and tiny pieces of rock made its way into sandals and boots alike. All the men wore helmets and armour and any extra clothing they could lay their hands on, even though it was incredibly hot. Sweat made the gritty ash stick to the skin, but all wore pieces of cloth tied across their lower faces so the stuff didn't get in their noses or mouths. He'd insisted that Julia wear a pair of men's long breeches under her skirt to further protect her legs. As all the helmets had been way too big for her, dropping down over her eyes to restrict her vision, he held a shield above her head to protect her from the rockfall.

They had torches, many of them, because almost fifty gladiators had decided to accompany them on this journey, including Taranis's old comrades in arms, Leod and Olin. The remainder of the gladiators had either gone into the city to seek out women they were involved with or fled in different directions. A few had even chosen to take their chance and remain at the barracks.

Behind them was total darkness, apart from odd flashes of flame which appeared to come from high up near the summit of Vesuvius. They'd come across a number of dead bodies, both human and animal. The men had cut free a team of oxen and a number of horses, which had been left strapped to wagons or chariots while their owners took off on foot without thinking to release the poor creatures. They'd watched the animals struggle from their tombs of enveloping stones and flee into the countryside following their natural animal instinct for survival.

The men had also come across a small group of scantily clad, overly made-up young women, most probably prostitutes, who they'd been only too happy to rescue along with other stragglers fleeing from Pompeii.

Taranis tipped his shield at an angle to rid it of its covering of pumice and looked down at Julia. She was covered in ash and grime but she was still struggling on determinedly.

'I could carry you?' he suggested, just as he had done a number of times.

'No.' She shook her head, her voice muffled by the

cloth across her face. 'We're almost there. Look.' She pointed just ahead.

Taranis saw a cluster of lights, and he could even feel a faint refreshing breeze coming from the sea. 'At last.' Slipping the shield strap over his arm, he picked up Julia and strode swiftly forwards.

Vesuvius was five miles north east of Pompeii and they'd travelled about three miles from the other side of the city, he thought, as they entered Stabiae, yet the dark cloud still hung above them. So how large was this strange phenomenon?

Many people were looking nervously at the large group of armoured men, laden with weapons, as they walked into the town. The refugees were everywhere, sitting disconsolately on the pavements, bursting out of the taverns and food establishments; even conscientious citizens had welcomed them into their homes.

'My mother's friend has a house close to the sea,' Julia said, as he set her down on her feet and heaved the shield across his back because, to his relief, the fall of stones had all but ceased now. Pulling his face mask down, Taranis took a deep breath. This close to the sea the air was a little clearer and he could see the white caps of the waves as they crashed against the shore. There were a large number of people crowded on to the wide beach. Clutching their most precious possessions, they waited for the bad weather to ease so that they could escape by boat, a number of which were anchored further out to sea. Judging by the flickering lights, there was also a number of larger vessels anchored even further offshore, perhaps rescue ships from the Imperial fleet.

Taranis regarded the waves. 'The sea is very rough. I don't think any of the vessels will be leaving yet.' He glanced back in the direction of Vesuvius, thinking that he would rather take his chances on the angry seas than remain here for much longer. Larger fires were visible now on the upper slopes, leading him to suspect that there was still worse to come.

Sirona had never known such fear; it had spread like icy tendrils through her entire body. As she lay naked, bound hand and foot, on the floor of the huge salon, she had to clench her teeth to stop them from chattering. Yet she was far from cold as the usually chilly mosaic floor was warm, as if the earth was heating up somewhere deep underneath them.

Aulus and his companions were making preparations for this bizarre, totally insane ceremony, which would ultimately end in her death, while outside Mother Nature was wreaking her destructive forces on all of them. No sacrifice on earth could stop what was happening, Sirona was certain of that.

The odd thing was that none of these people showed any concern at what was happening outside, they appeared to have totally placed their trust in Aulus Vettius's predictions that this would all end after her sacrifice. They had all stripped naked and were anointing each other with perfumed oils, their hands lingering suggestively on breasts and cocks, sliding between legs and buttock cheeks, as if they had all the time in the world to prepare for this ceremony.

Aulus was on his knees praying to Dionysis, begging the god to accept their noble sacrifice. There was another man with him, who was the same height and build as Lucius, with the same close-cropped dark hair. When he tied on his mask, Sirona at last knew for sure that she had been entirely wrong about her protector. Lucius had never been involved with this strange cult – it had been this man all along. Yet what good was this knowledge to her now? she considered in desperation, while a naked man began to play a flute and a woman discordantly clashed some cymbals together.

They broke open an amphora of Lucius's best wine, mixed it with a fine white powder and greedily gulped it down, consuming at least three or four goblets each. Dionysis was the god of wine as well as all sexual excess. Someone lifted her head and placed a goblet to her lips. She tried to resist but they forced open her mouth and poured it down her throat until she had to swallow or she would have choked.

Sirona shivered as the man, who looked so uncannily like Lucius, stepped towards her. Kneeling down beside her, he began to anoint her breasts with the strongly scented oil. The man caressed her like a lover would, stroking the underside of her breasts, kneading them gently and circling her nipples with his fingertips. A warm ache formed between her thighs as he leant forwards and delicately sucked on each teat until they stiffened into hard peaks. Then his fingers circled her belly, gently pressing down on the soft flesh above her pubic mound.

Someone untied her ankles and two women held on to them, forcing her legs apart. Kneeling between them, the man ran his hands up the soft inner skin of her thighs and through her pubic curls. He was breathing heavily and his cock stiffened, as his fingers eased open her pussy lips. Sirona's legs were trembling, half from terror, half from a bizarre kind of arousal, while a strange euphoria spread through her entire body. He leant forwards and delicately flicked his tongue against her clit, which had started to throb and burn. Slowly, he circled the tiny nub, then his lips fastened on it, licking and sucking until she wanted to scream with pleasure. She dug her teeth in her lower lip, trying not to utter a sound, fearing that her sexual arousal was somehow an integral ingredient in this strange ceremony. The skin of her belly tingled as the man carefully inserted three oiled fingers inside her vagina, slowly easing them deeper into her body, then sliding them back and forth while his lips still worked on her clit.

A soft moan escaped her lips, strangely she no longer cared about anything but her rising lust, as she shuddered and then climaxed quite violently. At once, the man drew away. 'She is ready now, master.'

The discordant music became louder, drowning out the sounds of the stones drumming down on the roof, as Sirona was lifted bodily and placed, belly down, on a padded stool. It was just high enough to allow her knees to reach the floor, and was so narrow that only her stomach was supported, and her full breasts hung down towards the floor.

A man stepped forwards and grabbed hold of her arms, keeping them straight, almost parallel to her body, while one of the women rolled on to her back and slid under Sirona until her entire face was directly beneath her breasts. She fastened her lips around one like a leech, pulling it deep into her mouth, nibbling, squeezing and pulling at the teats. Sirona's arousal magnified, despite the fact she'd climaxed only moments earlier. Wild sensual thoughts were all that filled her head now, the wine or whatever it was had somehow managed to extinguish all her fears. People were crowded around her, hands touching her body, fingers sliding into her pussy, others invading her anus. The rest were sucking, fucking and jerking off just as they had before. The myriad of sensations exploded into another equally earth-shattering climax and her body shook with the intensity of her orgasm, as her vision became hazy, as if they were all part of some erotic dream.

After she had climaxed, the people pulled away from her and Sirona felt a sharp searing pain as a lash hit her back. Aulus paused, allowing everything to come back into some kind of focus, before he hit her again. It hurt, yet the pain only served to intensify the delicious heat still simmering in her groin. With each painful stroke of the lash came a rush of pleasure, until her pussy became so wet that the moisture seeped from her vagina and ran down her inner thighs.

Sirona was way beyond anything she had known before, as she was overwhelmed by the conflicting sensations of pain and pleasure, until they combined into one perfect point of bliss buried deep inside her vagina. Each stroke now making her jerk and moan, as she soared towards orgasm again. Suddenly, the whipping stopped and Aulus knelt down beside her. The features of his gold mask swam before her eyes, as she heard him say, 'I always knew that you were a dirty little whore. Once I've come, I'm going to slit your throat.'

Nothing seemed to matter any more, as she felt his hands touch her buttocks. Despite the warmth of the room, his hands were chillingly cold, as was his cock, as it slid deep inside her.

Suddenly, from a great distance Sirona heard angry shouts. Aulus was pulled bodily away from her, and she felt someone untying her hands. She blinked in confusion, as Tiro placed a cloak around her naked body and gently pulled her upright. 'Can you stand, Sirona?' he asked. 'You have to try. You've been drugged.'

She nodded, unable to speak, her tongue refusing to work properly. Meanwhile, all around her, chaos reigned. There were soldiers struggling with the naked worshippers, who were biting and kicking insanely. So far, the soldiers hadn't used weapons but, after enduring a few moments of mayhem, some drew their swords in frustration and used the pommels to hit their insane attackers on their heads.

Meanwhile, Aulus and his masked companion had grabbed the two ceremonial daggers from the makeshift altar. The masked man screamed angrily, as he attacked one of the soldiers, while Aulus made straight for the man in command of the soldiers.

'Lucius,' Sirona gasped, able to speak at last, as Aulus, screaming like a man demented, flung himself at Lucius. He staggered back in surprise, as his stepfather tried to plunge the dagger into his throat. Lucius grabbed on to Aulus's wrist, trying to force the deadly blade away from his neck.

'Don't worry, Lucius will handle this,' Tiro said reassuringly, as Sirona stared at the two men struggling together.

The muscles on his arms bulging, Lucius forced the blade away from him and towards Aulus. Having no wish to kill his own stepfather, Lucius suddenly bent his head and butted him hard. Aulus slipped to the floor, while just above them came an ominous cracking sound. Lucius just managed to leap away from the falling beams, masonry and tiles, as part of the roof collapsed, burying Aulus completely. Three-quarters of the ceiling remained in place, but it looked decidedly dangerous, as if it were about to collapse at any moment.

Striding forwards, Lucius pulled Sirona into his arms. 'We have to leave now, my love.'

'The servants?' she just managed to say, as the full horror of all this at last hit her.

'One of my men is making sure that they leave with us right now, Sirona. I don't know how much time we've got to get to a place of safety,' he said gently, as he lifted her trembling body into his arms.

* * *

While Julia and Borax had gone to visit Pomponianus, Taranis and his companions had taken refuge in an abandoned villa. There was a reasonable amount of food and plenty of wine left in the house so they made themselves comfortable, relieved to have somewhere to rest for a while. The scantily dressed females they'd picked up en route were exceptionally busy and were all too happy to accommodate as many of the gladiators as they could. There were patient lines of men outside every bedroom of the villa.

Time passed and Taranis became concerned, as Julia and Borax had still not returned. The rockfall had resumed now but this time the stones raining down on Stabiae were heavier, denser and a dark-grey colour. Then the earth tremors started again. Ignoring the brothel-like moans and groans coming from the adjoining rooms, Taranis glanced anxiously up at the ceiling, as he heard the timbers creaking. The villa was fairly new and reasonably well constructed but some of the stones were large enough to smash the thick roof tiles and he knew that eventually the entire thing would give way under the combined weight of the stones.

He was just about to go and look for Julia when the door burst open and three people hurried through the atrium into the main salon. If the situation hadn't been serious, Taranis might have laughed, as all three of them had pillows strapped to their heads.

'Admiral Pliny suggested that the shield Borax was carrying might not provide us with enough protection. This was his idea,' Julia explained breathlessly as she untied the ribbon and the pillow dropped to the floor.

She sat down beside Taranis and he slipped an arm around her shoulder as he gave her an affectionate kiss on the cheek. 'I was worried.'

'We were invited to dine with Pomponianus and Admiral Pliny,' she explained.

'Galen?' Taranis exclaimed, as the third man unwound the flimsy scarf that had been covering his face.

'I was dining with the Admiral as well. It was quite by chance that I stopped here. I was planning to take a boat to Neaopolis,' Galen said, as Julia clutched nervously on to Taranis as the earth shook again.

'Better here than in Pompeii,' Taranis said, as Galen sat down on the floor opposite him.

'The Admiral and I compared observations,' Galen explained. Pliny was a famous scholar who'd written numerous books on a variety of subjects. 'We had both read of something similar to this happening in Sicily, but hadn't made the connection until now because the first phases of the phenomena had been rather dissimilar. Mount Etna has belched rocks, fire and eventually great rivers of red-hot matter on a number of occasions. Each time the destruction was terrible but Etna is in a relatively unpopulated area.'

'You think that might happen here?' Taranis asked, recalling the fires on the slopes of Vesuvius.

'Yes,' said Galen in all seriousness. 'I fear that might be so. Mother Earth is, however, highly unpredictable.' He put a hand to his head and rubbed it thoughtfully. 'Sulphur appears to play some part in this and I smelt sulphur earlier in the day.'

'Then damn the stones and the stormy waters, we must leave immediately.' Taranis sprang to his feet, pulling Julia up with him. 'Leod.' He saw the red-headed Briton standing patiently by the door of a bedroom, waiting his turn. 'Gather the men together, we must leave now. According to Galen, this could get worse, far worse.'

No one protested. If it hadn't been for Taranis, they'd all still be locked in their cells. After donning their armour and helmets, they followed him down to the beach. Most of the refugees were sheltering beneath strips of sailcloth or quickly constructed wooden shelters, as the stones continued to rain down on them. All of a sudden, the earth shook again and there was a strange cracking sound. They could not see more than a few arm lengths in front of their faces, but they knew that the roofs of the villas ringing the beach were collapsing one by one.

The fall of rock ebbed and flowed a shade, just enabling Taranis to see a small vessel bobbing up and down on the waves not that far out to sea. Ignoring the stones raining down on him, Taranis stripped off his armour and removed his helmet. 'Olin, Leod,' he called. 'We need to swim to that boat.'

Once they'd stripped down to their tunics, all three men battled through the waves crashing against the shore. They passed the foaming crests where the water became deeper, and they swam towards the small boat. It bobbed vigorously up and down on the waves and, as they climbed into the vessel, it began to sink lower and lower into the sea. Finding themselves almost knee deep in stones, they began to shovel as many as they could into the water. Once it was stable, they grabbed the oars and raised the anchor. They didn't have to row very hard before the waves caught hold of them and carried them swiftly towards the shore.

Taranis winced as he heard the bottom of the boat grate against the pumice, but the rock was reasonably soft and he hoped would do little damage. After jumping out of the boat, he ran towards his men.

'I have to leave you here for a short while,' he told Julia. 'I think all the large ships, further out to sea, are military vessels. The Admiral probably left men on board to guard the ships and to keep shovelling pumice off the decks to stop them sinking under the weight.' He beckoned to one of the more seasoned gladiators from Thrace. 'No armour, just weapons,' he ordered. 'Pick out at least a dozen of our best fighters and come with me.'

Taranis stood on the prow of his captured vessel watching the two small boats make their way back to shore through the rough dangerous seas. They'd commandeered another rowing boat because one was not enough to ferry his men quickly to this liburnium. They had encountered little or no resistance to their takeover of this vessel; most of the sailors had been too scared of the menacing-looking gladiators to even attempt to fight them. The ship had been listing dangerously, weighed down by the weight of the pumice, while the crew, bereft of any senior officers, had crouched below decks praying to the gods for deliverance.

There had been no need for Taranis to give his men any orders after they had secured the vessel. All of them had known exactly what to do. A couple had rowed back to the beach to pick up their comrades and find another small boat, while the others had started to shovel the pumice from the decks until the liburnium slowly righted itself. Now the vessel moved listlessly at anchor in a never-ending sea of stone.

All but the last few men were on board now, as well as the people they had rescued from the beach, along with the sailors who had chosen to remain on board the commandeered vessel. Those who had no wish to remain had been taken to join the Admiral on the shore. Taranis wanted no slave labour on this ship. If needs be, he and the other gladiators would work the oars. It wouldn't be easy, he knew that, but in the far north men had managed to navigate their way through seas nearly covered in ice, so why couldn't they make their way through a sea of stone?

'Taranis.' Julia moved to his side, doing her best to ignore the small lumps of pumice still raining down on them.

'I thought I told you to remain below deck.' He smiled. 'And where's your cushion,' he added teasingly.

They had passed Admiral Pliny on the beach when he had returned to collect Julia. The overweight, elderly Roman had looked a little comical with a cushion tied to his head. The man had stubbornly refused to let his boats put to sea carrying the refugees, insisting anxiously that it was far too dangerous. He had shouted and complained when he had realised that Taranis and his gladiator friends had appropriated a military vessel, but none of those with Pliny, not even the officers, had made any attempts to stop them.

'The colour doesn't suit me,' Julia said with a wicked grin.

Taranis removed his helmet and plonked it on her head. It was far too big and fell forwards, half-covering her eyes. 'Much better, we'll make a gladiator of you yet.' He didn't know how prophetic those words were because not that long into the future women would begin fighting in the arena.

He put an arm around Julia, holding her close. The rockfall was lessening again, just like it had before. 'The boats, will we be able to take on all the refugees?' Julia asked him anxiously.

'As many as we can, but Galen says that this must be the last trip. I trust his judgement, Julia. Next come the rivers of fire, so he says.'

The small boats were returning, packed to the gunnels with weeping women, screaming children and men trying to appear brave for the sake of their families.

'Look,' Julia said. The fires on Vesuvius were very visible now, even in the gloom, flickering orange-red sheets of flame pouring down the mountain towards Herculaneum.

Sirona would have left there hours earlier, Taranis told himself, as he watched Mother Nature take her revenge on the Romans. Meanwhile, gladiators were rushing to one side of the vessel to help the last load of terrified refugees on board. Above them, the sky had started to lighten a little as dawn tried to force its way through the enveloping clouds. With the light came more fire, sweeping down the sides of Vesuvius. Even from this distance, they could smell burning and the acrid odour of sulphur.

Leaving Julia to help with the refugees, Taranis walked to the rear of the vessel, knowing that it would take at least two men to hold the rudder in place. The gladiators joined the seamen at the oars, while a young boy moved to the drum and began to thump it in a steady beat. Terrifyingly slowly, the vessel turned away from Stabiae and headed towards the open sea.

Julia stood with Admiral Pliny's sister on the terrace of his villa, set high in the hills above the harbour at Misenum. Two days had passed since they'd docked here, the liburnium packed to the gunnels with traumatised refugees.

Taranis had found a small chest of silver coins in the captain's cabin and had distributed them among the gladiators. With luck, it would be enough to help them reach a place of safety, where they could live as free men again. Not knowing what else to do, Julia had suggested they stay with her friend, who was also called Julia. She'd welcomed them with open arms and they'd spent the last two days recovering from their ordeal.

No one in Misenum knew that Taranis was a slave, as Julia had introduced him as a citizen from Gaul. Everyone had been too swept up in the terrible events to question him or the fact she and Taranis shared a bedchamber and were obviously lovers. In fact, he had been publicly lauded for helping so many people escape.

Julia's friend had a son, Gaius Plinius, who was still only in his teens but was very close to his uncle. He had insisted on travelling to Stabiae on the first rescue ship to set out after the huge dark cloud had dispersed, and Taranis had volunteered to accompany him. The ship had docked not that long earlier and the two women waited nervously, as they watched Taranis and young Gaius climb the steps to the terrace. As soon as they saw their faces, they knew it was not good news.

Young Gaius was carrying a thick sheaf of papers they'd found on the beach – his uncle's carefully written account of the strange manifestations. 'He's gone,' he said sadly. Julia put a comforting arm around her friend's shoulders. 'It was strange, he just looked as though he was asleep,' young Gaius added, glancing up at Taranis.

'They all did,' Taranis added. 'All the people who remained at Stabiae perished. Galen thinks it was the sulphurous gases that killed them.' He turned to look at the distant mountain. The sharp peak had disappeared and now there was a deep hollow at the summit. 'As far as we could tell, both Pompeii and Herculaneum have been wiped from the face of the earth.' His voice faltered a little and she knew that he was thinking of Sirona and Lucius.

'Come, Gaius,' Pliny's sister said to her son. 'Let's sit a

while and you can tell me everything.' They walked off to mourn their loss together.

Once they were alone, Julia said, 'They'll have escaped, I'm certain.'

'You've had no news?'

'Not yet.' She had managed to remain far more positive than Taranis. 'Most probably they escaped by sea. People fled in all directions. It may take some time until we know they are safe.'

'Time I cannot afford, Julia,' Taranis said. 'More and more people are arriving from Pompeii, someone is sure to recognise me.'

'I know. We need to leave here soon. I have land in Spain. As soon as I can make arrangements, we can travel there.'

'You'd give up your life here for me?' He pulled her close. 'I can't ask you to do that, Julia.'

'But I want to,' she insisted.

'Julia,' Pliny's sister shouted anxiously, as she hurried on to the terrace.

Taranis tensed, as he caught sight of the people following her: a marine centurion and half a dozen soldiers. They made straight for Taranis, as Julia clutched nervously on to his arm. 'Run?' she suggested.

'Impossible,' he said regretfully, as the men grabbed hold of him.

'Taranis of Gaul,' the centurion said curtly. 'You are under arrest.' The centurion looked apologetically at Julia. 'We have reason to believe, my lady, that this man is an escaped slave masquerading as a citizen of Rome.'

Sirona shivered and pulled her cloak even tighter around her body. Three months had passed since they'd escaped from Pompeii and it was winter now. She'd never expected it to be so cold this far south. Pompeii was just a painful memory now and a lot had happened since then. Less than a week after they'd reached the safety of Rome, Lucius had been ordered to Illyrum to act as a temporary governor, until Titus had decided what changes would be made in his new administration. Sirona had gone with him, not knowing whether Taranis was alive or dead.

'It's too cold out here.' Lucius strode on to the terrace of the villa he'd rented on the outskirts of the city, looking very impressive in his military uniform. 'Come inside, Sirona.'

She followed him back into the villa, surprised as always that it was so warm. With its underfloor heating and glass windows, it was the height of luxury.

'Do you know when the ceremony will be?' she asked Lucius.

'No.'

Less than a week before, they'd returned to Rome because Titus had recently arranged a very auspicious union for his young protégé. Lucius was highly honoured, he was marrying into the Imperial family. He was now betrothed to Titus's youngest niece, Drusilla. Despite his affection for Sirona, Lucius had not thought to refuse the Emperor's offer, as his career was more important to him than anything else.

'Are you sure you won't change your mind?' he pressed. Lucius wanted her to remain his mistress. He'd offered to buy her a large house in the city so that their liaison could continue, albeit a little more discreetly.

'I can't,' she said sadly. Nothing between them was the same now, their relationship had changed the night that she'd betrayed him with Taranis, and it had never truly recovered. Even so, after he'd rescued her from

Pompeii, Lucius had been good to her. Life as a Roman governor's paramour had been quite enjoyable and their sex life had continued to be as stimulating as ever.

'I'll miss you,' he said sadly, as he tenderly stroked her cheek.

'And I you.'

Lucius pulled her into his arms and kissed her passionately. 'The Emperor has given you your freedom, Sirona. Now you can return home. All I hope is that you find happiness there.'

Sirona tried to stop tears from filling her eyes. 'And I hope that you'll find happiness with Drusilla.'

'Arranged marriages rarely turn out well.' He stared at her and she thought that he was about to tell her something of great importance. But she was wrong because he merely said, 'Your escort has arrived. They'll stay here overnight and you'll depart for Ostia at first light.'

'Then this is goodbye?'

'Yes. I have to go, Titus is expecting me.' Stepping back, he gave her a formal bow and then strode from the room.

Sirona stood there for a moment, thinking that their farewell had been far too brief, she should have been more affectionate and thanked him for all he'd done for her. However, in the last few days she'd felt that he had been trying to pull back from her, probably to stop their parting from being more painful than it already was. She made her way to her bedroom feeling sad that she was losing Lucius, but happy and a little apprehensive about returning home.

Dismissing her maid, she sat down on the bed that she and Lucius had so recently shared. It wouldn't be easy to accustom herself to the simple life back in

Brittania, especially as most of the people she cared for were either missing or dead.

There was a soft knock on her door and the slave girl, who'd been acting as her maid, pulled it open. 'My lady, the leader of your escort wishes to speak with you.'

'He does?' What would this man possibly want? Sirona wondered, rising to her feet, thinking that she'd speak to him in the main salon.

Suddenly, the girl was pushed aside and a man, wearing a long hooded cloak, strode into her bedchamber and slammed the door shut behind him. She was struck dumb with surprise, as he threw back his hood.

'Sirona!' Taranis pulled her into his arms, hugging her so tight he almost crushed her.

'Lucius knew?' she managed to stutter, as he took her face between his hands and stared lovingly into her green eyes.

'Yes, he and his sister arranged it.'

He kissed her, a hard raw kiss filled with so much passion it literally took her breath away. He held her tightly, his lips locked with hers until he was forced to release her through lack of air. Her body seemed to melt into his and she felt the hard line of his cock pressing sensuously against her belly.

As he gently pulled her towards the bed, he divested first her, then himself of clothing. She wanted to feast her eyes on his naked body, enjoy slow sweet hours of lovemaking, but the intoxicating pleasure of his presence drove this from her mind: she had to fuck him right now. Taranis seemed to be of the same accord, as he flipped her over on to her stomach. Lifting her on to her knees, Taranis buried his cock deep into her pussy and fucked her hard and fast, giving her far more pleasure than any other man could.

Sirona grabbed hold of the woollen coverlet, as his massive shaft thrust into her body. One of his hands reached for her breasts, while the other slid between her pussy lips to stroke her clit. In no time at all, she came, swiftly and fiercely, her orgasm overpowering her completely.

Taranis lay there watching Sirona sleeping. After he'd fucked her so roughly, they'd made love again. This time slowly and passionately, as he tried to convey all his thoughts and feelings in those long lingering moments of lovemaking. Exhausted and happy, she'd fallen asleep in his arms, while he had just lain there, unable to take his eyes from her, hardly able to believe that they were together again. He had to thank Lucius and Julia for this, the two people who had helped him were the same two people he would have expected to try and keep them apart.

Nevertheless, they had both been incredibly lucky, both to survive the devastation of Pompeii and to find each other again. After his arrest, he had been imprisoned for a few weeks then, eventually, when order had been restored in the area, he'd been taken to the gladiatorial barracks in Rome. Taranis had thought that he would be forced to fight in the arena again, but that had never happened. It was well known that he'd helped rescue many refugees from Stabiae and some citizens had said that he should be rewarded for that. However, he was also implicated in the escape of almost fifty slaves, all former gladiators. Most of them had not been recaptured, including Leod and Olin.

It had been some time before Cnaius had returned to Rome and learnt of his imprisonment. Cnaius had visited him and, to Taranis's amazement, promptly given him his freedom. Cnaius had then managed to arrange to have all charges against him dropped. By a strange quirk of fate, among the refugees he'd rescued from Stabiae had been Cnaius's sister and her young son, and freedom was his reward for saving them.

When the Emperor had heard what had happened, he'd insisted on meeting Taranis. He'd been fortunate to spend some time with Titus, and had got to know him quite well. Titus was a good man and Taranis hoped that eventually he might bring about positive changes in the Empire.

Once freed, Taranis had lived with Julia in her villa in Rome. However, freed slaves were not allowed to marry noblewomen, so she would have to leave everything and everyone she knew in order to be with him. Also, Taranis couldn't in all honesty think of marrying her when he still loved Sirona. He knew that eventually he would have to be cruel to be kind and leave Julia. Once she'd come to accept that, it was impossible for them to be together; she would soon find herself a new husband, especially as Titus had made a point of introducing her to a large number of rich and influential young men.

However, before he could carry out his plans, Lucius had returned to Rome to marry, bringing Sirona with him, and Julia had at last realised that she had no real future with Taranis.

'Taranis.' Sirona sleepily opened her eyes. 'What's wrong?'

'Nothing, my love. Go back to sleep, we have to leave early in the morning.'

She smiled and snuggled closer to him. Closing his eyes, he tried to relax, but it wasn't easy with her naked body pressed to his. He would keep the last surprise of all until tomorrow. Titus had freed her father and, when they reached Ostia, Borus would be there waiting for them.

Visit the Black Lace website at
www.blacklace-books.co.uk

LOOK OUT FOR THE ALL-NEW BLACK LACE BOOKS – AVAILABLE NOW!

All books priced £7.99 in the UK. Please note publication dates apply to the UK only. For other territories, please contact your retailer.

MANHUNT
Cathleen Ross
ISBN 0 352 33583 1

Fearless and charismatic Angie Masters is on a man hunt. While training at a prestigious hotel training academy, the attractive and dominant director of the institute – James Steele – catches her eye. Steele has a predatory sexuality, as well as a penchant for erotic punishment. By seducing a fellow student, Angie is able to sexually torment Steele. But Angie has a rival – the luscious Italian Isabella who is prepared to do anything to please him. A battle of wills ensues, featuring catfights, orgies and triumph for either Angie or Isabella. Who will be the victor?

Coming in March

CAT SCRATCH FEVER
Sophie Mouette
ISBN 0 352 34021 5

Creditors breathing down her neck. Crazy board members. A make-or-break benefit that's far behind schedule. Felicia DuBois, development coordinator at the Southern California Cat Sanctuary, has problems – including a bad case of the empty-bed blues. Then sexy Gabe Sullivan walks into the Sanctuary and sets her body tingling. Felicia's tempted to dive into bed with him . . . except it could mean she'd be sleeping with the enemy. Gabe's from the Zoological Association, a watchdog organisation that could decide to close the cash-strapped cat facility. Soon Gabe and Felicia are acting like cats in heat, but someone's sabotaging the benefit. Could it be Gabe? Or maybe it's the bad-boy volunteer, the delicious caterer, or the board member with a penchant for leather? Throw in a handsome veterinarian and a pixieish female animal handler who likes handling Felicia, and everyone ought to be purring. But if Felicia can't find the saboteur, the Sanctuary's future will be as endangered as the felines it houses.

RUDE AWAKENING
Pamela Kyle
ISBN 0 352 33036 8

Alison is a control freak. There's nothing she enjoys more than swanning around her palatial home giving orders to her wealthy but masochistic husband and delighting in his humiliation. Her daily routine consists of shopping, dressing up and pursuing dark pleasures, along with her best friend, Belinda; that is until they are kidnapped and held to ransom. In the ensuing weeks both women are required to come to terms with their most secret selves. Stripped of their privileges and deprived of the luxury they are used to, they deal with their captivity in surprising and creative ways. For Alison, it is the catalyst to a whole new way of life.

Coming in April

ENTERTAINING MR STONE
Portia da Costa
ISBN 0 352 34029 0

When reforming bad girl Maria Lewis takes a drone job in local government back in her home town, the quiet life she was looking for is quickly disrupted by the enigmatic presence of her boss, Borough Director, Robert Stone. A dangerous and unlikely object of lust, Stone touches something deep in Maria's sensual psyche and attunes her to the erotic underworld that parallels life in the dusty offices of Borough Hall. But the charismatic Mr Stone isn't the only one interested in Maria – knowing lesbian Mel and cute young techno geek Greg both have designs on the newcomer, as does Human Resources Manager William Youngblood, who wants to prize the Borough's latest employee away from the arch-rival for whom he has ambiguous feelings.

DANGEROUS CONSEQUENCES
Pamela Rochford
ISBN 0 352 33185 2

When Rachel Kemp is in danger of losing her job at a London University, visiting academic Luke Holloway takes her for a sybaritic weekend in the country to cheer her up. Her encounters with Luke and his enigmatic friend Max open up a world of sensual possibilities and she is even offered a new job editing a sexually explicit Victorian diary. Life is looking good until Rachel returns to London, and, accused of smuggling papers out of the country, is sacked on the spot. In the meantime Luke disappears and Rachel is left wondering about the connection between these elusive academics, their friends and the missing papers. When she tries to clear her name she discovers her actions have dangerous – and highly erotic – consequences.

Black Lace Booklist

Information is correct at time of printing. To avoid disappointment
check availability before ordering. Go to www.blacklace-books.co.uk.
All books are priced £6.99 unless another price is given.

BLACK LACE BOOKS WITH A CONTEMPORARY SETTING

| ☐ MANHUNT Cathleen Ross | ISBN 0 352 33583 1 | £7.99 |
| ☐ THE STRANGER Portia Da Costa | ISBN 0 352 33211 5 | £7.99 |

BLACK LACE BOOKS WITH AN HISTORICAL SETTING

☐ PRIMAL SKIN Leona Benkt Rhys	ISBN 0 352 33500 9	£5.99
☐ DARKER THAN LOVE Kristina Lloyd	ISBN 0 352 33279 4	
☐ THE CAPTIVATION Natasha Rostova	ISBN 0 352 33234 4	
☐ MINX Megan Blythe	ISBN 0 352 33638 2	
☐ DIVINE TORMENT Janine Ashbless	ISBN 0 352 33719 2	
☐ SATAN'S ANGEL Melissa MacNeal	ISBN 0 352 33726 5	
☐ THE INTIMATE EYE Georgia Angelis	ISBN 0 352 33004 X	
☐ SILKEN CHAINS Jodi Nicol	ISBN 0 352 33143 7	
☐ THE LION LOVER Mercedes Kelly	ISBN 0 352 33162 3	
☐ THE AMULET Lisette Allen	ISBN 0 352 33019 8	
☐ WHITE ROSE ENSNARED Juliet Hastings	ISBN 0 352 33052 X	
☐ UNHALLOWED RITES Martine Marquand	ISBN 0 352 33222 0	
☐ LA BASQUAISE Angel Strand	ISBN 0 352 32988 2	
☐ THE HAND OF AMUN Juliet Hastings	ISBN 0 352 33144 5	
☐ THE SENSES BEJEWELLED Cleo Cordell	ISBN 0 352 32904 1	
☐ UNDRESSING THE DEVIL Angel Strand	ISBN 0 352 33938 1	£7.99
☐ THE BARBARIAN GEISHA Charlotte Royal	ISBN 0 352 33267 0	£7.99
☐ FRENCH MANNERS Olivia Christie	ISBN 0 352 33214 X	£7.99
☐ LORD WRAXALL'S FANCY Anna Lieff Saxby	ISBN 0 352 33080 5	£7.99
☐ NICOLE'S REVENGE Lisette Allen	ISBN 0 352 32984 X	£7.99

BLACK LACE ANTHOLOGIES

☐ WICKED WORDS Various	ISBN 0 352 33363 4
☐ MORE WICKED WORDS Various	ISBN 0 352 34487 8
☐ WICKED WORDS 3 Various	ISBN 0 352 33522 X
☐ WICKED WORDS 4 Various	ISBN 0 352 33603 X
☐ WICKED WORDS 5 Various	ISBN 0 352 33642 0
☐ WICKED WORDS 6 Various	ISBN 0 352 33690 0
☐ WICKED WORDS 7 Various	ISBN 0 352 33743 5
☐ WICKED WORDS 8 Various	ISBN 0 352 33787 7
☐ WICKED WORDS 9 Various	ISBN 0 352 33860 1

To find out the latest information about Black Lace titles, check out the website: www.blacklace-books.co.uk or send for a booklist with complete synopses by writing to:

Black Lace Booklist, Virgin Books Ltd
Thames Wharf Studios
Rainville Road
London W6 9HA

Please include an SAE of decent size. Please note only British stamps are valid.

Our privacy policy
We will not disclose information you supply us to any other parties. We will not disclose any information which identifies you personally to any person without your express consent.

From time to time we may send out information about Black Lace books and special offers. Please tick here if you do <u>not</u> wish to receive Black Lace information.   ☐

Please send me the books I have ticked above.

Name ....

Address ....

....

....

....

Post Code ....

Send to: Virgin Books Cash Sales, Thames Wharf Studios, Rainville Road, London W6 9HA.

US customers: for prices and details of how to order books for delivery by mail, call 1-800-343-4499.

Please enclose a cheque or postal order, made payable to Virgin Books Ltd, to the value of the books you have ordered plus postage and packing costs as follows:

UK and BFPO – £1.00 for the first book, 50p for each subsequent book.

Overseas (including Republic of Ireland) – £2.00 for the first book, £1.00 for each subsequent book.

If you would prefer to pay by VISA, ACCESS/MASTERCARD, DINERS CLUB, AMEX or SWITCH, please write your card number and expiry date here:

....

Signature ....

Please allow up to 28 days for delivery.